Aurora's Gold

K. J. GILLENWATER

CHAPTER ONE

A roomful of eyes turned my way.

Ernie's Pub filled up nightly with sweaty, grimy gold miners, divers and drunks. Monday through Sunday. Not a night went by that some soused lout didn't wind up in jail for disorderly conduct, assault or just plain public drunkenness. Half the gold in the place probably went toward bail money or paying off fines for minor offenses. Worst part was, the best and most responsible divers (if you could call any of these lunkheads responsible) had already been snatched up well before the start of the summer gold season.

A half-Inuit woman with bleached blonde hair and an inch of dark roots gave me the once over. I encroached on her territory.

Men outnumbered women by a noticeable number in Nome, especially in the summer when dredge mining hit its peak. But that didn't mean women weren't competitive in this target-rich environment. Money came and went like the tide. A woman who lived off the crumbs of Nome had to flit from miner to miner to keep the free drinks and cheap bar food flowing.

The woman unbuttoned another button on her blouse, picked up a shot glass and tossed back a drink. My muddied jean shorts and faded Seahawks t-shirt along with my ratty hair and plain face probably convinced her I wasn't the competition. She turned back to a couple of shabby looking men with a wad of bills piled on the bar between them. Looked like it had been a good day for the pair of dredgers, and they seemed willing to share it with their new female companion.

Once the patrons of Ernie's Pub had recognized me and determined I wasn't flush with cash to buy someone drinks, they returned to their carousing. Rory Darling, daughter of Buck Darling, didn't slum around these parts. These guys knew I was off limits. A few curious stares followed me, but I ignored them and scanned the room. I had one goal in mind. Ernie's was the last bar in town, and I was determined to find what I needed.

"Hey, Rory, what can I get ya?" Bobby Sykes, former hockey goalie for the Nanooks at the University of Alaska in Fairbanks, tended bar most nights at Ernie's. He'd torn a ligament or something back in college. Dropped out of school. Came back to his hometown a decade ago to muddle his way through life as a dredge tender, mechanic and whatever else made him some money. He'd aged poorly since his return to Nome—beer gut, mostly bald, red-rimmed eyes that reminded me of one of those guys who drank too much and had a diet of Cheetos and corndogs.

I waved him off. "Not here for a drink." I needed to be on my game. "But maybe you can help."

Bobby cocked his head. "Sure, whatcha need?" He popped the top off a beer and passed it to one of the old time miners sitting at the bar.

"Got a line on any divers who might be looking for work?" I had a feeling it would be an impossible ask, but Bobby knew all the regulars and even the not-so-regulars. Plus, he knew, like most people, how dire my situation had become.

"I wish I had a lead for you." He chopped up a lime, avoiding eye contact.

Nome lived or died on the gold business. People's lives had been destroyed by one bad season, one bad decision, one bad piece of luck. I'm sure Bobby had had a dozen other dredgers ask him the same question in the last week. Trained divers were hard to come by. Although I could take a chance on a newbie, I didn't want to risk someone's life by hiring a desperate person with no experience under water.

"What about Clint Junior? You think he'd be interested in coming out of retirement?" Clint had been a good friend of my father's and had even worked for him twenty years ago when dredge mining had been less lucrative.

"He's back in the lower 48." Bobby waved at a couple of regulars who walked in the door and took their orders.

I don't know why I'd asked. I knew Clint had left Alaska a while ago. My mind reached for something, someone, anyone who might be able to help. The number of divers we'd worked with over the years became a blur of wetsuits and arguments. The dredging business could be filled with stress, anger, fights, fatigue. Divers who demanded more than their fair share of the gold haul. Divers who would throw a punch before they'd talk things out. Divers who pushed themselves too hard and ended up with injuries they never recovered from.

"How's your dad doing? I heard the news." Bobby had mixed up a couple of screwdrivers and handed them to the newly arrived patrons.

I took a deep breath. "He's still in the ICU." The question could bring tears to my eyes if I didn't stay focused. "Look, if you don't have any suggestions for me, I guess I'll ask around for myself." I scanned the dark bar once again. Maybe I could lure away a diver from another dredge with an offer of a higher percentage. Tonight I had to go home with someone ready to work in the morning. I had to figure out how to dig my butt out of a financial meltdown of epic proportions.

"You need a diver?" One of the regular pilots who flew between Nome and Kotzebue had been sitting on a barstool next to me.

I thought I recognized him. Nome was small enough that you felt that way most days. His name might've been Dave. But that could just be the fact that I knew three pilots named Dave, so the choice seemed like a good guess.

Bobby moved off to tend his customers, and I sat down to find out what information Dave the Pilot might have for me. "You know someone?"

"Guy flew in today from Anchorage looking for work." The man-who-was-probably-named-Dave tilted his brown baseball cap off his brow and nursed his beer. "I met him at the airport. I told him they always need divers this time of year. Seemed like he had some experience."

"Do you know where I could find him?" An experienced diver randomly showing up in Nome in the middle of the summer dredging season? This might be my lucky day. Unless someone else had snatched him up.

"He's over there." The pilot pointed to the back of the narrow bar.

In a dark, smoky corner sat a beast of a man. Scraggly beard, shaggy hair under a wool cap, broad shouldered, hooded eyes. My first thought was: how much of a rap sheet does this guy have? He looked like the type who had once been part of a biker gang. The only thing missing was a massive neck tattoo.

The Beast scratched his chin, which exposed an upper arm tattoo of an American flag and an eagle.

I smiled.

The Beast's gaze locked with mine.

I shivered at the black intensity and looked away. A pit formed in my stomach. The guy looked dangerous. I turned back to Dave. "What do you know about him?"

"Not much. Just that he said he was looking for work and was a diver. Thought he might make a few bucks."

"Got a name?" I imagined myself out on the water on the dredge with the Beast. Surrounded by 40-degree water, too far from shore to make a swim for it. Working a dredge was all about trust. I took a quick peek over my shoulder to get one more look. What would keep him from challenging me on his take of the gold for the day? The sluice box clean up could be fraught with opportunities to pick out any sizable nuggets while I was underwater running the suction hose.

"Ben something, I think."

"Thanks." I pushed back from the bar. It was now or never. I had no other choice. Either I convinced this Ben person to work for me, or I'd have to sell the dredge, and all the plans my dad had for our family business ended. My luck had run out. This was the last stop. Period.

The jukebox spooled up another AC/DC tune. The harsh guitar riff drowned out the din of human voices. I turned sideways to slither through a couple of beefy men in dirty t-shirts and faded jeans who were about to come to blows. Probably over a girl, or maybe over a not-so-great day on the Bering.

The tail of my jersey caught on the post of a chair. I turned, tugged it off and smacked right into a solid wall of muscle.

The Beast.

*

I don't have the best control over my mouth sometimes.

4

Especially when I'm embarrassed or stressed. Words pour out with a speed not seen since Usain Bolt ran the 100 meter dash in the 2016 Olympics. When I hit the Beast's chest, my brain stopped. For a full-fledged 10 seconds, I couldn't say anything at all. I'm not sure why. Maybe because he was my last chance. My only chance in this godforsaken place to find some redemption. To make up for the mistakes I'd made. To fix the whole messy pile that had become my life.

I looked up into the dark gaze of the one man in Nome who could quite possibly make everything right again. Up close, his eyes weren't black like I'd supposed. His heavy brow had masked the clear blue. Blue like the winter sky after a long snow.

His mouth stretched into a hard line. He smelled like gasoline and spearmint gum. A strange combination, but not unpleasant.

The Beast and I were stuck between two tables. We could only move forward or backward. No sideways. The AC/DC tune built to a crescendo making conversation difficult.

He narrowed his eyes, grabbed me by the elbows and spun me around to get past me. Empty chairs toppled over.

I opened my mouth and wanted words to come out. They weren't there.

The minute he'd swiveled me out of the way, he continued toward the door.

Goddamn it, he could not leave before he heard my offer.

I trailed after him and stumbled over work boots and empty chairs. I made a fool of myself. I probably looked like a lovesick school girl chasing after him. With the reputation I had in Nome that might actually be believed. I set that out of my mind. I didn't have the luxury of worrying about rumors any more. Life got complicated. Time to grow up and figure a way out of it.

"Hey!" I called after the Beast's hulking figure headed across the muddy main street.

Even though it was late, the sun still hovered in the sky. The long Alaska summer nights might make it easier to dredge long hours under the water, but it also made it harder to get a good night's sleep.

The Beast didn't even give me a glance.

I took off at a jog to catch up to him. "Hey, Ben, I'm talking to you." I'd almost called him *Beast* instead of Ben.

He stopped. "Do I know you?" His words were dark and accusatory.

I questioned, once again, the logic of partnering up with an unknown entity. So many things could go wrong. "I'm Rory Darling. I own the *Alaska Darling*, a dredge. I need a diver. Heard you might be looking for work." Maybe an offer of employment would take the dour expression off his face. I had a hard time imagining him with anything but a scowl.

"Maybe." He stood apart from me. His body language told me not to get any closer. "Where'd you hear that?"

I nodded toward Ernie's. "Pilot. He met you at the airport." I shivered in the cooling air. My shorts were still damp from a day spent tuning up the dredge. "I can offer you twenty percent. That's a better deal than most out here would give you." I hoped Dave the Pilot hadn't made it clear how desperately divers were wanted. The Beast probably could've found someone eager enough to give him thirty percent.

"Twenty-five."

The low light from the summer's midnight sun created a shadow across his face. My expression would be in plain view with the light shining in my eyes. I knew I didn't have a very good poker face. He must've sensed weakness or the pilot had given him a good indication of the scarcity of divers.

"You got your own gear?" I sized him up. Probably six-foot-three or so. "My wetsuit probably won't fit you." My dad and I were about the same height and shared a suit, and Kyle had taken his stuff with him yesterday.

Kyle.

I really didn't want to think about Kyle at that moment. I bit my lip.

"Yeah, I brought some gear."

"Dredged before?"

"No."

"But you've dived before, Ben...?" Teaching someone to dredge wasn't really what I wanted, but I didn't have much choice.

"Ben Abel." He gave a nod. "And yes, I've dived before."

"I can do twenty-five." I calculated my breakeven point for a day's work. Probably 1 or 2 ounces of gold. "But the first couple of days, until you figure out how to handle the equipment, I'll give you twenty." A new dredger generally didn't know what to look for under water—the right kind of cobble, what was worked ground and what was virgin ground. If he was sloppy at the beginning, he might put me in the red.

He laughed. "Never heard of a lady gold miner before. You sure you know what you're doing?"

I bristled. He was the newbie, not me. "Do you want the job or not? I can find someone else…"

"No, you can't."

I couldn't believe my ears. What an arrogant, horrible, beastly jerk. I wanted to use every swear word I knew. Lay it out for him I was the one in charge here. It was my dredge, my business, my deal. But the worst part about it? He was right. I had no other alternatives. I could try working with one of the notorious drunks who roamed the pier occasionally hoping to find a boat willing to let them work to buy their next fifth. Or I could scavenge a decent diver from another dredge, but he'd likely ask for more of a cut. Something I couldn't afford with my responsibilities.

"You are a bastard." I gritted my teeth, holding back the word I really wanted to call him.

"Yep."

"Fine. Twenty-five percent." Not the best way to start a working relationship—with a loss. "Meet me at the docks tomorrow at 5. The *Alaska Darling*. Blue hull with white trim, gold lettering on the side. You can't miss it."

"Aye-aye, Captain." He saluted me.

I headed to my truck parked outside Ernie's as my new diver made his way down the street. Who knew where the hell he was staying. One of the flea bag motels probably. As long as he showed up tomorrow on time with gear in hand, I'd be fine.

Maybe.

CHAPTER TWO

Five a.m. in the middle of July in Nome sure looked a lot like noon in most of the world. My brain wanted me to be back in bed, but the bright light told me the day had only just begun. Although I needed to keep my attention fixed on the dredge equipment to prepare it for a day on the water, my peripheral vision distracted me. Every movement on the docks caused me to shift my focus from the sluice or the air compressor or the radio.

Not good.

The condition of the equipment meant life or death. If any of the systems failed, a diver could die. Carbon dioxide could get sucked into the air pump, the comms could conk out and leave a diver in a world of cold and silence, motors could fail, fuel could leak. The worries were endless. Although I'd dredged with my father for years with these possibilities, today they were all my responsibility.

If I made a mistake, I could kill someone.

Dredge mining out on the Bering Sea required at least two people: a tender and a diver. The tender worked all of the controls above water—communications, air pump, hot water line, fuel levels, and sluice—all the while keeping an eye on the location of the dredge to ensure it remained centered over the gold and didn't stray off the public claims into someone's private domain. A diver had to brave the murky, cold depths of the arctic waters off Nome to locate the gold amidst the sand and rock while handling a heavy-duty suction hose that could rip off an arm if he wasn't paying attention.

A diver had to trust his tender with his life. Without trust, the whole operation could fall apart.

I wondered if my new diver would show or if he'd been snatched by someone else on his way to the docks. That had been known to happen. Loyalties were fleeting in Nome, especially if a dredge captain couldn't bring the gold.

As the only woman in Nome who ran a dredge, I had more obstacles to overcome. The assumption was Buck Darling had given me a leg up because I was his daughter, not because I'd earned my way to the top. I knew how to operate the machinery, and I'd built up the stamina to dive in the cold water of the Bering for hours at a time. With my dad beside me, I'd been protected from what dredgers really believed about my abilities and my work ethic. But after his accident, the patronizing comments and expectations for my failure didn't remain behind closed doors any longer.

"Rory, didn't think I'd see you out here." The familiar voice turned my blood to ice.

Keep it cool.

I looked up from refueling my equipment. Nate Frazier stood on the pier. "I don't want to talk to you."

He looked bad, worse than when he'd left the dredge last summer with a broken nose and a pocketful of pickers from the sluice box. Yes, his nose had a decided bent to it. But his cheeks had hollowed out, his once thick hair had thinned considerably, and his skin looked the same color as lye soap. Not the robust diver I remembered.

"Your dad owes me." He took a step onto my dredge. It dipped at the additional two-hundred pounds of weight. Dredges weren't the sturdiest of things. Built for hauling gold from the sea floor, not for sailing the open waters. Too much wind, and you had to head to town to avoid being sunk. Top heavy with equipment, flat bottomed and typically loaded with second-hand, and sometimes third-hand, motors and machinery—the money went into the fuel most of the time, rather than replacing stuff. "About twenty grand for my half of the business, if I've calculated right. Told me he'd pay up after ice season. Now it's July."

Nate knew my situation, and he wanted to take advantage. I had no idea if the conversation had even happened between my father and him. I'd been the dutiful daughter, not really paying attention to the business end of things. I ran the comms and other topside equipment, bought the fuel with cash my dad gave me, kept us in tuna fish and peanut butter sandwiches, did some of the diving, but my father had been the one with his hands on the bank account and the business. Not me.

Only in the last week or so did I know how bad things were, how much my father had hidden from me. Either he didn't want me to worry or he thought he could dig himself out of a financial hole before I knew anything about it. Knowing my father, it was probably the latter.

"That's between you and Buck." I kept my gaze on filling the generator, checking to make sure I didn't spill any gasoline. I could barely afford what I put in and couldn't waste any due to inattentiveness. "I don't know anything about owing you money or you owning half the business. As I recall, Buck let you walk off of here with gold that wasn't yours to begin with."

My peripheral vision caught movement. Nate stood over me. Although he'd lost weight and only had me outsized by a few inches, my gut clenched. I remembered the dark look that had settled over his features when he'd walked off the dredge, nose dripping bright red blood.

"He owes me." He wrapped his hand around my forearm and forced me to look at him directly. "Half this dredge is mine."

"Hey." I flinched and curled my arm inward. "You think I've got that kind of money on me?"

Nate twisted it. "Maybe." He leveled his gaze with mine. His brown eyes flashed in the morning sun.

I felt as if he was reading me. Gauging my honesty. My arm hurt, but I didn't show it. Fear nibbled around the edges of my brain.

He let go and leaned casually against the navigation wheelhouse. "I heard you have a new diver. Some military expert."

I didn't have time to deal with this creep. When he mentioned my diver, my hackles went up. "Where did you hear that?"

"Around." Nate took a toothpick out of the left front pocket of his plaid flannel shirt and stuck it between his teeth.

I brushed past him into the wheelhouse to turn on the Aquacom equipment. "Hm." I busied myself with the dials, knobs and switches. I turned over in my mind Nate's claim that he owned half the dredge.

"Not sure what a jarhead knows about dredging. Sure you know what you're doing?" He gave me the smile of a Class-A jerk—cold and insincere. "Did you get Kyle's okay?"

"Guess you didn't hear *all* the news. Kyle's not working on the *Alaska Darling* anymore." The emotional wound still hurt. He and my dad had been close. But that relationship didn't override what had happened.

Nate spat on the deck. "I always thought he was a pussy." He grinned and showed his crooked teeth.

"I need you off my dredge. I've got work to do." My focus should be on finding gold today, not thinking about my father, Kyle or anyone else.

Where was that damn diver?

Nate shrugged. He pushed off the wheelhouse with his shoulders, hands in his pockets. "If you have a good day out there, you know I'll come knocking. You get in touch with Buck, ask him. He knows what the situation is." He headed aft.

Unsettled emotions welled up inside. Fear, sadness, loss.

Screw Nate for breaking my focus. I didn't have time to be a girl today. I needed to suck it up and get out on the water.

The dredge dipped and swayed. Nate finally left. Who knew if any money was owed. My dad and I had done so poorly over the ice season, we only had enough cash to get us through our winter rent payments and grocery bills. I didn't have twenty thousand bucks laying around. And even if I did, I'd have a hard time forking it over to a lowlife like Nate. But he'd be back. Not only did he know my dad was out of the picture, Nate had learned Kyle was gone. I probably looked like an easy target, despite the right hook I'd delivered to his nose last year.

Nate had rattled me. He didn't have the best reputation in town. Well, comparatively speaking, he had a better reputation than half the Nome miners. But his penchant for drunken brawls, angry explosions, and occasional theft worried me. He'd gone out of his way to be here at 5 am. Most likely he'd been out carousing the night before with Lola Chang—a floozy who flitted from miner to miner during the gold season. Rumor had it Lola had cultivated a pretty wicked drug problem last winter and might be dealing. She'd been picked up by the local police for assault not too long ago, if I remembered right, and had spent a few days in the drunk tank.

Having seen Nate with Lola in the past, I knew it couldn't be good. If he'd picked up her habits (and his altered appearance suggested he may have), he could be more dangerous than he'd been last summer. He'd made a point of coming to see me rather than sleep it off in his yurt near the beach.

The dredge rippled again. Was Nate back for more?

I rushed out of the wheelhouse in mid-yell, "Get the hell off my dredge."

Ben, my brand new diver, stood on the deck, a full pack of gear on his back. "I thought we had a deal."

Shit.

My mind blanked. I couldn't think how to answer him.

"So? Do we still have a deal?" Ben had shucked off his pack and stood, arms akimbo, looking like a combination between the Jolly Green Giant and Paul Bunyan.

If I didn't say something, he might walk. I found my voice. "Yes, deal still on." Last thing my new diver needed was the sense his dredge captain was a raving lunatic. "I wasn't yelling at *you*, just so you know."

He shrugged and glanced at Nate who climbed into his broken down Jeep.

Guess Ben's stint in the military had accustomed him to being yelled at. Compared to Nate and his unpredictable outbursts of anger, a man with a calm, cool demeanor was exactly what I needed. Although last night I'd been uncertain about Ben's character based on his size and appearance, he exuded a steadiness I liked.

"You can stow your gear in the wheelhouse while I get the engine primed." Ben wasted no time and slipped past me, depositing his pack next to a bench in the rear of the wheelhouse. "Then we can shove off, and I'll explain to you how this all works." I waved my hand at the controls.

I headed aft to the outboard motor. I squeezed the gas bulb, put the shift lever in neutral, pulled out the choke, and yanked on the starter rope as hard as I could. The motor roared to life on my first attempt.

Thank goodness.

My dredge had been sitting unused for about five days. The *Alaska Darling* wasn't the newest boat on the water, and sitting cold in the harbor the motor could give inconsistent results. Would've been quite embarrassing to have trouble starting it in front of my new employee.

I slipped the rope off the mooring and pushed away from the pier. It would take us a good 20 minutes to get to our mining location.

Ben stepped into the wheelhouse.

I sat in the 'captain's chair'—really a torn up padded stool from a massage business that had gone under a decade ago—and switched on the GPS unit. As it came to life, I navigated around the other dredges tied up at the pier and made my way to the open water. The marked spot on the display made my stomach queasy, but there had been good gold there. At least an ounce an hour the day of the accident, Kyle had told me. I hoped this early in the day the chance of running into other miners on the public claims would be minimal.

Ben took a seat on the beat-up plaid couch.

I kept my eyes on the waves in front of me, set us straight on course, and tied off the wheel. We'd be fine for a few minutes, before I'd need to head us south toward the claim we'd be mining.

"Let me show you how all of this equipment works." I leaned against the plywood that made up the wheelhouse walls. "Before we do any diving I need to make sure you know what you're doing."

"I know how to run a generator…and an outboard."

"There's a lot more to running a dredge than a generator and an outboard."

He snorted.

I knew what he was probably thinking: dumb girl what does *she* know about this equipment that I don't know already? He probably thought he could run circles around me topside. "My dad and I have been running this dredge together for more than a decade."

"Really." He sized me up. "So, what, you were ten when you got started?"

I knew my answer wouldn't instill a lot of confidence. "Twelve."

"Your parents let you operate a dredge—dive in the Bering Sea—when you were twelve?"

"I didn't dive, but I did run the equipment."

"All righty, *captain*." Ben sat back and crossed his arms. "Tell me everything I need to know about your amazing watercraft."

Lord, I really did not need the sarcasm. I wanted a diver who could find me gold, not challenge my authority in the first five minutes. But what did I really expect when I hired the Beast last night in the dark, out on the street?

It wouldn't be easy convincing him I could run the dredge. Women weren't supposed to be mechanical, weren't supposed to be interested in this stuff. I should be at home, sitting on the couch, painting my toenails while binge watching something on Netflix.

Well, I was not that woman. He'd have to learn.

"This is the wheelhouse. We've got an underwater radio system." I pointed out the Aquacom radio and handset next to the steering wheel. "Works just like a CB radio. Looks like you might be old enough to remember those."

He raised an eyebrow. "Is that how this is going to go? You're too young to be doing this; and I'm too old?"

Good, I'd gotten a dig back at him.

I continued without skipping a beat, "Topside has to keep up good communications with the diver. Do not leave the radio, unless you have an emergency. It's only the two of us out here, if something goes wrong, we have to rely on each other."

"Got it." His sudden seriousness told me he understood.

"If you aren't getting a response from me, try a double click on the receiver." I picked up the handset and pressed on the button twice. Static-filled clicks sounded. "If you still aren't getting a response, the next step is to tug on the hose. I'll show you that outside in a minute. We also have a GPS unit." I pointed at the screen, which displayed various dots and lines labeled with latitude and longitude. "Whenever we find good gold, we mark it in the GPS. That way, if we run out of daylight or the weather turns, we know where to come back to the next day. Very important."

"Check."

"We also have spare parts and tools back by the cooler." I squeezed past his knees to the back of the wheelhouse. "Hoses, clamps, fuses. Stuff like that. I don't have a lot here, you really can't plan for everything, but our little stash has come in useful in the past. I've got some screwdrivers, a wrench—the usual."

Ben had gotten up and seemed to be taking a mental inventory of the parts. He picked up a roll of duct tape and smiled. Then, he systematically pawed through the cardboard boxes and a cabinet my dad had built in the corner. "Gas?"

"Tied up behind the wheelhouse outside. I always bring three or four cans, more than enough to get through a full 14-hour day running the genny and the outboard." What he didn't know is, I'd only filled half the containers. I didn't have enough cash for more than that. I depended on today being a decent day, even if I had to be the one who spent the most time under the water.

"I've got sandwiches and drinks in here." I opened the cooler.

He nodded.

I turned over the plan in my mind. Earlier I'd envisioned myself being the first to dive. I knew what I was doing down there. Ben was brand new and had no clue about dredging. But I wasn't so certain this was a good plan after the dust up with Nate. Maybe I should stay top side and keep an eye on the sluice box. I needed every grain of gold dust I could find. And what did I know about Ben anyway? Not much.

"You're going to be diving first." There. I'd done it. Changed my plans at the last minute. I had no idea if Ben even knew how to find gold, much less dive in Bering Sea conditions. "What kind of experience do you have again?" I realized I hadn't even asked last night. I'd just been happy to find anyone willing to dive for me.

"I was a Navy Diver for eight years. Pretty much done it all—salvage, rescue, maintenance."

"Military. I think Dave mentioned something about that." I hoped he'd open up a bit about his past. Help me gauge his trustworthiness.

"Dave?"

"The pilot." I stepped out onto the deck. "You flew in from…?" I sent out my bait, hoping he'd bite.

"Right. You mentioned him."

Hm. Guess he wasn't interested in talking much. "All right. "We've got some pretty important pieces of equipment up here. When you're working top side, your responsibility includes taking care of the air compressor—we don't use pressurized tanks, since we only dive about 10 or 15 feet down at the most. Sometimes 20. We use an air hose and a compressor to keep the air flowing to you under water."

Not sure if he knew that's how we did our diving out here, but in this day and age he could find pretty much anything online. I hoped he had an interest to find out a little bit about what he was getting into before he flew up here from God knows where.

"Then there's the hot water. We pump hot water into your suit so you don't freeze to death. The water out there, even in summer, is only about forty degrees." I pointed to the exhaust system on the dredge motor. "We use the dredge pump to suck up the water, and this heat exchanger runs water through the mixing tank and into the hose. The hose connects to your suit below. We tape the air hose and the hot water hose to each other, so you don't get a tangle problem."

Ben hovered over the dredge motor to see how it worked. Something else he didn't know. Funny how knowledge leveled the playing field. I might not be his expectation of a gold dredger, but I knew my stuff.

"Have any questions?"

"How do you find the gold?"

I held in a smile. I thought he'd ask about the air lines, the hot water. Of course he'd ask about the gold. He was a newbie after all.

"Oh, yes, I forgot about the most important part, the suction hose." I picked up the 6-inch hose we'd be using to suck up sand, rock and, hopefully, gold down on the ocean floor. "The dredge runs the hose. It's got a lot of force, so you have to be careful and keep your hands away from the mouth." I held up the hose for him to see how large a 6-inch opening actually was. I put my hand inside. "See how easy it is to get stuck?"

He took the hose from me, feeling the heft of it. "Guess that'd make it kind of hard to come back to the surface."

I nodded. More than one diver had died over the years due to accidents with the suction hose.

He handed the hose back.

"What you want to find is what we call cobble. Not just flat sand. Gold won't get trapped in the flat sand. You're looking for rocks and pebbles where the gold can hide, where it gets caught and settles to the bottom." I held the suction hose by the handles on either side. "You're going to grab a hold of the hose and suck up the cobble, move the bigger rocks and then target the stuff underneath. You might even get lucky enough to see some nuggets."

"That'd be nice."

I noticed our distance from shore. "Let me check on our position. You can change into your wetsuit."

"Sure."

His answer carried a waiver of uncertainty.

I grinned at the Beast's ability to have any amount of uncertainty. Didn't seem the type. "You gotta learn some time. Looks like the conditions should be pretty good today—calm water, hopefully clear down there." We both entered the wheelhouse. "You'll be fine."

"Hope I don't disappoint." Ben shucked off his t-shirt and jeans. In his jockey shorts he wrestled his wetsuit out of his pack.

I meant to turn back to the GPS, worry about our position, get us over the gold. My gaze roved over his well-built physique—hard planes of muscle, tanned skin, another tattoo of an anchor on one thigh. I also couldn't help but notice a jagged scar on his muscular back. I gulped. Visions of the Beast making mincemeat out of terrorists overseas during his military stint flashed through my head. Or was there something I didn't know about my newest diver?

CHAPTER THREE

Ben had been down at the bottom about three hours, and I'd barely heard a peep once I'd talked him through the basics of the air line, hot water line and suction hose. "How's it going down there?" I spoke into the handset and attempted some dialogue with Ben. Maybe it was time to check the box to see if any gold sparkled. "Did you find the ridge I mentioned?"

"I think so." Ben's voice over the comms had a garbled quality that was typical with the system. "I think I found that big rock you were talking about."

The last time the *Alaska Darling* had been out on this claim it had not been a good day, although Kyle had admitted they'd been on great gold before the accident. The fear and confusion I'd felt pushed back into my brain. I bit my lip.

Stop. Stop. Stop.

If I didn't think about something else, I'd turn into a blubbering mess. I needed to be strong, tough. As captain of my little vessel I had to focus on the work at hand. No use fretting over things I couldn't change.

"Good." I tamped down my runaway emotions. I took a breath to calm myself and provide some guidance to my new diver. "You should see some ground that looks worked over, disturbed." In my mind's eye I imagined the pile of tailings next to a deep groove in the ocean's floor. A sure indicator of the path of a dredger's hose.

I liked being underwater. Insulated from the noise up top, I could concentrate my energy on guiding the suction hose back and forth through the cobble. Sometimes I could see the flecks of gold in the sand and gravel under my hands. The sun streaked its way through the cold waters of the sound and glinted off the finest gold flakes yards below the surface.

"I think I see some!" Ben's excitement came across the comms.

I jumped off the stool. If we were on the gold it would be the perfect antidote to distract my mind. "Let me check." I dropped the handset and let it dangle from the shelf by its corkscrew cord. I examined the sluice to watch the material Ben sucked up from the ocean floor—pebbles, some sand, a few larger rocks—dump into the box.

"There's a trail here. I'm gonna follow it." Although the generator made quite a bit of noise, Ben's voice managed to reach me out on the deck.

A torrent of sea water poured over the riffles in the tray, which deposited heavier material in the special carpet underneath. Gold was nineteen times heavier than water and more than seven times heavier than dirt. Although it seemed impossible, even the lightest flakes of gold would sink into the carpet.

Frigid water sprayed my face. I wiped the back of my arm across my brow to keep my eyes clear. A few glints of gold winked at me from the box. Relief flooded through my limbs and made them tingle. Although our day had just begun, we had many hours ahead of us to push the bank account well into the black. I felt more like myself—in control of the outcome because I'd stuck to the plan.

Be out on the water as often as you can for as long as you can.

Buck Darling's mantra. He'd repeated it to me my first summer up in Nome. I'd grabbed onto him the minute he'd met me at the airport. I had been all skinny legs and wild hair at twelve, but I had his same green-gray eyes. That's how I knew he was my father. The eyes. He'd given me a big hug, and I'd hugged back twice as hard. I think he liked that. A chortle had erupted from deep inside his lean body when my arms had tightened around him. I had wanted to be loved, and Buck had had no issue with that.

"Got a problem." Ben's voice came over the comms and knocked me out of my thoughts. "I lost suction."

I trotted to the handset. "You probably sucked up a rock, got a jam. Can you knock it loose?"

If a diver wasn't careful, he could easily suck up rocks and debris too large for the hose, causing a clog and blocking the gold from reaching the sluice.

"How?"

He'd have to learn to deal with a clog sooner or later. "Follow the hose, knock it hard every few feet. See if you can jiggle it loose. That usually works."

If the rock wasn't too big, the method I'd described would work and would send the debris up to the surface and into the sluice. A little rough for the sluice box, but nothing detrimental.

"Got it."

Through the receiver, I could hear a muffled, repeated sound that indicated Ben's attempts to fix the problem.

Maybe he'd been down there long enough. A new diver unused to the conditions could get fatigued easily. A diver had to learn how to sway with the tide, while holding onto the suction hose and working the ground. Until underwater dredging became routine, the list of things that could go wrong was enough to overwhelm even the most experienced diver who tried dredging for the first time.

After Ben let fly a few curse words, I decided he'd had enough. "Why don't you come on up? Get a break. Let me do some diving. I can probably fix it."

He agreed.

As I waited for him to surface the wind picked up. The *Alaska Darling* dipped as the waves grew in size. I shrugged it off. We'd be okay. We could handle a little bit of rough seas. I needed results today. Ben had done admirably for his first dive, but I couldn't let on that his pay was in jeopardy or he might split for the next needy dredge once we hit the dock.

Ben, in the short time he'd been in the water, had proven himself to be a fast learner. Although the gold in the box had been minimal, rookie divers had been known to bomb with their first few dives. Ben had an eye for the work. He could turn out to be the avenue to saving the business before I ran out of time.

Other boats who'd clustered around their own gold spots headed in. Some less experienced captains didn't know how to handle the weather change. I'd seen my father hold off on heading to the docks with waves worse than this. We'd be fine.

We had to be.

*

Ben surfaced. He swam to the edge of the dredge. Once he got a grip, he pushed off his diving mask. "I think I found a good streak. But who knows, maybe I was just seeing things."

I gave him a hand to help him onto the deck. "Let me show you the box."

Ben shook out his shaggy hair. Wet strands flapped like a dog after a dunk in the lake. He pulled off his diving mitts and unzipped his suit. "Sorry about the clog."

"Don't worry about it. It happens." I didn't want to tell him it was a typical rookie mistake. He'd done a good job for a first dive, and I didn't want to discourage him. But it did help me suss out his character somewhat. He didn't get frustrated, argue with me, or question my knowledge. Suppose that was the good thing about hiring a diver with no dredge experience and no knowledge regarding the doubts of some about my true capabilities.

He'd peeled back his suit so he was bare chested. Easier to move and, out of the water, a wetsuit could be uncomfortably tight.

The sight of his slick athletic body took a hold of me for a second. I gave myself a mental slap. He might be nice to look at, but I had work to do.

I shut off the water feed to the sluice box. The blockage had completely jammed the hose. I gestured for Ben to come closer so I could show him what he'd found during his few hours under water. "See this here, between the mat fibers? That's gold."

"You're shitting me." He leaned closer to the box. The bits of gold flake twinkled in the summer sun. "Whoa. That's nuts."

Ben's demeanor shifted completely. The hulking Beast I'd seen last night transformed into something different. He broke out in a wide smile. His eyes, which I'd perceived as 'dark' last night, glinted bright blue. For a split second I sensed someone I could maybe see as a friend. A person I could trust out here.

"Yeah, you did all right for a rookie diver."

The gruffness returned. "I'm not a rookie."

I'd only meant it as a joke, but Ben took it seriously. Guess I assumed too much about that smile. Instead of pressing the matter, I moved on. "You think you can run things up top while I dive? The water's starting to get a little rough out here. I want to make sure we go home with plenty of gold in the box before we have to head back."

Ben scanned the small waves causing the dredge to bob about. "Rough? You call this rough?" I would have called what he did a

21

laugh, but to my ears it sounded more derisive than anything. Not worth calling a laugh, more of a critical sound.

I could surmise from his background he'd probably dived under much more dangerous conditions while in the military, but the *Alaska Darling* was a different operation. We weren't out on the water to run a mission with military equipment made for rough-and-tumble operations, we were on my father's dredge—a light, flat-bottomed platform 'boat' of sorts that could be easily swamped when the wind picked up beyond five miles per hour.

"This is my dredge. I know when it's safe and when it's not." In a huff, I ripped off my t-shirt and stepped out of my shorts, stripping down to the faded two-piece bikini I wore under my suit when diving.

Ben glanced away.

I tossed my clothes in the wheelhouse. They landed on the comms system instead of the couch where I'd aimed.

I ducked inside, grabbed the wetsuit I shared with my father, and pulled it over my legs.

Ben followed me. He grabbed my clothes with pincer fingers and tossed them at me. "Yes, I think I can handle things up here." He studied the GPS screen. His blue eyes had turned back to that dark shade I remembered. The door of friendship had closed. He clicked on the handset a few times, and annoying static echoed in the wheelhouse. "What about the blockage?"

I zipped up my suit, grabbed my mask, and headed to the bow where I'd attach myself to the heat and air. "I'll fix it. I've done it a million times." I quickly tied my hair with a rubber band to keep it from getting swept into my face while I worked. "Keep an eye on the fuel levels." I tapped on the generator running my air and heat. "Turn on the sluice when I tell you, and if the waves start cresting over the bow, let me know."

I couldn't read Ben's expression. The glare of the sun obscured my view. I knew he could hear me, though, because we weren't that far away from each other. I climbed down the rusted steps my father reattached to the side of the dredge almost every summer. I'd have to get something new soon, as they'd corroded pretty badly in the last few years. I floated in the cold Bering Sea, spat in my mask to keep it from clouding up, and prepared to dive.

I trusted Ben only slightly more than when I'd found him the night before. I'd have to dive knowing I was the only one who had my back. Sure, Ben would tend the equipment and stay in communications with me, but for the first time since I'd been working on my father's dredge, I had no one who cared about me working up top. Ben only cared because I was a paycheck—a means to an end. Kyle had cared about me when we'd worked together, as would be expected from a boyfriend. My dad for sure cared about me and would baby me a bit, even after I got dive certified.

This would be my very first dive where I'd be truly alone.

I let the water lap against my face. The familiar sting of ice cold salt water hitting my cheeks comforted me in a strange way. Since I was twelve, the dredge and the water had been a second home to me. A place where I'd found refuge from all the hurt and disappointments in my life. My father had cocooned me in Nome even with all of its roughness and dirtiness. I'd been his precious daughter—lost and then found. Something special to take care of. He'd watched over me, held my hand when I'd been afraid, encouraged me when I couldn't screw up the courage myself and, eventually, turned me into his business partner. We'd been a solid team. Our work had been a joy. Even when we weren't finding much gold, I'd loved it. But what young girl cared about money? Not until the accident did I get forced from my cozy place and made to care, made to take responsibility of some kind.

I dove under the choppy waters, and the murky sounds of the ocean enveloped me. I turned inward and ignored the problems waiting for me on the surface. The water covered me up with a quiet rush. I set my worries in the back of my mind while my body took over. Going back to old routines and skills I'd built since I was eighteen. I used the suction hose to pull myself further down and searched for the clog.

About eight feet from the end of the hose I found the problem. I fisted my hands together and beat on it a few times. With the suction turned off, I could feel the rock loosen and slip out of its wedged position. A few more whacks ought to do it.

A good sized rock tumbled out and rolled to one side. With the jam gone, the suction could go back to work.

"Kick on the sluice," I called to Ben. "Got rid of the clog."

"On it."

As I waited for Ben to turn on the sluice and start up the suction, I surveyed his work on the ocean floor. He'd done all right. He wasn't exactly where I'd wanted to be, but at least he hadn't tried to suck up straight sand. We'd had an inexperienced diver or two who never quite learned gold didn't sit in sand, it hid under and around rocks and boulders. Gold was heavy. You had to find places where the gold got trapped. Untouched places. That meant looking for undisturbed cobble and helter-skelter rocks and boulders. If you found a perfect line of cobble, you were most likely working someone's tailings—the stuff a sluice spit back into the water after a dredger had sucked his way through an area and found all the gold. Tailings looked like they had potential if you were inexperienced. But someone who knew what they were doing looked for the undisturbed bottom and stayed away from sandy stretches.

I hauled the hose closer to the area my father had been working last week. He'd been at this for decades. Well before I ever came to Nome. He was a methodical diver with excellent recovery skills. He had a nose for the gold and could clean out an area faster than a man half his age. I'd been chasing his abilities since the very first day I qualified to dive.

I straddled the suction hose, grasped the end by the handles and settled in for a long day of dredging. The choppy water worried me, but what else could I do? I had to make the most of the day. Get as much gold as possible. The huge air ambulance bill I split onto two credit cards would arrive in a matter of weeks. I didn't have time to think about a little bit of weather interfering with my dive.

Ben could handle it.

"Hey, your cell's ringing. Should I pick up?" Ben's voice came across my comms.

My first thought was: the hospital is calling. "Yes." My heart raced. I needed to control my breathing when diving. Steady, slow breaths. Calm thoughts. I focused my sights on the untouched ground in front of me.

"Ok." The mike clicked off.

Maybe I should've told Ben more about my situation, or at least the situation with my father. I didn't even think about phone calls and treatment updates. "Hey, if it's the hospital in Anchorage…" He should take some notes for me or get a person's name or number. I'd heard so little out of them in a week's time. Hard to keep up-to-date when I was 500 miles away.

"It was your sister. She wants you to call her back ASAP. She didn't sound happy."

Crap.

Zoe. My half-sister. She must be back home finally after some work seminar or whatever. I'd left a message with Henry, my stepfather, about Buck. I'd been in a panic. All the words I'd left on his voicemail and then spoken to him when he'd returned my call had come from a place of pure fear. I'd hurt his feelings. Again.

"Okay. Thanks."

Why couldn't I just be left alone to find gold? I wanted maybe one day to go by without drama and tragedy. First, it had been Nate with his threats and odd behavior and now, having to deal with Zoe.

I positioned the suction hose right under a large boulder and cleared away the cobble and bits of sand. Glints of gold twinkled. A stream of gold dust swirled up and into the hose. Far more satisfying to stay down below than deal with the hot tempers flaring above the waves.

CHAPTER FOUR

"Hey," Ben's voice filled my ears. "You told me to let you know if the waves were coming over the bow."

My arms ached from holding the suction hose. I'd been working the bottom for five hours straight. My stomach growled, but I'd ignored it. No telling when conditions might turn. And Ben's update told me I'd made the right decision. "I'm coming up."

I left the hose on the bottom and swam for the dredge. We'd made good progress on the patch of untouched cobble, but I'd noticed the visible gold had been harder and harder to find.

When I surfaced the skies had changed. An additional layer of dark clouds had gathered in the distance. I prayed the incoming storm would blow by overnight and clear us for dredging tomorrow. The chop had grown strong with whitecaps as far as the eye could see. I scanned the horizon—not another dredge in sight. My stomach lurched.

Ben gave me a hand, and I hoisted myself onto the deck. "Thanks." His palm warm against mine. I unzipped my suit, shook off the sensation, and headed straight for the anchor. "Could you pull up the suction hose and shut off the genny?"

"Got it." Ben quickly turned off the generator and hauled up the hose.

He worked as if he'd done it many times before. I couldn't believe how lucky I'd gotten at Ernie's last night. I'd really assumed I'd be attempting a one-man dive today—incredibly dangerous—but in desperate times one took desperate measures. Not only did Ben figure out how to get on the gold, he had some mechanical know-how. That twenty-five percent I'd promised him seemed well worth it in hindsight.

A wave smacked the side of the dredge. I fell against the wheelhouse and barely kept my footing. "Damn it." Seawater flooded the deck. "We've gotta get out of here. Now." I started up the motor while trying to maintain my balance. The wind picked up.

Ben instinctually headed for the controls. "I'm on it!"

The engine roared to life.

"Get us to the jetty. I'll take care of the sluice." The waves might wash out the gold we'd collected all day.

Ben hauled the craft hard to the left to bring her around and headed us toward the safety of the little harbor behind the man-made jetty. "Should I've called you up sooner?"

I quickly removed the riffles from the sluice to get at the carpets underneath. The end of the sluice closest to the edge of the dredge had been washed clean of material. "Shit." I rolled up the mats as quickly as I could and shoved them into the five gallon buckets we used for transport. A hard wave hit from the starboard side, and an empty bucket slid across the deck and into the water. "Goddamn it." I crammed the last mat into an already full bucket and then dragged both into the wheelhouse.

"We lost a bucket," Ben pointed out.

"Don't you think I know that?" I snapped. "It's lost now. We need to get to the dock ASAP. The wind is only making things worse. I should've never left you alone up here."

Ben's face grew mottled. "I've been on this boat for less than a day and you're gonna blame this on me? What about you? How the hell was I supposed to know your crap dredge can't take more than a two-inch wave? Who built this piece of shit anyway?"

I wanted to grab a wrench from my dad's tool box and swing it at him. "I thought Mr. Soldier had it all under control. '*I've got my own gear.*'" I mimicked his deep, gravelly voice. "Guess I thought I was hiring an experienced diver, and I got stuck with a dud."

He gritted his teeth. "I was in the Navy," he ground out. "I'm no grunt. The Army's for people that couldn't hack it anywhere else. Don't insult me."

"Then don't insult *me*. My dad built this dredge with his own two hands and never once did we swamp it. Lucky you, you get to be the first." I picked up one of the heavy buckets and moved it deeper into the wheelhouse to keep it safe. Maybe my decision to hire an unknown, scary-looking stranger had been a huge mistake after all. I went back for the second bucket. The dredge heaved, and I was knocked sideways into Ben, landing in his lap.

He raised up his hands, clearly bewildered by his predicament. "Hey!"

"Oh you love this, I'm sure." I rolled my eyes and disentangled myself. I still wore my wetsuit rolled down half way and a bikini top. "Probably the closest you've been to a woman in a long time, honey."

"Wait, you're a woman? Could've fooled me." A small smile tweaked his lips.

I growled. What a chauvinistic...jerkish...nasty... "Argh!" I stormed out of the wheelhouse to take out my anger on anything I could get my hands on. I thought Nate had been badly behaved last summer. Ben, however, took the cake. How in the hell was I going to work with this horrible, terrible, pig? My few thoughts about his attractiveness made me embarrassed.

I ripped off my wetsuit so violently I slipped on the wet deck. I fell on my ass—hard—but I pretended it was purposeful. I tugged one leg of the wetsuit until I got free. I wouldn't give him the satisfaction of seeing how absolutely livid I was. I wanted to scream at the sky to get rid of all the negative emotion building inside.

So I did.

The noise of the motor masked my words and the strong winds carried them away. I uttered a stream of curses along with some choice adjectives. I had to get along with Ben. I had to find a way. I had no one else. Last night had been the end game for me. Every avenue searched, every possibility tracked down. Ben had been the only person left.

I stayed out on the deck for the rest of the trip back. I needed to burn off steam. The wind cooled my heated face and brought my emotions down to a more reasonable simmer.

Ben managed to steer us around the jetty. I had to give him that. Under these conditions, with no experience on the *Alaska Darling*, it was admirable.

"I'll take over now. Thank you." I stood in the doorway of the wheelhouse. Calm. Cool. Collected. A business woman in charge. I wasn't going to let any of it bother me.

"Sure." Ben stepped away from the wheel. "Feeling better?"

I took the wheel and slowed us down to approach the dock. "Shut up."

"Aye, aye, Captain."

*

Ben and I lugged five-gallon buckets to my dad's truck. The mats were laden with sand, gravel and, I hoped, a decent amount of gold. My hands, chapped from the cold water and biting winds, hurt. I chose to say silent.

When we'd docked, I'd set aside my annoyance and chalked it up to stress. I'd thought for a moment to offer up an apology, but lost the courage. Plus, wouldn't that be typical female behavior? My dad wouldn't have apologized.

Cleaning out the dredge was no simple operation. I'd spend the rest of my evening covered in dirt and grime, but the results were so worth it. Since I needed to build trust with Ben, I wasn't quite ready yet for him to take part in the process. Most divers were present for the clean-up. That way, everyone knew they were being treated fair and square. But for some, after a long day of diving, they wanted to bail and go to the bars or get some sleep before work began the next day. So sometimes the clean-up would be remanded to the captain and one of his more trusted crew.

I'd been cleaning up mats with my dad since I was a kid. At first, it had been Buck and Nate with me as the tagalong. Nate didn't like it, but my dad had insisted. He'd wanted me to learn everything about the 'family business.'

We came up on my dad's truck. "You need a ride somewhere?" My attempt at a truce.

Ben hefted his bucket into the bed and then climbed up to help me load the second bucket in. "Nah, I'm good." He nodded his head in the direction of a beat-up ATV about fifty yards away.

Wonder where he'd gotten that from?

I thought over my next words carefully. "Why don't I take you to breakfast tomorrow?"

My pantry stood nearly empty. Either I'd be eating some frozen peas and Potato Buds in the morning, or I could splurge and get a short stack at the Polar Cafe. Besides, I needed to start things out on the right foot tomorrow. Today had been rough for both of us.

He set the bucket down, stood there for a minute, and looked up at the faded blue sky. "I suppose I could do that."

"I'll pick you up at 5:30." I hoped he understood I'd offered him a white flag. "Where are you staying?"

He landed on the gravel with a bound. "I'll just meet you there."

"All right. It's next door to the Post Office on Front Street."

He wiped his hands together. "Hey, looks like I got some gold." His lips parted.

A few teeny, tiny gold glints twinkled on his sandy hands.

"Keep it." I climbed into the truck. I'd left my window rolled down halfway to keep the interior from heating up and stinking like seaweed and dead fish. An inevitable smell if you were a diver. The scent of the sea—salty, cloying and foul— clung to everything.

"Don't forget to call your sister." Ben gave me a salute and hopped on his ATV.

I'd completely forgotten she'd called in the rush to get the dredge back to shore. "Oh, yeah, thanks."

A stranger to Nome, he must be staying at one of the few motels in town. But where did he get the ATV? A quick purchase after he'd arrived? Seemed a strange thing to do. The piers were about a half mile from the center of town. It'd take ten minutes or less to walk the distance. Why go to all the trouble of getting an ATV?

Ben drove up the road. But instead of taking a right to head back to town, he took a left toward the airport and points unknown.

I waited a few seconds. I wanted to follow him and find out where he went. But I knew if I didn't call Zoe back, it would upset her further to make a second phone call. She'd probably found out about the message I'd left for Henry—I'd been begging for a loan. Thousands of dollars to fly Buck on an emergency medical flight to Anchorage. Henry and I had had it out a few hours later. I'd been rebuffed.

Although I understood my stepfather's stance, Buck wasn't his relative by any stretch of the imagination and had been his wife's lover for a time, I thought Henry's love for me—strained though our relationship might be—would override his feelings about Buck.

I hit Zoe's number on my cell.

"Aurora, I appreciate you calling me back." Zoe's words were cool. Not many people called me 'Aurora.'

"I just got back to the dock a little while ago." I didn't know what else to say. She'd never approved of me staying in Nome after my mom had run off. She thought I'd abandoned Henry—or 'dad' as she would call him. Probably because she had been a young adult, and I had been a child, when our world fell apart.

"So John's in the hospital?" Zoe would never use my father's nickname. I suppose she found it distasteful or maybe a type of disloyalty to Henry. "I'm sorry to hear that. Dad told me."

"Yes, it was a heart attack." The words were hard to say. It made it more real, truer. I bit my lip. "Something went wrong while he was diving." I couldn't bring myself to relay all the details.

"Dangerous work. I'm surprised he'd made it this long without an accident." Zoe's words settled on me like a stone. "So I suppose you had to sell the dredge to pay for the flight."

"No, I managed to scrape the money together, no thanks to Henry." I couldn't help the dig.

"Wow, Aurora, really? You blame Dad for this?"

"I thought possibly he could be a human being for once and help someone in need, but then again, I'm not his real daughter, am I?"

Zoe snorted. "Why did you think Dad would put up his own hard-earned cash to help John? Whatever gave you that idea? It's not his problem. It's not someone he cares about. A man John's age is too old to be chasing some stupid dream of getting rich. Where's the millions, Aurora? Where's all the money and success he promised you?"

We were headed back into an old pattern. Zoe was always quick to remind me that I'd bet on the wrong horse. Steady Henry Pomeroy with his good accounting job, nice retirement account, and paid off three-bedroom house. I'd turned away from him and decided to take up with my biological father—someone I barely knew—to chase some idiotic dream about finding gold.

My muscles felt weak. I could've gotten all worked up like I usually did. But I wasn't up to it today. "Why did you call me?"

"What?"

I'd taken her off guard. "Why did you call me? Did you actually have something to say, or was this all about 'I told you so'?"

Zoe let out a long rush of air before answering. "You really hurt Dad's feelings. I thought you should know."

"Great. Thanks." I wanted to hit the red button on my phone and hang up on her.

"He loves you, Aurora." Her tone quieted. "He wants you to come home. When he saw you calling last week, he thought you wanted to talk to him. After last year—well, it got his hopes up."

Henry had had his hopes up ever since I'd told him at twelve I wanted to stay in Nome. I don't know why he wanted me around so badly. I'm sure I only reminded him how my mother had treated him. How she'd never been serious about their marriage or being a parent or any of it. He'd been used.

"I *am* home, Zoe. Maybe one day the two of you will understand that." I ended the call. I had nothing more to say. In my time of need my 'family' had let me down. That's all I needed to know. I might be in debt up to my ears, but I was going to succeed. If Buck had taught me one thing, it was to keep a positive attitude. When things looked the worst, that's when you found that streak of gold under a rock. Never failed.

And this time, I would come out on top, too. I was sure of it.

CHAPTER FIVE

The phone call with Zoe had rattled me. Although I was curious about my diver, I was too tired to do much with it. I hesitated at the intersection. Ben's ATV had kicked up the dust and had disappeared over a rise in the road. Maybe I'd learn more tomorrow when we met for breakfast.

In my rearview mirror I caught sight of a familiar vehicle: Nate's black Jeep. A beat up piece of crap with a huge dent in the hood. He'd had it as long as I could remember. And each year it looked worse and worse.

My instincts told me it wasn't coincidence Nate turned up right behind me. Had he been waiting for me all day? Did he think he could strong arm me into handing over some of my gold? He'd made it clear he thought my father owed him money for his stake in the dredging operation.

When I had been younger, my dad had a habit of calling Nate 'partner,' but he'd never given an indication to me Nate owned any piece of the *Alaska Darling*. Buck had scraped together the funds to build her and maintain her all these years. Nate had been a trusted worker who stuck by my dad through thick and thin. I'd thought they'd work together forever. Until last summer when Nate had turned into something new, meaner, more out of control. The incident on the deck, while my dad had been under water, had been the last straw.

Nate flashed his brights at me.

He wanted me afraid, maybe wanted me to pull over. Another

confrontation on the road side.

Well, I wouldn't stop.

Annoyance boiled over.

I'd be damned if I let Nate bully me.

He must've thought he had a chance to intimidate me with my dad out of the picture and sick in the hospital. He saw me as a sitting duck. He remembered the young girl Buck had brought on board all those years ago. A girl who wanted to please, wanted to earn her keep.

Not anymore.

I kept driving. I gripped the steering wheel to keep my emotions under control. My hands grew sweaty.

Although I wanted to clean up our gold, this new wrinkle made that nearly impossible. Nate knew I had gold on me. His demeanor on the dredge earlier today disturbed me. In his state of mind he might try anything.

I thought about my options. How could I get away from him?

I made a calculated decision and drove past my turn. I'd stop by Kyle's. A stop I didn't want to make, but with Nate on my ass, it might be the safest option.

I checked my mirror. Nate inched closer to my bumper.

Jerk.

I made the last turn to Kyle's. Nate peeled off. He knew where I was headed and didn't want to follow through on whatever threats he had in mind—not with Kyle around anyway.

Coward.

My hands trembled on the steering wheel. I didn't think Nate had scared me, but clearly he had. My mind fired on all cylinders. I needed a drink.

Kyle lived in a Quonset hut on the east side of town. It had been some gold dredger's winter storage place. The previous owner had converted some of it into a live-in with a small kitchen, a rudimentary bathroom with a shower right out in the open, and a small loft for a bed. Kyle rented it from the owner who'd retired from gold dredging and had settled in a retirement village in Florida.

Although my father had his own clean up equipment, he'd stored it all at Kyle's place for the last couple of years. Kyle had a better spot for doing clean-up work, and, besides, I'd been living on-and-off with him. After our break-up I had yet to pick up everything. If I took the equipment back to the apartment, I'd have to store it inside and then haul it out every time I wanted to use it. A big pain in the butt. I hadn't left things all that great between us. In fact, I'd accused him of wanting to kill my father. Probably not the best way to break things off.

I'd moved out last week. The same day my father had been loaded on an emergency medical flight to the hospital in Anchorage.

Kyle had left me a few messages since then, asking when I'd get the rest of my stuff. I hadn't been sure if he'd meant the clean-up equipment or the odds and ends I'd left behind—or maybe both.

We'd had a few fights in the past. I'd quit him before, running off to my father's place to cool off and think things through. But this time had been different. I'd been, well, meaner. Said some things Kyle probably didn't deserve. I'd made a huge mess of it all.

Kyle's little gray Toyota pickup sat out front. I'd heard another dredge snatched him up after our falling out. He was employed within hours of my impetuous firing.

My treatment of Kyle would likely embarrass my father if he knew. As if Kyle were no better than any of the other gold dredgers in town. A diver with a dream. Just one of many.

Kyle had been different, though. He'd been smart, adventurous and driven when my father met him. He'd been a commercial diver in Louisiana and heard a good diver could make big money in Alaska. He'd bailed on his boring 9-to-5 job and took on the feast-or-famine life in Nome. I'd heard something about a family connection to Nome, but we'd never talked about it.

My father should've known I'd fall for Kyle. He had all the makings of my perfect boyfriend: He could dive, he looked good in a wetsuit, he didn't mind my rambling mouth, and he didn't treat me like a girl. That last one had been very important to me at the time.

I knocked on the faded green door, but kept an eye on the road behind me in case Nate changed his mind.

"Kyle, it's me." I had no idea what I'd say to him. Nerves gathered in my stomach like sour bile. "I've got some clean-up work to do. Was hoping I could use the equipment."

I knocked one more time.

Maybe he'd decided to walk to one of the bars in town.

No answer.

My heartbeat slowed. Maybe I wouldn't have to confront him after all. I had a key, but it seemed wrong to let myself in without Kyle knowing. I pulled out my phone and texted him about my plans.

There. Guilt alleviated.

I put my key in the lock.

The dark, warm interior enveloped me. A bit stuffy. I could smell Kyle had burned some bacon earlier. In the small kitchenette at the back of the place, greased-stained paper towels rested on the counter. He hadn't even bothered to set them on a plate before he'd dumped out his bacon. I broke off a piece of the remaining bacon strip—the unburned end—I was hungry.

Not bad.

Under the kitchen counter I found a few plastic grocery store bags. When I saw something of mine, I chucked it into a bag. I'd rather get as much as I could now, then arrange with Kyle a time to stop by for anything I'd forgotten.

My phone beeped. Kyle had texted me back.

I'll be there in fifteen minutes.

Shit.

I skipped around the living spaces, grabbing clothes, shoes, hair products, and other random items one brings over to a boyfriend's place when she sort of moves in. I also grabbed a couple of things I identified as my father's from the dredge: a tool box, a cardboard box full of replacement parts, and a few moth-eaten wool blankets that came in handy on the colder dredging days.

I climbed into the sleeping loft. I couldn't help but make the bed. That had been my ritual every morning. Made me feel more like a good girlfriend. Heaven knows I hadn't been a good housekeeper, but at least I could make a bed. As I shook out the sheets a book fell to the floor: *Seven Signs You Should Break Up.*

I'd never seen the book before. Although I suppose one wouldn't put such a book out in public view while the object of said break up is present. I paused. Before my blow up last week, I didn't think anything had been wrong with our relationship. And, besides, I didn't think of Kyle as the type of man who would take advice from a self-help book.

I laughed, picked it up, and set it on his makeshift nightstand— a stack of milk crates with a piece of broken plywood as the top and a battery-powered lantern acting as a lamp.

I sat on the bed for a minute. This had been my view most

mornings for the past eighteen months. A great view of the whole hut. Near the front, a broken down speedboat sat, all its guts spilled out on the concrete floor. A project Kyle had started before I'd arrived and still hadn't finished. In fact, it looked identical to the day I'd moved in. One large rolling tool chest stood next to the boat, and several small toolboxes spread around it like children following a parent. A couple of garbage cans were near the side door opposite the kitchenette. Too risky to keep trash cans outside. I'd cleaned up enough animal-strewn garbage—either wild or semi-tame animals—to refrain from complaining about the stink of garbage when the cans were full and no time could be found to take them to the dump. A set of metal shelves ran from floor to curved ceiling next to the garbage cans and were filled with cardboard boxes, books, electronic parts, diving gear, industrial size containers of cereal and other dry goods. Cheaper to buy in bulk when you received the annual PFD—Alaska's Permanent Fund Dividend. Kyle had qualified for his first PFD this year, and he'd celebrated by buying corn flakes and canned beans in quantity.

For a long time, I'd really thought he'd been perfect. We'd been such a good diver/tender team. Seemed natural that we'd go from teaming up on the dredge to teaming up in bed. I'd been naive to think that was all it took to make a relationship work—teamwork. The quick dissolution of everything in a matter of hours, in the middle of a crisis, taught me a lot about what makes for a good relationship.

Oddly, I hadn't cried many tears over the break up. Maybe I'd been in shock. Maybe I'd still been dealing with my father's accident. Or maybe I was just a cold bitch—that's what Kyle had called me that night. "You are one cold bitch, Rory."

He'd said that right after my father's emergency flight had taken off.

Those words hurt. They were familiar words. But not words spoken to me. Words I never thought I'd hear used against me. I'd done everything—or so I'd thought—to avoid anyone accusing me of being cold or unfeeling.

I climbed down and carried my full grocery bags to the truck. Then, I made a couple more trips with my father's stuff. I set it on the floorboards in front of the passenger seat just as Kyle came walking up the road. He wore the Coors Light ball cap that he only took off when diving.

I took a breath and steeled myself for whatever he was going to sling at me.

*

"Never did ask you for my key back." Kyle, rangy and wearing a t-shirt and jeans, carried a six pack and a loaf of bread.

From where I stood I couldn't read his expression. His words came out clipped, monotone.

"Help me load my dad's equipment in the truck, and I'll give it to you." I'd been hoping to clean my concentrates here at the hut and move the equipment another day, but Kyle had derailed that plan.

He headed toward the door and eyed the back of my truck. I knew he saw the gold buckets in there. "Need to do a clean-up?"

"I can handle it." I slammed the truck door and leaned against it. He knew better than to poke the bear.

He leaned over the edge and checked out my haul. "Did I offer to help?"

"You were going to."

He turned his hat around backward. A habit of his when he was ready for a verbal battle. "You don't know me very well, then."

I bristled. Those were the same words he'd used when I'd heard the story about my dad. I didn't need his crap right now. I had debts to pay. "So are you going to help me load the spiral machine and the trommel in the back or what?" I'd lug it and load it in the truck myself if I had to, but I hoped Kyle would be decent. No matter how we'd left things the last time I saw him.

He squinted. "I heard you found a new diver."

Word traveled fast in Nome. "Yep."

"He any good? Heard he was green."

"Why do you care?"

He raised his hands in a mock surrender. "Just a question. No need to get all mad."

"I'm not mad." But Kyle knew me better. He'd ruined my plans to sneak in and sneak out. He knew it, too. He'd probably seen me load my stuff into the cab of the truck.

"So, it must be some crap material, huh? That sucks."

"Kyle, I don't want to fight with you. I've got enough on my plate. We both said some nasty stuff last week. Can we bury the hatchet for one night?" I wanted to clean up the concentrates, get home and get some sleep. Either I'd be doing it behind the apartment complex as the night got cooler and the rowdy types spilled out of the bars, or I could make nice with Kyle. "Would you let me do the clean-up here tonight? I can come get everything another day."

Silence settled between us. In the distance a motorcycle revved down the street.

He shrugged. "Whatever."

"Thanks."

Without a word, Kyle climbed into the back and handed me a bucket. I lugged it to the door. Kyle followed behind me with the other one.

We had a truce for now. Maybe he felt sorry for me. More than likely he was thinking of my father. Everyone loved Buck.

I was a harder person to love.

*

I stood over the propane powered stove and dried off the gold flakes and small nuggets we'd separated from the sand and dirt.

Kyle cracked open a beer. "I know why you came over here tonight."

"Oh?" Clean gold shined prettily in the cheap dollar store pan. I never tired seeing the end result of even the worst day out on the water. I stirred my finger through it.

"A booty call."

"What?" I almost burst out laughing. "I'm not your girlfriend anymore."

"So?"

"You think pretty highly of yourself." I kept my eyes on the gold. "No, I didn't come here for sex. I'm came here for my stuff. It's in my truck, Kyle."

"Why else would you show up when you thought I was home?"

He did have a point. His truck had been outside the Quonset hut when I'd arrived. I couldn't have known he'd walked to the store. It did look rather suspicious. "I needed my equipment. That's the only reason I stopped by."

He sighed and shrugged. "If you say so. I'm gonna shower and then make a sandwich. You hungry?"

Kyle stripped off his shirt, dotted with sand and other debris, and then unzipped his jeans.

I blushed. "Hey." We were over, done, kaput. What was he thinking?

Kyle had a lean, slick body. Not a hair on his chest anywhere. My gaze swept over his bare upper torso. "Keep your pants on, please." A very distinct memory of our last sexual encounter flashed through my mind.

"What difference does it make?" He headed to the free standing shower beyond my view. "You need to get over yourself, Rory."

I wanted to tell him off. He'd been the one to ruin things. Not me.

I turned my focus back to the task at hand. Wasn't worth the emotional effort to get so upset. If Kyle wanted to make a fool himself by strutting naked in front of me, then I should've let him do it. It would've been more humiliating for him to see I felt absolutely nothing. We were over. Done. Period.

The last of the moisture dried up in the pan, leaving pure yellow gold. I turned off the stove and set the pan aside to let the contents cool. Judging by experience, it couldn't be more than three ounces. After expenses and paying Ben his 25% that'd leave me with an okay chunk to put toward some debt and still be able to run the dredge. My heart sank a little. I had a running tally in my head that had haunted me for the last week. This had been my first opportunity to get back on the water, and I'd been hoping for a lot better.

But what could I expect from a two-person team and one half of that team never having dredged before?

Kyle whistled in the shower.

For a moment I considered asking Kyle to come back to the *Alaska Darling*. I'd been upset when I'd found out about my father's accident. But maybe I'd been hasty. Kyle had been a good diver. He'd learned quickly and had become a reliable gold hound. I doubted I had time to teach Ben enough before the summer gold season ended.

My relationship with Kyle was over, but maybe I could salvage our professional relationship. He'd just helped me clean up without asking for a thing. Somewhere in there he still cared.

The gold had cooled enough that I could pour it into a mason jar. I took an old newspaper, rolled it into a funnel and then carefully poured every speck into the jar.

I could've had twice as much gold if Kyle had been with me today.

The shower shut off.

"Hey, Rory, can you bring me a towel?"

I quirked a smile. Same old Kyle.

I left the jar on the kitchen table and grabbed a towel from the laundry basket. "Heads up." I tossed it over the shower curtain.

CHAPTER SIX

One would be hard pressed to find a tourist in Nome, Alaska. After more than a hundred and fifty years since the town had been first established, it hadn't changed much. Gold seekers had lined the beaches sluicing for any ounce of gold they could find. They'd braved the wind, cold, rain and snow to eke out a living in the unforgiving landscape. The canvas tents, which had lined the beaches, gave way over the decades to rough-hewn storefronts, saloons and hotels to house the ever-growing population of gold miners, native Alaskans and missionaries. But even with the dawn of more advanced techniques and the modernization of gold recovery, the character of Nome remained rough, bleak and indifferent.

I shivered as I got out of my truck. Even in the middle of July, Nome didn't get much above 60 degrees on the hottest of days. Mostly we were stuck in the mid-50s. Sure, everyone adapted to the climate after about a year, but I hadn't felt what I'd call 'hot' since I left Washington State.

At 5:30 in the morning, a chill wind blew from the shore covering my arms in goosebumps. I grabbed my hooded rain jacket, one of the items I'd recovered from Kyle's place, and headed into the Polar Cafe.

A few older miners at the tiny counter drank coffee and gassed up for a day on the water. A couple of cops, likely eating breakfast before their shift, sat in the corner. I recognized one as Mr. Isaacs, the father of a former school friend. I waved and smiled. He nodded in recognition.

Like most diners in Nome, the decor left something to be desired. It was a boxy space with local art hanging on beige walls, which ranged from simplistic to surprisingly good. Even a small town like Nome had its artists. The tables and chairs were the folding type. At least the seats were padded. Every time I ate here, I felt as if I were in a church basement sitting down for a potluck. A mishmash of new and stained tiles made up the ceiling, and a dingy ceiling fan gave out most of the light.

"Hey, stranger!" Stella, my closest female friend, waved at me from the ordering station tucked up next to the kitchen's swinging door. "Take a seat. I'll be with you in a minute."

She rung up the two grizzled figures with beards, overalls and dirty boots. Hard to tell if they were dredge miners or placer miners. We had both in Nome.

Ben sat by the window at a 4-person table. He perused the paper menu and hadn't noticed me yet.

I took a chair across from him. "Hey."

He looked up. "Good morning." He frowned and pointed. "Can't believe the prices."

"Well, then, you're lucky I'm buying." I set a plastic container filled with an ounce-and-a-quarter of gold on the table. "I owe you something. After expenses, of course." Didn't seem like much to the average person, but it was worth close to fifteen hundred bucks.

Ben scooped it up. "We did this?" He twirled the tube between his fingers. The gold shifted in the container like sand in a snow globe. His astonishment reminded me of his reaction to the gold in the sluice yesterday—a child-like wonder.

Before I could answer, Stella approached our table.

My best friend, her dark, curly hair tightly bound in a ponytail at the back of her neck, tapped a pencil against her order pad. "You and—*your friend*—ready to order, Rory?" Stella did her best to compel me to identify the stranger with me.

"Ben Abel, this is Stella Hansen. Stella, this is Ben, my new diver."

Ben's mouth curved up in a slight smile. He reached out a hand. "Hello."

Stella blushed and shook his hand. "Hello, *Ben*." She held it a few too many seconds more than necessary. "Do you know what you want? I'd recommend the reindeer sausage. Really good. Right, Rory?"

A funny feeling settled in me. Maybe it was the genuine smile Ben gave to my oldest and dearest friend, but had yet to give to me. I shook it off. I was being ridiculous. Who cared what the Beast thought of me or my friend? "I'll take the House Special with pancakes and bacon." I'm sure my order signaled to Ben how I felt about reindeer sausage.

"Sausage and Cheese Omelet." Ben handed Stella the menu with a twinkle in his eye.

A goddamn twinkle.

"You got it." Stella grabbed both menus and gave a toothy grin. "Coffee?"

"Please," I said.

Stella raised a brow. I knew what that meant, girl code for: *you need to tell me everything about this guy.* She took off at a clip to enter our order.

"She's friendly." Ben remarked.

"Yes, she sure is." My words came out laced with a bitterness I didn't intend. To cover for it, I pulled a piece of notepaper out of my pocket and flattened it with my fingers. "Here's the totals from last night with the expenses laid out, so you can see."

Ben looked it over.

"Usually I pay in a check or cash, but I wanted to make sure you got paid for your first day. I know you just got here. Wasn't sure what your situation was. The assayers don't open until 9. If the weather's good I hate to waste time in their office trading gold for cash. But I can show you how to do that, if you'd like." I put out my hand for the vial.

I scanned his face. Although he'd given Stella a smile, he had mostly an unreadable expression on his face. Dark, maybe. He hadn't caused me any trouble yesterday—except for not knowing when the chop was too strong for the dredge, a newbie mistake. He'd done well for a first-time diver.

"Gas is pretty pricey up here." He read through the expenses list. Mostly fuel and a few spare parts I'd added to the pile of what we had on board. Lunch had been on me.

"Did you drive past the Bonanza Express off Seppala when you came into town?" Seppala Drive would've been his route this morning, if he'd stayed somewhere east of town last night. "Gas is more than six dollars a gallon."

Ben nodded. He didn't confirm whether or not he'd come into

town. "Looks good to me." He handed me the slip of paper and held up the tube of gold. "This is fine."

"Eventually, I'd like your help with the clean-up." Kyle had packed up all the equipment in my truck last night after we'd cleaned all the concentrates. I wouldn't be relying on him anymore to help. It had been an unspoken moment between the two of us last night. Our relationship, not on great footing to begin with, had been irrevocably damaged by last week's events. If I had to sit out back behind the apartment complex and refine the concentrates in a more public setting, I'd feel better having the Beast on guard with me. "Most divers like to be involved so they can keep an eye on the totals."

"Makes sense."

Stella arrived with a pot of coffee. "I know you take it black, Rory. Ben, how do you like your coffee?" She flipped over the mugs and poured steaming coffee into each.

He grabbed two packets of sugar from the little bowl by the window. "Been trying to cut back on the sugar, but can't seem to keep it out of my coffee. Tastes like dirt without it." Ben glanced across the table.

His hooded gaze penetrated me. Those eyes of his. Brightest of blue one moment, black the next. I took a long sip of my very black, very strong coffee. I shivered, but brushed it off as a reaction to the hot coffee entering my slightly chilled body.

"You don't look like you need to worry about sugar." Stella's gaze roved over Ben's muscular build.

Ben said nothing, ripped open both sugar packets simultaneously and dumped them into his coffee. I could feel the weight of his gaze on me. Something about this man made me want to run away. Yet, on the dredge he'd been nothing but helpful. Sure, he'd gotten my dander up, but nothing worrisome. And, besides, the whole thing hadn't really been his fault.

"He'll burn it off today out in the Bering." I wanted to lighten the mood. I didn't like how he made me feel exposed with just a look. I needed to remind myself I was the one in charge here.

"Order up." The cook called from the window between the dining room and the kitchen.

"Probably yours." Stella left us and went to pick up the plates of food steaming in the pass-through window.

The silence that settled between us unnerved me. Ben drank his coffee, stared out the window and watched as beat up trucks and ATVs drove past. In the summer, if you weren't a hard core bar fly, you got up early. Got to the docks. Got out on the water before the weather could turn sour. The water tended to be calmer in the early morning.

"So, gold dredging," Ben said. "Doesn't seem like every little girl's dream job. How'd you end up doing that kind of work?" He slowly stirred his coffee.

"My father, Buck. I moved up here when I was twelve." I shrugged. Everyone in town knew my story. Wasn't often anyone asked me about my past. "That's what he did for a living. So his thing became my thing."

He took another sip of coffee. "And your mom? What's she do?"

My insides chilled. No one—*no one*—asked about my mother. "I've got no idea. She skipped out on me when I was a kid."

"Oh." Ben's voice quieted. "That's kind of a raw deal."

"She wasn't much of a mom." My new employee didn't need to know the sordid details of my sad childhood. I didn't share much even with people who had known me for years. "I'm good with it."

"But you've got a sister. Zoe?"

A beat up van drove past. Nome was starting to wake up.

"We're not very close. She's quite a bit older than me."

He nodded. "So just you and your dad then?"

"Yep. The two of us against the world."

"Sorry he's not well." His expression turned pensive. "I lost my grandfather not too long ago. He'd been sick a long time. Hurts to see someone you love in pain and not be able to fix it."

I felt the tears welling up.

God, I didn't want to look like a weak, blubbering baby in front of him. "He should be waking up any day. The doctor's very hopeful."

Stella handed our plates to us. "Be careful. They're hot." She placed silverware rolled in paper napkins next to each of our orders. "Anyone need ketchup, hot sauce…?"

Ben shook his head.

I took the opportunity to dab at my eyes.

I didn't want to talk more about my life, my past, my father. I'd been doing my best to tread water in the whirlpool I'd found myself in. "So what's with the scar?" I couldn't help myself. Instead of asking something normal, I went for the biggest question in my head. "War wound?"

His gaze settled back on me. His eyes hollowed out, and his face paled ever so slightly.

His eyes begged me to take it back.

*

I was grateful Ben had his own vehicle to get to the docks. Spending more time with him in silence would have been difficult. I couldn't believe what an idiot I had been in the cafe. I knew he was military. We were still at war with Afghanistan. I had no idea what he'd seen or done, what kinds of assignments he'd been given. If any of his buddies had been wounded or killed.

Idiot. Idiot. Idiot.

I rested my head on the steering wheel for a few minutes.

I knew what it was like to have secrets you didn't want to share. Wounds you didn't want to discuss. But yet I plunged right in without thinking to get the focus off of me. What a mistake. I hoped we could work together without awkwardness.

My phone blinged. I had a text from Stella.

Ben sure is cute.

Not really in the mood for girl talk I sent her back an emoticon—eye roll emoji:

😑

We could discuss the finer points of my new diver's attractiveness at a later date.

I'd paid the cafe tab out of the couple hundred in cash Kyle had traded me for a 1/4 ounce last night. Some of the gold I'd given him was in payment for helping me with the clean out, even though he hadn't asked for compensation. Seemed the right thing to do. The rest I'd traded for whatever cash he could spare. The assayers office was only open daytime hours, and I intended to be on the water as late as possible today. Surely, there would be a day soon with bad weather or crap conditions for diving, and I could turn in all of my gold and get some money in the bank.

With a credit card payment coming up soon and rent due in a few days, I'd have to find some time to get my butt there. Luckily, the gas station in town knew my father and was willing to trade gas for gold. Probably didn't get the best exchange rate, but beggars couldn't be choosers.

I followed Ben's ATV to the docks. Fog hovered over the water. The air was still, the waves nonexistent. Another stellar day for dredging. Several boats had beaten us to the punch, but from where I stood I couldn't tell if any were in our spot. The gold had been good yesterday. My dad had been right. Some untouched areas still remained in the public mining area with good gold—maybe even the mother lode he believed was out there. My father always had a knack for it. Better than any other dredger I knew.

I wouldn't be surprised if Kyle passed along the news of my success to the new outfit he worked for. I'd forgotten to ask who'd taken him on. Maybe the *Goldfinger*, Jerry Sterling's dredge. I'd heard they were short a diver. All Kyle had to do was point out my dredge on the water, and they could do the rest. I didn't own a lease. I had no right to the discovery. Every man for himself out here.

Ben and I would need to move quickly to do some uninterrupted diving and set the boundaries. Dredging in the public areas could turn into a dangerous mad house if someone thought another dredger had found a good streak. Although the rules stipulated dredges must stay 75 feet away from each other, not everyone followed them—especially under water. However, establishing your own spot was part of the game.

I parked in the gravel. I half expected Nate to show up. My nerves were a bit on edge after yesterday morning's strange encounter and my suspicions that he'd followed me last night to rattle me. But I shook it off. Nate was nowhere to be seen. Maybe he'd gotten over whatever it was that had set him off.

Ben retrieved the refilled gas cans from the back of my truck. It impressed me he thought to do it without my direction. He paid attention.

I grabbed the empty buckets.

"What's this?" Ben looked under a tarp in my truck bed.

"A trommel and some other equipment."

He nodded and dropped the tarp.

"I'm sorry." I couldn't hold it in anymore.

"What?"

"Back there. At the cafe." I had a hard time meeting his gaze. "It was none of my business to ask about your scar."

"I came to Nome to get away from bad memories, but I guess

I'm finding out I can't run away from them." He put the strap of his duffel bag across his chest, full of diving gear. "It's part of who I am."

"A lot of people come to Alaska for some of the same reasons."

We headed to the dock. I had the buckets, he hefted the gas cans.

"Makes sense," Ben said. "On a map it looks so far away."

"Nome ends up as a last stop for some."

"Was it a last stop for you?" he asked quietly, as if he were testing the waters.

No one had ever asked me before about my decision to stay in Nome. "Of a sort."

"Sounds like you've got your own memories you want to forget."

"Doesn't everyone?" I set down the buckets.

Ben put the gas cans next to the other ones on the deck. "I suppose so."

Strangely, it felt as if we had worked together for years. Seamlessly, he joined my struggling operation and fit right in. I wasn't particularly easy to get to know. I didn't have many friends. Only God knew why Stella had stuck by me through thick and thin, fights and tears.

"Anyway, it was none of my business," I said. "I won't ask questions like that anymore. Promise." For some reason I needed more from Ben. A recognition that things were square, that I hadn't set up a block between us. I'd pushed away enough people. I needed him until the season ended. I knew how it worked. Someone shrugged when really they harbored all kinds of ill feelings toward you that bubbled up to the surface at some point, and eventually bit you in the ass. Not this time.

"I'm over it. Really."

"Ok."

We loaded our gear. He checked fuel levels in the generator and dredge engine and sloshed gas into the open tank.

In the wheelhouse I put the three peanut butter and jelly sandwiches I'd made at Kyle's place last night into the cooler along with a couple of sodas, a few water bottles and a six-pack of beer with three beers missing. I'd noticed yesterday Ben had dug around in the cooler looking for something else after we'd had a late lunch. Big guy like him probably needed a lot more fuel. He'd eaten every scrap of his mega omelet, and I'd noticed him eyeing my leftover pancake at the cafe.

Across from us, a few dredges motored into the bay. I wondered where were they headed and whether Kyle was on one of those boats. I turned on my GPS. The screen lit up, and the purple dot appeared that I'd set in the system last night. Slightly further south than where we'd started yesterday. We'd follow the trail of gold beneath the waves until it disappeared.

I'd been in charge of the GPS a few seasons after I'd moved to Nome. My father had showed me how it worked: how to find a location, set a point, store it in the memory, so the spot could be found again. That first summer the GPS and the lunch cooler had been my two tasks. I made the sandwiches, ensured they got into the cooler, filled it with enough drinks for everyone. Nate had tolerated me pretty well those first few years. I'd been a goofy kid who took over some of the more mundane jobs he hated. If my father had asked me to do something, I did it with rarely a complaint. Nate liked to order me around when my father was diving, as if I was a private in his own personal army. But I'd done what he'd asked.

I'd wanted nothing more than to be useful to Buck and his partner. I didn't want him to send me back to Seattle. I couldn't go back.

When Henry, my stepfather, had told me the truth—that my mother had run off again and wasn't coming back—he'd had a perpetual hurt look on his face. Wrinkles in his brow. Worry weighing him down like gravity on Jupiter. The gravity there was three times the strength of gravity on earth. And that's just what Henry had looked like—as if he were walking around on Jupiter. The weight of it dragging him down.

Zoe, my half-sister, had believed every word my stepfather had said. My mother was a tramp. She didn't want a family. She'd run off to live free of us. Free of the chains of her children and her husband. She'd done it before, he said. Before I'd been born.

I grabbed a beer before I shut the cooler. It had been my father's rule that no one drank while driving or tending. The beer was reserved as a reward for a job well done. For some reason, I wanted it. Six-fifteen in the morning, and I wanted a beer. Made zero sense, and I knew Buck would disapprove, but I didn't care.

I snapped the top.

Ben looked at me from the foredeck.

I stared right at him as I took my first sip. I don't know why. It was a defiant, childish thing to do. I was the boss. I should be modeling the behavior I wanted on board the dredge.

Ben turned back to his work.

Without Buck around, I was losing it. Had I ever been as confident as I believed? Had I ever been good at doing any of this dredging stuff? Or was it all made up crap by Buck? A surprise daddy who'd been blessed with a gap-toothed 12-year-old when her mother up and split. Maybe he'd felt sorry for me.

I set my beer next to the comms system and headed aft to start the motor. "Let's get moving. The weather report didn't sound too good for this afternoon."

The motor roared to life. Ben finished filling up the equipment and tied the gas can to the others.

I steered us out of the dock area. My gaze focused on my competition. About five dredges had hit the water ahead of us. Most turned north toward a different open mining area. But I didn't let it fool me for a minute. Kyle had seen my gold last night. Either he was the best ex on the earth and would keep it to himself, or he went blabbing. Gold secrets didn't last long in Nome.

"I'll dive first today." I gathered my hair into a quick ponytail, the tie between my teeth. "You think you got it up here?"

Ben sat on the couch behind me. "Not that much to worry about."

"Today might be different. If any of these other dredges get too close, let me know." We hadn't had anyone on our ass yesterday. But, then again, yesterday I was silly Rory, Buck's kid, trying to run a dredge by myself. No surprise the competition didn't see me as a threat. "And keep an eye on those clouds." I pointed to the gray mass gathering on the horizon. "It could mean the wind'll pick up some."

I navigated toward the open water. I'd finished about half the beer. My stomach turned queasy. I slid open the plexiglass window opposite the doorway to the deck. The cool breeze made me shiver. I dumped the remaining contents of the can into the sea. I crunched it and tossed it into a bucket I used as a garbage can.

"Can you take over while I suit up?" I stepped away from the wheel.

"On it." Ben checked our location on the GPS and steered us to the right spot.

I'd left my dive suit drying on the deck, the black neoprene cool to the touch. I stripped off the striped t-shirt and rolled up jeans I'd found at Kyle's. My mind wandered back to last night. I thanked my lucky stars I hadn't taken him up on his offer of sex. That would've been a major mistake.

He was a good guy. He really was. Not bad looking with his lanky, lean body and rock star hair. Physically, it had worked. We both had a love of dredging and diving, but that was pretty much all that we had in common. Our conversations revolved around our work life—diving stories, gold recovery numbers, discussions about new equipment and techniques, debates over the best way to keep one's toes and fingers from freezing when doing ice diving. Our arguments were generally mild and not all that interesting. I suppose most people would be happy to have uninteresting arguments, but I guess I wished for something a little more challenging. Kyle gave up too easily.

After the accident, it had been surprisingly effortless to let go of him. I'd dumped all my fears and anger on him, his actions or inactions, and made that as a reason to leave. But I knew the relationship had been failing for some time. Like all of my relationships had in the past. I used the accident as an excuse to break it off in an obvious way that made sense to most.

Kyle thought we were back to our old games again. Where I'd sleep with him and stay over for a few nights and then go running back to my Dad's place when I felt like it.

Not this time.

I looked out over the dark blue waters of the Bering Sea. I wanted to bury myself in mining, forget about all these problems, these confusing thoughts. Love, hate, fear twisted inside my head making me tired.

CHAPTER SEVEN

The gold streak lay before me like the Yellow Brick Road. I followed it for hours. Not really keeping track of time. My air line was clear, the heated water kept pumping to my suit, and I hadn't gotten a jam in the hose all day. Great dredging. Yesterday's haul had been pretty good. Today's should be even better. I didn't know how long the gold would last, how long I'd have before it ended.

I added up my debts in my head. Buck's flight to Anchorage had totaled thousands of dollars. Shocking, to say the least.

I hadn't been prepared to handle it.

The phone call to Henry had been mostly about processing the cost and figuring out what to do. Instead, it became a conversation about loans and money and was just plain horrible. Henry had been too practical to talk me down out of an emotional flare up. He was a brass tacks person. Facts ruled. Decisions were based on weighing the options, carefully considering the outcomes, choosing the best path.

I'd just wanted to get Buck on a plane to the hospital so he wouldn't die.

Needless to say, Henry and I had clashed on the phone. I'd hung up. In desperation, I had dug into my father's glove compartment and had found his 'emergency' credit card with a $6,000 limit. If this didn't constitute an emergency, I don't know what did. We also had another card with some room on it and $2,000 in the bank: Our profits from the summer dredge season so far after rent, food, and some debts had been paid off.

Buck had looked so pale and helpless when he'd been loaded on the plane. The heart attack had nearly killed him. They'd shocked him back to life at the clinic in Nome, pumped him full of drugs, and then urged me to get him to Anchorage as soon as it could be arranged.

Now I not only faced a huge credit card debt with mega interest, but the hospital had called me about Buck's medical insurance: limited. With a high deductible plan, he had to come up with $25,000 before his insurance would cover anything. For now, the debt was racking up, but the bill would come eventually, and I'd have to be prepared. The whole event would equal a year's worth of earnings.

Zoe had suggested I sell the *Alaska Darling* to cover the debt. It was the one asset Buck owned that had some value. Dredging equipment was not cheap, and in Nome, new miners were eager to invest in a get-rich-quick opportunity. They showed up every summer with big dreams and typically went home poorer than when they arrived. Dredging was not for the faint of heart or the inexperienced.

But the *Alaska Darling* was my legacy. The one thing Buck had been proud of, besides his daughter, and the one thing he'd never let go of, no matter how bleak our financial picture had been over the years. There'd been hard times before when his usually good instincts didn't pan out, but Buck had never considered selling his dredge. Not once.

I lifted rocks and guided my hose under them. I sucked up the sand, gold and gravel underneath. The work was routine after six years of diving. A diver got a feel for what good ground looked like, and this was good ground. The right mix of cobble and larger rock. But letting my mind wander too much could be dangerous.

I noticed my hot water and air lines had twisted around my legs. I'd been following the streak in whichever direction it took me, even if that was in circles. I kicked free. As I did so, I could see in the murky distance another diver and dredge. They appeared to be the correct distance away, but it still didn't make me happy. This could be Kyle's new employer. They might've found the continuation of my hot streak. In another day or two the gold could be played out. Even more divers could show up. They could muscle in on my find.

The urge to work my ass off and get as much of the gold as I could took over. The tide pushed at me. The force of it difficult to work against. It became harder and harder to stay in place and continue following the gold. I knew those clouds, and likely a squall, were drifting in quickly.

"Ben, how's it looking topside? Starting to get rough down here."

Suddenly, breathing grew difficult. My air supply had been cut to a trickle in a matter of seconds. Without thought I gasped and bucked backward, dropping the suction hose to the sea floor.

"Shit." Ben in my ear. His one word to me said everything.

I was in trouble.

Instinct kicked in. My lungs burned as the air ran out. The air had cut off so quickly I hadn't had a chance to get one last breath. I couldn't help but think of my father's accident. With a quick movement, I released my weight belt and headed toward the surface fifteen feet away. Twice the depth of a swimming pool. The water felt like mud around me. Thick, impossible mud. The surface glinted high above, just out of reach.

I was a strong swimmer. I'd played games before with my friends. Swimming across the Snake River in the height of summer. Rapid breathing ahead of time to super saturate the oxygen in the blood. Hyperventilating. Then, I'd swallow a big gob of air into my lungs. I'd dive down, down, down as close to the rocky bottom as I could and kick like an otter, arms along my sides. I'd glide through the cool water to the other side.

This was not like those childhood games. This was real.

I wanted so badly to breathe. A few more feet, and I could surface. The sun bright above me. The white hull of the dredge was visible through the water. The lines tangled around my legs. I imagined for a flash they would drag me back down. As if they were living, breathing creatures who would swirl around me until I'd been bound up and immobilized. Trapped by the lines of air and heat that had been keeping me alive below.

My hands stretched for the surface. My fingertips cleared first.

The pain in my lungs was unbearable. I wanted so badly to take in air where none existed. I wanted to pull off my mask, but knew if I did I'd open my mouth, and the sea would rush in. The cold, cold salt water. Gagging me. Filling me.

I panicked. I flailed. I couldn't kick anymore.

The sun. There it was. Right there. Through the veil of water. I reached for it.

Strong arms wrapped around me. Tugged me to the surface. My mask ripped from my face.

I coughed.

Air filled my lungs.

The rush of oxygen overwhelmed my other senses. I couldn't see, couldn't feel, couldn't hear. I took in lungful after lungful. Over and over and over. Coughing and sputtering between gasps.

A hand held mine. Very tight grip. Squeezing occasionally.

"Rory, can you hear me? Are you all right?" Ben's voice cut through the fog in my head.

I grew limp. My energy sapped. I could barely think much less coherently answer. So I nodded.

I realized I was on the deck. I don't know how I got there. The last I remember Ben had grabbed me out of the water and hauled me to the surface.

How had he gotten me up on the deck?

"Just take it easy." He wiped strands of wet hair off my forehead.

I'd replaced all the hoses after my father's accident in a bit of an emotional haze. For a moment it did cross my mind that maybe I'd messed up, putting my own life at risk.

"The air compressor stalled out," Ben said. "I think a fuse blew. I'm so sorry."

I managed to sit up. A never ending series of coughs took over before I could speak. "That's ok." The air compressor had crapped out once before when Nate still worked for us. Maybe it had been a fuse problem, but I couldn't erase from my mind the possibility I'd missed something. "It's not your fault."

Ben sat back on his haunches. Soaked to the skin and shivering. He'd dived in after me in his t-shirt and jeans. He looked emotionally exhausted. A deep wrinkle set between his brow.

"I'll be all right." I didn't want him to worry. I didn't want to talk about the similarities to my father's accident or think about how close I'd come to giving up. I took deep breaths. "Something like this was bound to happen sooner or later." I coughed some more. My voice sounded weak and strained. "Ask around town. Air compressors going bad, running out of gas, getting tangled in hoses. There's so many things that can go wrong down there."

I wanted to wrap up in a blanket and take a nap. But we were a mile or more from shore, and it would take us some time to get in.

Plus, we were on good gold. Crazy thought after I'd almost drowned, but that was the heart of a miner.

I looked up at the sky. The fog had cleared some. Although the current underneath had grown to a steady ebb and flow and had been difficult to work with, the surface didn't appear too turbulent.

"If you're up for it, there's still time to get some diving in." I unzipped my dive suit to my waist. The cool air on my body was invigorating. It made me feel alive. Exhilarated. Some sort of adrenaline high, I guess, after my harrowing experience.

Ben's teeth chattered. "Hell yes."

"Maybe we should warm you up first."

Ben shrugged out of his shirt and grabbed a beach towel off the bench on deck. "I'm fine."

Yesterday I didn't know what to think about my new diver. He was monster-huge, looked like he belong to a motorcycle gang and barely spoke more than two words to me at a time. But today, Ben saved my life, and I would never doubt him again. After something like that, trust was an automatic.

"I've gotta fix the compressor."

"Let's have some lunch first."

He helped me to my feet, and we both headed into the wheelhouse. Peanut butter and jelly never tasted so good.

*

Ben had done an admirable job his second time out. Although the ocean got a little rough near the end of the day, and we'd have to cut back to shore before I'd planned, I felt good about what we'd accomplished. Oddly, the catastrophe I'd experienced was barely a blip in my brain. All I needed to do was look at the gold in the box, and any fears or remaining bad feelings I had about running out of air 15 feet underwater instantly disappeared.

Ben bobbed to the surface, pushed up his mask and hauled himself onto the dredge before I could even offer a hand. He was so strong. Amazing, really. I still didn't know how he'd managed to get me onto the deck so quickly. Like the speed of light.

"Looks like that other dredge may have wiped it out while I was working on the compressor." Water droplets clung to his beard. He ran a hand over his chin.

"Crap." I'd worried about that. Right before my air cut out, I'd seen that other dredge. A good distance away, but it had been where we were headed. South-southeast.

Once a miner found a streak, she followed it. The worst was not having any streak to follow, because then a miner had to go back to prospecting. Out on the free claims that could be incredibly difficult. These areas had been worked over by amateurs and pros for years. Although a lot of untouched areas remained, they could be hard to find. Usually a miner hoped to find some tailings that were poorly mined by someone without experience.

"You got some other hot spots?" Ben unzipped his wet suit and peeled it back to his waist. He grabbed a towel and roughly dried his mane of hair.

"Not sure. My dad might have some notes somewhere."

"I thought you did this for years?"

My hackles automatically went up. "I have." I didn't want to be irritable, but Ben had hit a soft spot. Most of the dredging community assumed my Dad had been covering for me. The notion had been helped along by Nate who had bad mouthed me after being fired last year. "But my dad had been the one who chose the spots, tracked them, made notes on different places and which ones might be good for exploring."

I don't think Ben even realized he'd set me off with his comment. "Oh, okay."

To smooth it over and keep my diver hungry I added, "He did tell me about the rumors, though."

"Rumors?" Ben sat on the bench.

"About big gold. Lost out there." I gestured at the dark blue-green water. "Nuggets the size of quarters."

"What do you mean, 'lost?'" He looped the damp towel around his neck and held both ends. His attention fully mine.

"My dad used to say an old miner had found a huge pay streak, but he died before anyone could find out where."

He raised his brows. "Like an Alaskan *El Dorado*."

I smiled. "Something like that." My dad loved to tell me all kinds of crazy stories. I never knew which were real and which were for fun. "You ready to head in?"

"Let's do it."

Ben crossed to the port side and pulled in the suction hose and other hoses. Even though he had two days of experience dredging he seemed to know exactly what to do and when to do it. Not sure if he had good instincts or what, but I was happy not to be ordering him around like I'd had to order Kyle. Ben did things without being told.

Kyle, although he'd been a good diver, didn't have a lot of initiative. Drove me nuts sometimes. I'd acted like his mother, carping about this chore or that chore left undone on the dredge before we got back to the docks.

Maybe Ben's attitude came from his military training. They say the military taught people how to work as a team.

I shut off the sluice, the air compressor and the heat exchanger. Ben coiled the hoses into neat piles on the deck. I slid the buckets over to the sluice and removed the riffles that not only trapped the larger gold but held the miner's moss in place beneath. I rolled up the mats and carefully set them into the buckets.

When I finished, Ben grabbed them and carried them into the wheelhouse.

The waves grew stronger and broke across the bow of the dredge. "We'd better get moving before we end up in a repeat of yesterday." I took the wheel and set course for shore.

Ben grabbed a beer out of the cooler, set one next to me on the dash and stood behind me.

I scanned the horizon as we turned toward town. Half the dredges that had been out on the water earlier today had returned to the dock. Smaller dredges couldn't take this kind of chop.

Buck had made the biggest dredge he could afford when I'd been about sixteen. His original dredge had some rot problems and some of the equipment needed total replacement if he'd wanted to mine the next summer. Ice dredging didn't require a dredge, so he'd worked his ass off that winter. He and Nate had taken some risks to ensure he'd have enough to put together a better dredge by June.

I remembered how rickety that original dredge had been. Even a five-mile-an-hour wind had been too much for the original *Alaska Darling* to keep from capsizing.

Some of our competition continued to dredge. It burned me to see that. I knew they were on good gold—our gold. My father might've stayed out another hour or two, but I didn't want to risk it. Ben needed to learn more about safe versus unsafe conditions. He depended on me to make educated decisions based on my experience. I didn't need him rescuing me twice in one day.

"I'd like to teach you about the clean out process." I relished the sharp tang of beer on my tongue. After a long day on the water, it soothed my nerves and relaxed me a bit. "It'll take a few hours' time, but I'll feed you."

I mentally scanned my refrigerator to remember what I might have to whip together as a decent meal. Maybe a block of cheese. Some bread. Possibly a can of peaches. More beer.

"Sounds good. You said this morning it was part of the job, and I want to be able to do my job." His voice rumbled in my ear.

I didn't realize he stood so closely behind me. I could feel the heat of his body on my back. He still wore his rolled down wet suit, the expanse of his muscular chest exposed and radiating warmth.

I straightened my spine. "Not very hard to learn, just time consuming. But then I can pay you your share tonight."

I sensed a loss of heat. Ben had moved toward the open doorway. He braced between the frame and leaned into the wind. "I love that smell. Don't you?" He took in a lungful of sea air.

"You mean the rotting seaweed and bilge water?" Although sometimes the air could be fresher on the water, it usually depended on the breeze. If it blew from shore to ocean, it typically had a foul, dank smell. Like rotten fish or wet tennis shoes.

He laughed. The first time I'd heard him laugh. A rolling deep sound from deep down inside. It rumbled through me. Down to my bones. "Kilgore used to say the same thing."

"Kilgore?" I asked.

"My dive buddy in Dive School. He was from Iowa. Never had seen the ocean in his entire life." Ben faced me. "Seems funny, doesn't it? Some farm boy wanting to be a diver? He knew how to swim. But he'd never been in anything deeper than a swimming pool."

I could see it in my head. A typical American farm boy, probably freckled and tan with a wiry frame developed from years of hefting bags of seed and fertilizer.

"He'd been disappointed when we moved from the pool to the open water. In the pool you can see everything, clear, clean water. Bright lights. Out on the ocean, miles from shore?" He whistled between his teeth, burly arms crossed casually. "You're dealing with oil patches drifting on the surface, decaying seaweed, and then the dark under water." His voice drifted off, as if he was lost in a memory. Ben pointed at the bay in front of us. "This stuff we dive in? Ten, maybe fifteen feet? This is like a training ground for me."

I nodded. Most scuba divers felt that way in Nome. They'd had experience diving down to depths of twenty, thirty, forty feet or more. What we did here was baby stuff to them. The dredging apparatus and the long hours in the cold were the challenge. Especially during ice diving season. Not only did a diver have to deal with the typical dangers inherent in underwater ocean dredging, she had to worry about frozen air lines or getting trapped under a foot or more of ice.

Scuba divers typically had trouble with the tethering, the hoses and lines a dredge diver had to worry about. Both scuba experienced divers and dredge divers had to be cautious about how deep they could operate. A diver could end up with the bends if she weren't careful with her depths. The bends, or decompression sickness, derived from too much nitrogen entering the bloodstream. When a diver got below 15 or 20 feet nitrogen would build up in a diver's tissues. If the diver surfaced without a slow, stepped ascent, the pressure would decrease and the nitrogen, which had dissolved into body tissues, would leave the body. The bends caused blocked blood flow and disrupted blood vessels and nerves. The symptoms of the bends were so mild, it could be hard to tell, at first, what the issue was—tiredness, pain in the joints and muscles, dizziness or confusion. More severe symptoms like paralysis, loss of consciousness, or pulmonary problems could send someone into shock and possibly be fatal. Scuba divers were trained to pay attention when surfacing to avoid the bends, but most dredge divers stayed within the 10 to 12 foot depths that meant a diver didn't have to worry about the nitrogen build up and, therefore, did not train for a regulated ascent.

As we neared the docks, I kept an eye out for the dredge I thought had been operating near ours. The one I was pretty certain Kyle now worked on—the *Goldfinger*. They had also begun to return to shore. I could see the name of the watercraft scripted across its side in bright yellow paint outlined with black. Most dredges headed in now, as the wind had become steadier and the whitecaps taller.

"Ready to tie us up?" I jockeyed for a spot between two older vessels that had left a big enough gap between them for my smaller dredge to slide right in.

"Yup." Ben grabbed one of the lines attached to the dredge on the starboard side and got up on the lip of the dredge, ready to make a leap when we got close enough.

I slowed the motor down to a crawl to avoid a collision.

Ben leapt like an elk from the dredge to the dock. Amazing a man with such a solid, tall frame could jump so gracefully. He whipped the rope around the closest cleats. The dredge bumped gently into the dock, the float tied to the side, which protected both my dredge and the dock. I shut off the motor and headed to the second line attached at the fore and tossed it to him.

As Ben pulled on the line to tie us more securely, other dredgers hauled smaller, lighter boats ashore and set them atop trailers. Inexperienced, young guys who had no money and no sense had put these dredges together. They'd show up every summer with cash in their pockets, likely from selling their car or everything of value they owned, just for a stake in gold fever. Either they'd buy up the leftovers of someone else's broken down dredge or put one together out of plywood and dreams, not realizing their little dredges couldn't make it too far out on the water and were reduced to working only a hundred yards offshore. With undersized motors and weighed down decks full of rusted and broken equipment, they'd never risk going out too far.

The competition out in the public areas had been cramped enough, but closer in to shore, the little dredges fought for any scrap of gravel they could find. Usually tailings from the previous years' dreamers.

I said a quiet prayer thanking God that my father had left me with a good dredge with relatively reliable equipment.

"Hand me the buckets." Ben stood on the dock.

I picked up one heavy bucket at a time and carefully passed them over. I grabbed the trash out of the wheelhouse, locked it with all of our gear inside, and let the *Alaska Darling* have her night's rest before more dredging tomorrow.

I missed where the *Goldfinger* had docked. But why did I care? Our buckets were full, we'd had a productive day. It was inevitable someone was going to find our spot before too long. Kind of sucked it had been Kyle.

Ben headed to my truck laden with two buckets. I carried a third, which I left at the side of my truck. Then, I went toward the dumpster at the other end of the parking lot to dump the trash. When the heavy lid clanged shut, I turned to see Ben engaged in conversation with Kyle.

Red alert.

Not good. Kyle was a decent guy, but I worried about anyone

poaching my diver. Better to keep Ben's skills a secret and make people think he was a typical dredge rookie.

I hustled back to the truck.

"Hey, Kyle." He wore a t-shirt I'd given him a couple of Christmases ago. "See you met Ben here."

Ben set the last of the buckets in the truck bed.

Both men turned my way at the same time. Kyle lanky and thin; Ben monstrously huge and intimidating. An odd emotion rushed through me—something like pride? I was inwardly glad that Ben, scary, muscular Ben, had agreed to be my diver.

"Yeah, he was just telling me about his background a little bit." Kyle knew that would bother me. "Navy diver. Impressive."

Kyle said those last words as if he really wasn't impressed. Not sure what he thought about Ben, but it didn't seem like the usual, relaxed Kyle I knew. He was tense. Defensive, maybe, about being replaced by a stronger, bigger man.

I nodded. Not sure what else to say.

Ben's expression remained blank. His hooded eyes were dark, which reflected the darkening gray skies above.

I wondered if, in the few minutes I'd been gone, my relationship with Kyle had come up. I don't know why I cared if it did, but I did. I squirmed at the thought of Kyle revealing to Ben where I'd been last night. It might appear as if we were still together.

"Looks like it's going to rain." I jangled my truck keys. "We'd better get going."

"Right." Kyle's lips curled up slightly at the corners. He knew I was uncomfortable. "Weather doesn't look too good for the next couple of days. But maybe we both need to spend some time scouting for new ground."

The signal that, yes, Kyle had been aboard the *Goldfinger*, and that the streak we'd been following could possibly be played out. I took my smart phone out of my pocket. "I thought we were supposed to have a few clear days this week." I hadn't looked at the latest weather reports. I swiped to get to my weather app.

"Winds at 25 miles per hour, rain."

My weather app displayed exactly the forecast Kyle described. "Damn it."

"No diving tomorrow?" Ben asked.

I might have been slightly better today at reading his immutable expressions—possibly a bit irritated or disappointed we couldn't go dredging. Maybe if he were clean-shaven I'd have a chance, but with his full beard it made it hard to know if he was angry, sad or bored.

I slipped my phone back into my pocket. "Doesn't look like it."

Kyle nodded. "I'll be at my place tonight, in case you forgot anything, Rory."

Shit. Shit. Shit.

I told myself to keep it cool. "I think I got it all." I patted the tarp. "We're good." I hope that saved me. Maybe Ben would think Kyle's reference was about the equipment he'd seen in the truck.

Kyle laughed. "Gotcha. All right. Just didn't know if you might need something." He winked then, giving a very lascivious feel to the whole thing and left.

Ben stood in silence. I didn't know what he thought of the exchange, maybe I didn't want to know.

"Follow me," I instructed. "We'll head back to my place. No rush on the clean up now, but I can take you to the assayers in the morning, so you can get your gold turned into cash, if you want."

"Sounds good."

Kyle drove off in a wave of dust and gravel.

I was grateful Ben said nothing about Kyle's statements. "I'm in town. Not too far from the Polar Cafe."

"See you there." Ben climbed on his ATV, started it up and waited for me.

CHAPTER EIGHT

Nome had several streets lined with aging, decaying buildings. Most were various shades of brown, tan and gray. Due to the harsh weather conditions during most of the year and the direct pummeling by wind, rain, snow and sea water from the Bering Sea, the exteriors didn't remain in good shape for long.

I pulled up in front of my father's apartment. Ben parked behind me.

We lived on the second floor of an ugly, brown, two-story apartment building with six apartments. My father had rented the place for about a year. We'd started out in a house outside of town. He'd shared it with Nate for a while before I showed up. I had ended up with my own bedroom, and Nate had moved out into the insulated garage space.

When he and Nate had their falling out last summer, we'd moved into the first place available. My father didn't plan things in advance. There'd been the ruckus with Nate, and we'd needed to get out. My dad had moved us into the apartment within days. I hadn't spent much time here, though, as most of my nights I'd spent at Kyle's.

"Come on in." I unlocked Buck's apartment and snapped on the lights.

As one-bedroom apartments go in Nome, it was the typical saltbox boring square—living room and kitchen combo in front, one window next to the door looking out at the street, a bathroom on the same back wall as the bedroom. I slept on the pull-out couch when I stayed here.

Unfortunately, I hadn't bothered to make the bed the last time I'd slept in it. My dirty clothes were strewn across the rumpled sheets and couch cushions lay on the floor.

"Um, let me clean up a little bit." I scooped up the clothes and dumped them in a half-full laundry basket near the bathroom. Then I quickly folded the bed into the couch and replaced the cushions.

Ben handed me the last seat cushion. "You don't need to go to any trouble."

I rushed over to the recliner my father usually sat in and removed an old newspaper and an empty Chinese food container. "This is the best seat in the house." I patted the worn leather. "I'll make us some grilled cheese sandwiches."

I hustled into the cramped kitchen. An L-shape that ran from the bedroom door around the outside corner of the apartment. I grabbed the bread and a frying pan. I started the stove, and then hunted in the fridge for the block of cheese I knew was in there. If I didn't have any other food in the house, I could usually find cheese in the fridge, bread and peanut butter. Sandwiches were mostly what I was good at making. Buck hadn't been much of a cook when I was younger—or even now—so I'd learned out of hunger how to make a few things I liked. Beyond that, I was hopeless.

"That'd be fine." Ben tipped my father's chair back and let out a sigh. "Not bad."

I cut slices of cheese and put some butter into the heating pan. "My dad's." I put two slices of white bread in the pan and topped each slice with the cheese. I was grateful for the company of someone who didn't know my father, didn't ask more questions, didn't wonder about what happened.

I got a beer out of the fridge and offered one to Ben.

He held up his hands as if to receive a football pass.

I threw the can to him underhand.

"Thanks." He popped the tab of the beer. Foam hissed out and leaked over the edge of can into his hands. "Damn." He held the can over the laminate floor. A few flecks of foam landed on the dark planks.

"Here." I tossed him a roll of paper towels.

The roll spooled out as it flew through the air.

He caught the mess of paper towels and ripped off a few from the tail end. "Thanks." He wiped up the mess.

"Sure." I opened a can of beer for myself and leaned back against the counter sipping while the sandwiches fried. I topped them with more bread and turned down the heat so they'd brown and not burn.

"So you said you've been working on the dredge since you were a kid?" Ben balled up the soaked paper towels and set them on the coffee table.

"That's right." I opened the cupboard and took out the second to last can of peaches, opened it, and dumped them into a big cereal bowl with a serving spoon from the dishwasher. "My dad taught me everything I know. About diving, running the dredge…"

"Seems dangerous." Ben took a gulp of beer and ran a hand through his shaggy hair.

"When I was younger I just worked up top." I left the sandwiches frying, scooped up the heap of wet paper towels and dropped them in the kitchen trash. "Didn't start diving until I was, oh, maybe sixteen, seventeen."

"Impressive." Ben said.

"I'm sure your training was a lot more rigorous than mine."

"It had its moments." Ben stripped off his sweatshirt "Is it hot in here?"

The tattoo of the eagle and the flag on his bicep caught my attention. "So you got that when you were in the Navy?"

"What?"

"The tattoo. It's pretty cool."

He nodded. "Yeah, my dive buddy and me. Matching ones." His jaw tensed.

Somehow I'd hit a nerve with a simple question. "Did it hurt?"

He shrugged. "We were both blitzed."

I stepped closer to get a better look at the artwork. "Is it okay…?" I wanted to roll up the sleeve of his t-shirt to get a better look at it.

"Go ahead."

I pushed up his shirt sleeve to expose the whole piece of art. "Wow. This is really well done." I traced along the edge of the eagle, its wings spread wide. It clutched the American flag in its talons.

"Got it in Florida right before we shipped out to Iraq."

Iraq. Interesting new tidbit of information. My mind flicked to the scar and what may have happened to Ben. I pulled away. Too intimate. Too close.

"After we eat, I'll show you how I set up for the clean out," I explained. "We don't have any space in here, so we have to do it out back in the alley. There's a hose back there we can hook up to." Although cleaning up the concentrates outside was not my ideal, I didn't have any other choice tonight.

Ben brushed down his sleeve. Something strange hovered in the air between us.

I returned to the kitchen to flip the sandwiches. Both had a nice golden brown color on them. I added another pat or two of butter to the pan.

Whatever that was—that moment—must've been my imagination working overtime.

Ben joined me in the kitchen. He appeared even bigger in the apartment than he did outside. Maybe because I was used to my dad's size. Buck was only a few inches taller than me—maybe 5'9" or so.

"Jeez, you are one big dude." I handed him a plate and then flipped a hot grilled cheese onto it. "Peaches?" I offered him the bowl. "Hope one sandwich will be enough. I don't think I have enough cheese to make more."

"This is fine." He took a huge bite. The sandwich was half gone. "Gotta fork?"

The peaches slipped around his plate. He set it on the table next to my dad's recliner.

"Here." I handed him one.

I put the other sandwich on my plate, turned off the stove, and scooped peaches. A barstool stood near the kitchen sink. I have no idea why. I didn't remember putting it there. I slid it over and munched my food. "So the first step is going to be moving the equipment from the truck to the alley. Then, we have to clean the concentrates out of the mats, so we have material to run. Then I'll show you how to set up the spiral. That will separate the gold from the black sand."

Ben had finished his sandwich and had moved on to the peaches. Beer and peaches didn't seem the best combination, but he ate and drank them together anyway. "I guess I thought it was more of a one-step process. Seemed like the stuff in the sluice was pretty refined."

"It takes a lot of work to go from sluice concentrates to refined gold." I ate the crusts of my sandwich first, saving the cheesy, crunchy middle for last. I'd eaten grilled cheese that way for as long as I could remember. "But the hard work is definitely the dredging part. The refining is the reward."

"But tomorrow, no dredging?" He'd finished what was likely a meager meal for his body size and set his plate next to his beer.

"Not if this weather doesn't change. Too dangerous." I took out my phone and tapped on it to look at the weather app one more time. I prayed that somehow the weather forecasters had made a mistake and, really, the conditions would be clear and sunny tomorrow. "Nope. Still bad. At least three days of downtime."

"I like to keep busy," Ben explained. "Not good when I have too much time on my hands—to think."

We all had our secrets, didn't we? Things we didn't want to share. Embarrassments. Disappointments. Mistakes. With Ben's military background and time spent in a war zone, I'm sure his history was much worse than mine. He had been kind enough this morning not to press the issue with me about my mother, I offered up the same courtesy to him and let his statement lie with no response.

"Unfortunately, with the weather looking as bad as I think it's going to be, we can't risk going out there." I took both our plates and set them in the half-full sink. If I was going to be living here full-time, I needed to start doing the housekeeping. "But you're more than welcome to meet me in the morning, and we can go to the assayers' office together. I can show you how that part works. Nome might accept gold as payment, but if you want to spend your earnings anywhere else, you'll need cash."

"Sounds good."

"Let me throw on some pants and a sweatshirt, and we'll get going." I glanced over at the sweatshirt he'd left on my father's chair. "You might want to do the same." The change in the weather pattern also meant colder temperatures in the evening. Although a native Nome resident wouldn't think twice about wearing shorts and t-shirts in the middle of summer, I still couldn't handle the evening's drop in temperature when the wind shifted. I paused. "Do you want to borrow one of my dad's jackets? We might be out there for a few hours."

"I'll be fine." His eyes crinkled up at the corners.

I thought he might chuckle at the notion. But just as quickly as the expression appeared on his face, it disappeared.

I snatched some clothes from one of the cardboard boxes I

used as a dresser and slipped them on over my t-shirt and shorts right in the middle of the living room. "All right. Let's get this done."

*

I'd gotten a small bonfire going in the shared fire pit out back. The evening air had a crisp snap to it. Even though it was late July, I could feel autumn racing toward us. Soon enough ice would begin appearing in the Sound, and we'd be racing against the clock to haul in our last gold for the summer season.

After that it would be months before the ice grew thick enough to gear up for ice dredging. These remaining days and weeks of summer were so important to the overall financial picture for my dad and me. The loss of several days of mining due to weather hovered over me like a dark cloud of doom.

I held my hands to the heat of the fire and reined in my scattered and frightening thoughts. I had no time to worry.

Ben had helped me set up the Spiral Wheel Concentrator or, as most miners liked to call it: the Spiral. The main piece of the machine was a green dish-shaped wheel with a spiral of tracks starting on the outside and working toward the middle. In the middle of the wheel was a hole. A small container attached at the back. Gold would accumulate in it as the wheel spun and gravity did its magic. The Spiral sat at a slight angle and, once the water turned on, spun at a slow speed a bit like a water wheel. Gold, being heavier than dirt and sand, remained in the tracks and moved toward the hole in the middle with each turn. The lighter material washed away. At the end of the process, the container would hold all of the gold. I clicked the wheel into place on the stand and then made sure the collection container was securely in place.

We'd beaten our neighbors to the hoses. A split valve existed so we could run two hoses at once and share the water pressure. Out of the six residents of our apartment complex, half of us were dredgers.

I turned on the spigot. The flow coughed a couple of times before the water sprayed into the Spiral as it turned.

"So what next?" Ben appeared eager to learn and understand the process.

Most people I'd worked with over the years showed up for the diving and then sat slack-jawed while my dad and me ran the refining equipment. I appreciated his interest. "Get that first bucket for me,"

70

I instructed.

We'd already rinsed out the mats inside the buckets and now had fine gravel, sand, and gold dust all mixed together that needed to be separated.

"We take a scoop of concentrates." I took a trowel and dug into the bucket. The hose put out a steady stream of water into the Spiral, which spun slowly. I added concentrates a little bit at a time at the top using the trowel. "As the wheel turns, the water flushes the lighter material away, and the gold remains on these tracks." I pointed to the swirl of ridges that made up the wheel. Then, the gold ends up back here."

Ben peeked behind the wheel.

I liked his curiosity.

I added another trowel of gold-filled concentrates. "Watch. As the wheel turns, the heavier materials—like gold—moves around and around traveling to the center of the Spiral." I indicated the catchment box in the back. "The lighter material, like the sand and gravel, get washed away."

Already a stream of tailings ran toward the ditch that drained into the alley. We apartment dwellers had to clean out the ditch occasionally to keep the water flowing away from the clean-up area we'd created. Old piles of tailing surrounded the fire pit area. A lot of times we used the tailings to fill in potholes in the dirt driveway and parking area.

It was hard to believe such a simple contraption could work so well. But these gold panning wheels had been around for a while and were very reliable. Larger versions existed, which the big operations used. They could be fed more material more quickly, but for our purposes, the size of my father's Spiral worked well.

Ben stepped back.

I took a small scoop of concentrated material and let it fall a little bit at a time into the turning wheel. In a matter of seconds, a small line of gold dust was visible, working its way from the outside Spiral riffle to the center hold with each spin of the wheel.

"Well, I'll be darned." Ben peeked in the catchment box. "So weird to think about gold being heavier than rocks."

"Hard to believe a labor-intensive job like this one is connected to the Table of Elements." I remembered learning all of the weights of the various elements in Mr. Begay's class in high school. "Did you ever take chemistry?"

"Probably." Ben laughed. "I wasn't the best student. Football had been much more important to me at the time."

Giving him a sideways glance, I asked, "So you were always this big?"

He shrugged. "I just always was better at physical things than sitting still and learning stuff that didn't seem to matter."

I fed the wheel another trowel of concentrates. "Well, if you were designing gold refining equipment, paying attention in chemistry would've helped."

He smiled. "No doubt."

He had a great smile. I had the urge to tell him so. His smile was so genuine, so pure, it made me want to elicit it more often. He had an easy, relaxed grin with a flash of bright white teeth between full masculine lips. Even though he had a shaggy beard, his smile did not get lost in it. I smiled back. I couldn't help it.

"What's this do?" Ben peeked under the tarp in the bed of my dad's truck.

"That's my dad's trommel. They use that in regular placer mining where you're stuck with a lot more dirt and junk. The beauty of dredging is, you weed out some of the heavier materials right on board the dredge using the sluice."

"Gotcha." He let the tarp fall.

"If we're lucky, we'll have a few nuggets in here." I scooped up another trowel of sand and gold. "Gold dust is great, but nuggets are always a good sign when you do a clean out." I handed him the trowel. "Do you want to try it?"

"Sure." He scooped material into the bottom of the wheel and watched as the machine spun its magic.

The gold dust trail grew wider and longer with each scoop. Ben added more concentrates into the Spiral.

We stood together in the dim light of a mid-summer Alaska evening, enjoying each other's quiet company, watching the gold spin ever higher into the cup, and building a gossamer web of friendship between us.

A shiver ran through me, and I chalked it up to the cooler air and salty sea breeze blowing inland. I inched closer to the fire.

"I gotta take a quick break." Ben said. "Can I get the key to your apartment?"

"Sure." I dug my keys out. "It's a little tricky. If it won't turn, jiggle the knob."

"Got it."

His fingers brushed my palm.

Our gazes met.

"Anyone ever told you your eyes look like the ocean?" Ben asked in a low, quiet voice. "They're so green."

Something dark and secret burned inside me. Something I hadn't expected or wanted. I tamped it down. "Not that I recall." My words came out stiff and unwelcoming.

Ben backed away a few paces and smiled, as if he were happy with my discomfort. "Green as the waves on a cloudy day." He skipped, turned his back and disappeared around the corner of the apartment building.

I mused for a moment. What had that been all about? I surely didn't need a flirtation between me and my new diver with everything I had on my shoulders. But inwardly I was pleased as any normal woman would be. I felt anything but attractive when working the dredge or cleaning up gold. Dirt, grime and the stink of the ocean didn't make a girl feel pretty. But those few words did. And even if Ben had said them to butter me up, I didn't care. I locked them away in the back of my brain and let warmth fill me.

I scooped more gravel and sand. The street out in front of the apartment building grew quiet. Most miners were back home by now and either looking to go out for a drink or settling in for the evening. The sun rode the horizon, still high enough to make it seem closer to mid-afternoon than almost 8 o'clock at night.

A Jeep roared down the alley toward me—one I recognized. My stomach bottomed out. I didn't want to deal with Nate Frazier again. Once had been enough, and the way he'd followed me last night had spooked me. I didn't want to be alone with him. I silently prayed for Ben to hurry back. Then I hoped Nate would drive right past me.

Nate stopped his Jeep, a few feet from my set up, and hopped out. "Looks like you had a good day out there." He scratched his arm and sniffed violently a few times. His scraggly hair under a ball cap looked as if it hadn't been washed in a few days.

I focused on my work. "Maybe." Nate wasn't worth my time. He'd proven to be volatile and unwilling to be reasonable.

I sensed him coming closer too late. He yanked on my arm and forced me to face him. "You think I'm stupid?" His pupils had dilated so much his irises had been reduced to small rings of brown.

I pulled free with a jerk. "Don't touch me, Nate. You don't want to go there." Although I sounded confident to my own ears, inside I felt more like jelly.

He loomed over me. "You owe me. Your father owes me."

"I told you yesterday, I don't owe you anything." I grasped the trowel like a knife, ready to use it if things turned ugly.

"Call up Buck. He knows. That dredge is half mine. I spent more than 20 years working with him." His face twisted into a mask of anger. "Side by side. Even when he couldn't pay me. Even when I had better offers."

Although Nate had always had a short temper, it rose to a level of threat I'd never seen. The rumor about Lola Chang and a possible drug problem seemed more and more likely.

"My father is ill, Nate. Very ill. He's in the ICU in Anchorage. They don't even know if he'll make it through the surgery he needs. You think I give a flying fuck about you or your problems?" All of the worry and fears about my dad poured out of me. I had reached a point past mincing words. I probably would enflame Nate, but I didn't care. Goddamn it, I just didn't care. "My father might die, and you're worried about half the dredge? A dredge you never put any of your own money into?"

Nate's face turned purple. "You think I'm gonna let some pansy-ass daughter of his take what's mine?" He grabbed my sweatshirt at the shoulders and twisted the thick material in his hands.

I reared back and mistakenly dropped the trowel. "Let me go, Nate." Fear had caught up to me. I'd gone too far. He'd snapped.

He shook me hard.

My teeth rattled in my mouth. My head snapped back, and I bit my tongue and tasted blood.

"You are a fucking bitch, Rory. A fucking bitch." He tossed me aside. "Looks like you've got plenty of gold to share."

I landed hard on one hand and a knee. My face scraped the rocks around the fire pit. I scrambled away before he could kick me.

His boot missed my midriff by inches, glanced off the leg of the Spiral and knocked it over with a crash.

I curled up in the fetal position and covered my head with my hands in a defensive move. I wouldn't be able to avoid his kicks for long.

A deafening roar filled my ears. Loud, guttural, black as night.

As if a demon had been loosed from hell.

CHAPTER NINE

I heard the body blow before I saw it.

Ben had appeared like an eagle dive bombing its prey. The punch must've hit square in Nate's gut. He'd doubled over by the time I'd come out of my fetal ball next to the fire pit.

Ben's face held no emotion. I chalked it up to his military training. Reactions automatic. Defensive and offensive moves were robotic, perhaps, for someone with his background.

Nate took a step or two back, clutching his midsection, but remained on his feet.

"What is your problem?" Ben bellowed. He shook out his fist, opened his fingers and let the tension dissipate. "Didn't your mother ever tell you not to hit a girl?"

Nate coughed. His voice was strained. "Just here for what's mine. Wait 'til she screws you over, too." He backed toward his Jeep while keeping an eye on Ben's position.

"So you're a big tough guy, huh?" Ben's fist tightened up, and he did a fake out move, as if to strike again.

Nate recoiled and hopped into his Jeep. "Ask her about last summer. She's not so innocent." He started up the engine and focused his attention on me, "This isn't going away. We're not settled yet. Your bodyguard can't be around 24/7."

Nate pressed on the gas. His Jeep fishtailed in the gravel. The wheels kicked up dust and rock. He disappeared so quickly down the alley that he was gone by the time Ben helped me up.

"What the hell was that guy's problem? Are you okay?" Ben

gave me the once over noting the scrape on my face and my bloodied palm. "Want me to call the cops?"

The cops. As if that would fix anything. Nate would end up in jail for a few days, I'd get a restraining order, and he would still come after me. His anger had been raw and real. A court date would only anger him more. I had to figure out another way to deal with him.

"I'll be all right." I wiped the dust off my jeans.

I saw relief on Ben's face when I rejected the police. I tucked that away for later. I'd ask him about it when we were in a different mood. Right now, we both had our adrenaline pumping, I'm sure.

"Let me see." Ben reached for my hand.

Although I tried to hide my injury—I didn't need someone babying me—Ben got hold of my hand and turned it over to reveal the bloody wound from landing hard in the dirt. "I'm okay. It'll be fine. I just need to clean it off."

The touch of his fingers was electric. I shrugged it off as part of the injury. My hand was particularly sensitive, and pain radiated in waves from the hard thud I'd taken.

"Come here." Still holding my hand, he made me walk over to the hose, which had been knocked loose from the Spiral. He forced me to put my hand into the flow. The cool water soothed the injury and cleaned off the dirt and bits of gravel.

Once the wound was clean, I pulled back my hand. "Thanks." I shook off the excess water. Blood oozed.

He touched the scrape on my cheek. "That looks like it smarts."

I leaned my head away. "It's fine." Touching my hand was one thing, but the gentle touch on my cheek made me feel uncomfortable.

"You need a bandage." He gestured at me to follow. "Let's get something on that. I'm sure you've got gauze or something in your apartment."

"We can't leave the concentrates out here." I pointed at the tipped over Spiral with gold spilled on the ground. As much as I'd like to believe the citizens of Nome would leave someone's gold haul alone, I knew her people better than that. Nate was the rule, not the exception, when it came to greed and violence.

"Hold up. I'll be right back." Ben trotted between apartment buildings. "If that jackass comes back, you run."

"Got it."

As I waited, I set the Spiral on its stand with my uninjured hand.

My knee throbbed. I'd probably have a good bruise there tomorrow. I touched my fingers to my cheek. When I drew them back a bit of blood stained them.

My mind raced to comprehend what had happened. In all the years I'd known Nate, I didn't remember him as someone who was dangerous. Sure, he had a temper, and he'd scared me the other night when he'd followed me to Kyle's. But he'd never been quite this physical. If he had, my father would've fired him years ago. Clearly, something had changed in Nate's life to push him to such a level. If it had been anyone else who'd attacked me, I'd be calling the police. But I knew the man. He'd actually taught me a few things about tending on the dredge that I still used in my day-to-day gold mining work. The idea Nate had gone from slightly weird and touchy business partner to raging lunatic didn't make sense.

Nate must've had a momentary lapse in judgment. Although I didn't get a whiff of any alcohol on him when he'd grabbed me by my sweatshirt, his dilated eyes told me he could've been high on something. Coke? Meth? I didn't know much about illegal drugs. Even though an underbelly existed in Nome along with a contingent of drug addicts, I didn't encounter them on a daily basis, nor did I know any personally. I stayed away from the bars where they tended to congregate and kept to the nicer, more populated parts of town.

I'd heard drugs typically were kept outside of town limits, on the fringes where they were easier to hide and people could avoid law enforcement. However, every year at least one dredger or another OD'ed. I remember one diver who drowned while high. Not the better dredges run by friends of my father, but the newer ones, the small outfits put together mostly by those who showed up in the summer hoping to get rich. Usually, people looking for fast money had a habit they needed to fund.

I'd gotten the wheel set up and added the concentrates to the feeder scoop by scoop with my left hand instead of my injured right one. We'd nearly finished emptying out the first bucket.

Ben returned.

I was glad to see him. The emptiness of the alley and the growing twilight unnerved me.

Ben had a roll of duct tape and a couple of napkins. "Couldn't find any Band-Aids, but I did find this." He held them up for me to see.

The skepticism I felt must've been apparent on my face.

"No, really, it works." He reached out his hand. "Give me your palm."

I set the trowel in the bucket and offered him my injured hand. "It's really not necessary." The cut was clean, but blood had started to flow again.

"Enough," he said. "Let me do this for you."

For such a large Beast, he acted gentler than I would've expected. He tore off a piece of napkin, folded it a few times, and laid it on the wound. The oozing blood stuck to the napkin, keeping it in place. He took the duct tape, bit it with his teeth and ripped. Then, he carefully wrapped the chunk of tape around my palm, making sure the napkin stayed in place.

He wound it around a few times, and then stuck it down with an easy press to my palm. When he'd finished he held onto my hand a few seconds longer than necessary.

"Thanks." The protection of the napkin and the pressure of the tape honestly made it feel better.

"You're welcome." He tossed the tape next to the buckets. "Back to work?"

I nodded.

He picked up where I left off, adding more concentrates to the Spiral. The collection container filled little by little with more refined material.

Nate had scared me. Maybe I should ask Stella for some advice. She knew Nate well enough, and her family had a long history in Nome. She might be able to offer an idea that would end the dispute without any more violence.

I thought about how much gold I'd need to pay the mounting bills and to set me up for the dredge-free months. I might have to see if they needed another waitress at the Polar Cafe or a server at Ernie's or another bar in town. I'd done that in the past when the gold was lean. Not my favorite thing to take orders and serve people—I wasn't a friendly, social type of person like Stella. But I could do it if I had to.

My father always managed to figure things out in the lean times. I don't know how, but I never remembered us going into winter without enough of a cushion to see us through to ice season. He'd taken care of me no matter what. Now it was my turn to take care of him.

"So you never did tell me what that dude's problem was with

you." Ben continued to feed concentrate into the spiral, while I sat by the bonfire to keep warm.

"That's Nate Frazier." I tossed another chunk of punky wood on the fire. "He worked with my father as long as I can remember. Last year, we had to fire him. I guess he still harbors a lot of anger about it."

"That's one way to put it." Ben kept his gaze on the gold-filled tracks of the Spiral. "Why'd you fire him?"

"It's a bit of a long story."

"I've got nothing but time and another bucket."

"All right." I picked up the roll of duct tape and slipped it over my hand like a bracelet. "Well, it goes way back. My dad and Nate had dredged together for years before I came along." The flames crackled orange and yellow in the fire pit. The smoke drifted up and up. I spun the tape on my wrist. My gaze blurred as I recalled their history. "They had a few extra divers they'd bring on from time to time, but Nate and my dad were thick as thieves. I guess that's what happens when you go through a lot of crap together—you bond."

Ben kept up a rhythmic scoop.

"My dad put every red cent into the dredge we have now. Nate came up with the design, sourced the equipment—he didn't have any money really to put into the business, so he felt his contribution was the manpower, the loyalty. It gets pretty competitive up here for good divers." I smiled to myself. "But I'm sure you figured that out." Even though I'd only just met Ben, I knew he wasn't stupid. He'd sussed out very quickly he was a hot commodity and had pressed for a better deal than I'd wanted to give. After what happened with Nate, I was glad to pay Ben the extra 5%. Already he'd given me some kind of loyalty that I'm not sure I deserved.

"Last summer, something changed between him and my dad. I don't know what drove the arguments, but they started to get on each other's nerves. Nate would gripe about something, then my dad would poke back at him. Like two brothers fighting, you know?"

The fire popped and sizzled as it consumed the half-rotten wood I'd added.

"One day, Nate showed up late. We were supposed to be shoving off around 6:00. Kyle had the day off, I was going to tend the boat, while Nate and my dad did the diving. That's how it usually worked. I'd fill in some of the diving time if it was a particularly long day, but most of my work was above water. Nate suddenly appeared an hour late, drunk as a skunk, and griping about everything—the work, the dredge, how he wasn't appreciated. My dad had heard it all before. Didn't think anything of it. We took off for the mining grounds we'd scoped out, and my dad suited up. He'd be the first to dive while Nate sobered up." I absentmindedly stroked the duct tape bandage with my fingers. Not even Stella knew the whole story about the day Nate was fired. I swallowed. "My dad loved Nate. He really wanted the best for him. Sometimes, though, he was too forgiving. Maybe he should've kicked Nate to the curb that morning, but he didn't. He wanted to give the guy a chance to sober up, straighten out, get over whatever demons he had going on and get back to doing the work he was good at."

Nate had been self-taught, just like my dad, but he had some sort of magic when it came to diving and dredging. He could swim like a fish. He had no fear—even during ice diving season when the risks escalated. I understood why he and my dad had been so successful. Nate had pushed my father to do things he maybe wouldn't have done on his own. Crazy stuff that ran on the edge of safety. But they'd always pulled it out.

"While my dad was diving, Nate and I were alone up top. I hadn't been paying any attention to him or his moods. I'd seen it before—or so I thought. I'd been more interested in making sure the equipment was working, keeping the dredge where my dad wanted it, doing the comms. That kind of thing. Nate was supposed to be resting up for his turn. Then, out of nowhere he starts ragging on me. Calling me names. Telling me I was an idiot and didn't know what I was doing. That I'd almost killed him once or some such crap. He suddenly backed me into a corner of the wheelhouse. Screaming in my face. I acted on instinct and punched him in the nose."

Ben paused what he was doing and gave me a look of surprise.

"I don't know where it came from. I'd never hit anyone in my life." The memory of it still seemed so bizarre. As if my hand acted on its own without my direction. "I broke his nose somehow. Blood everywhere. But it got his attention. He backed off. I immediately got my dad to surface—I was worried what might happen far from shore, the two of us alone. I had no idea if Nate would retaliate. But when he heard me call my dad on the comms, he quieted down. He sat on the couch until my dad came up."

The Nate I saw tonight had been different, more volatile, and seemed to have no boundaries. If Ben hadn't showed up when he did, the anger in Nate seemed so strong as to overpower his reason. I might've been more badly hurt.

"I think he knew he'd done wrong. Knew he'd pushed it too far. My dad had been his touchstone in a way. The one who kept him grounded and on the right path. Dredging is full of people with a need for adventure, excitement, risky behavior. My dad is one of the few dredge owners with a healthy mix of risk and reality. Nate knew that. He'd experienced my dad ignoring his worst ideas and selecting his best—when if Nate had been acting alone, he probably would have pursued them all."

By the time my dad had surfaced that day, Nate knew what was coming. His posture told the story: slumped shoulders, wouldn't look me in the eye, quiet.

"I met my dad at the rail and told him what had happened. My dad fired Nate on the spot, and we headed immediately back to shore. Whatever disagreements there were between them apparently included me. Last summer I had no idea Nate felt my involvement with the dredge was a threat to him. I had no idea he believed he'd earned some kind of ownership of the business that had never been given. I guess with my father being gone…"

"Sounds like your dad tried to do right by the guy." Ben set the trowel down. "Some people are just destined to screw up their own lives."

"Thanks for saying that." Not even my dad had acknowledged Nate's downfall had been coming for some time. "A lot of old timers blamed me for breaking up the team."

"Forget about them. What do they know?" Ben sidled up to the fire to warm his hands. "Now I can understand a little bit where Nate's coming from. Might help if he tries something like that again."

"I think the loss of my dad's friendship was the last straw. Over the last year, I've seen him slipping further away from life, reality." I needed to process everything, talk to Stella, think of what to do. Maybe it was a mistake not to include the police. My father had been too soft on Nate for years and look where they'd ended up. But deep down, I knew it would be what my father would want. No matter how their relationship had ended, he wouldn't want Nate in jail. He'd want the best for him, hope that he could overcome his problems and find his way back.

"Yeah, I've known a few guys like that." Ben held up the second bucket and tipped it toward me to show it was empty. "Now what?"

I shut off the Spiral and detached the container. I handed him the refined concentrates—mostly gold dust and little bit of black sand.

"Hell, yeah." He took it eagerly. His enthusiasm was infectious. "That's probably the coolest goddamn thing I've seen in a long time."

Benjamin Abel confounded me. A Beast one moment, a boy the next. I was grateful for his protection, but wary of the power he could wield. I had a feeling he'd held back when he attacked Nate. Something about the quiet calm of him, the emotionless look on his face made me wonder about giving Ben my complete trust. For a moment I thought about would happen if he decided to turn that power on me.

Before I'd been worried Ben would find another dredge with more gold once Nome's miners found out his skillset. Lured away from Buck's nutty daughter who thought she could run a dredge for a promise of something better. No longer was that foremost in my mind. He'd settled in with me easily. Eager to learn. He'd stepped in as my rescuer, my protector. He barely knew me, but yet he had been willing to shoulder some of my burden for no purpose I could see. I decided to keep my trust loose and pliable. Maybe I needed Stella's help to find out more about my mysterious new diver.

"Let's meet at the assayers tomorrow around nine, and I'll show you how to turn gold into cash," I said. "That way you know I'm on the up-and-up." The last thing I wanted was another angry diver who accused me of owing him money.

He handed the box to me. "Aye-aye, captain."

His eyes glinted in the firelight. My heart took a leap.

I shook the feeling loose and let it drift away. The last thing I needed was a romance-gone-wrong. My life was hectic and messy enough without doing something stupid like crushing on my new diver.

CHAPTER TEN

I woke up to my phone ringing. I really need to change my ring tone—some hip hop song Kyle had liked. He'd added it to my phone a few months' back, and it aggravated me. He and I were over, over, over. I needed to put him in the rearview mirror, ring tones and all.

I recognized the number—the hospital in Anchorage. My fuzzy mind sobered instantly. "Hello?"

"This is Dr. Leskiv, your father's cardiologist."

"Oh, yes, Doctor, is my father doing all right?" Buck hadn't been fully conscious since he'd been flown to Anchorage. Some tests had been done to evaluate the reason for his coma-like state. He could respond to simple commands, but hadn't tried to fight the breathing machine and had been unable to speak, as a result.

"He's slowly coming out of it, and we've been waiting until he shows enough strength for the surgery. He's had a pretty large trauma, as you know, and it wouldn't be prudent to put his body through surgery until we felt he could handle the stress."

"I understand." I had a hard time imagining my father, in his late 50s, in such a state. I avoided taking a trip to Anchorage to see him because of that fear—and the extra expense for a flight I couldn't really afford. I felt like a coward. As if I'd let my father down. But it had been easier for me to put my head down and do the work he'd taught me to do: dredge for gold. Since I first came to Alaska he'd instilled in me the same zest as he had for the business. The rush of discovery. The risk and reward. The ups and downs. I loved it all. My father had never given up, never quit. And I wasn't about to quit while he lay flat on his back in the ICU.

I thought about how Buck hadn't known I existed until I was in the 6th grade. When I took my first trip to Nome after my mother ran off, I latched on for dear life. Buck had needed someone, too. He'd forgotten what it meant to have someone love him, really love him all the way through. When I'd made the decision to stay in Nome, Buck dove into the role of 'dad.'

Buck had told me that I'd be the 'only woman in his life.' We'd shaken hands on it. A bit strange to reflect on—a girl and her father shaking hands over something so silly. But it had felt right at the time—his calloused palm warm against mine. I'd felt safe. Secure. And I wanted nothing to change about that feeling.

The doctor's words brought me back to reality. Life was nothing but change. As an adult, I knew that to be true. The wishful thinking of pre-pubescent Aurora had been silly. Now it was my turn to fully dive into being a grown-up daughter.

*

The wind blew more strongly today than it had the afternoon before. The view of the waves from the landing at my apartment building revealed large whitecaps. A lone dredge worked the grounds, but it was an unusual dredge—a large excavator mounted on a barge, which scooped gold bearing material from the sea floor into its monster-sized sluice. The *Blue Dragon* could handle the rougher seas. No divers needed. When conditions were crappy for a smaller dredge like the *Alaska Darling*, the *Dragon* could still mine for gold. Theirs was a multi-million-dollar operation, however. Most of us miners in Nome didn't have the means or the know-how to run such a dredge.

I glanced at my watch. Ninety minutes until I'd planned to meet with Ben at Alaska North Assayers. Hopefully I'd have enough time for a chat with Stella while I ate some breakfast. My refrigerator, as evidenced by last night's meager dinner, lacked anything I'd call 'breakfast material.' Although I was watching my pennies, not only did I need a good meal, I needed my friend's advice. Worth the $15 or so I'd spend on an omelet and some coffee.

I double checked the seal on the Tupperware container I used to transport my gold flakes and dust we'd collected last night. I tucked it into my largest bag—an old straw beach bag that had seen better days. The weight of the gold pulled on my shoulder. Still surprised me how heavy even a small amount of gold could be.

I zipped up my father's windbreaker, which fit me better than it fit him, and texted Stella.

U at work?

A gust of wind barely above freezing cooled my cheeks. I tucked my hands and my phone into my pockets. Wouldn't make sense to buy breakfast, if I didn't get to chat with Stella. I prepared to walk the extra half-mile to the Safeway to buy a few groceries. Wasn't worth it to spend the gas on such a short trip.

My phone buzzed.

Yep. Slow morning. :-(

I answered:

Not anymore. Be there in 5.

She sent me a GIF of a kitten clapping its paws together.

I smiled and finished my stroll, sailing into the cafe on a burst of wind.

Stella stood by my favorite table near the window with a pot of coffee ready to pour. "Two days this week. What gives?"

By the time I sat down my mug was full. I unzipped my windbreaker and pushed my windblown hair out of my eyes. "Empty pantry."

"Ah, the usual. Are you meeting another hottie for breakfast?" Stella tapped her pen against her order pad and studied me.

Blushing was not my thing, but if it were, I'd be as red as a beet. Last night's situation had been more than just trouble with Nate, it had made me see Ben in a new light. But I stuck to the real question on my mind. "Actually, I wanted to get your opinion on someone else."

She raised an eyebrow.

"Nate showed up last night during our clean out. Behind the apartments."

Stella slid into the seat across from me. Only a couple of customers to take care of. She didn't seem worried about what her manager might think. "Stirring up something?"

"He'd stopped by the dredge a few days ago. Really angry." I circled my cold hands around the warm mug of coffee. "Said my dad owed him money or something."

My oldest and dearest friend nodded. She'd heard about last summer's confrontation, the firing. Maybe not all the details I'd shared with Ben, but she knew the basics.

"Anyway, I brushed him off. Then, later that day I think he followed me back to Kyle's."

"You went to Kyle's?" Stella's eyes widened in her round face, like two tarnished pennies.

I couldn't hold back a sigh. "Listen. That's not the point. The point was Nate tailgated me all the way from the marina to Kyle's. It freaked me out."

"Understandable." Stella relaxed and crossed her arms. "And last night he showed up at your place? What did he want?"

"Same story. But this time—well, he came at me." A chill ran up my back at the memory. "Tried to really do some damage. If it hadn't been for Ben…"

Stella's brown gaze caught fire. "Ben came to your rescue?"

I knew where she was going with it—getting me off track again. "He got Nate to leave." I swirled the dregs of my coffee absently. "What I wanted to know is, have you heard anything about Nate and drugs? I know he's been hanging out with Lola and those types over at The Glacier." The Glacier was a well-known dive bar on the east side of town. Lowlifes and druggies of all types congregated there. Maybe because it was rumored the owner's son had access to any number of illegal substances. "When he showed up last night he was all hopped up. I mean, the guy's got problems, but he'd only been a mild alcoholic when I knew him."

"Hold on. I need to get Rusty his bill." She got up from the table. "You want me to put an order in?"

"Ham and Cheese Omelet. Side of hash browns." If I ate a huge breakfast I wouldn't have to worry about lunch.

Stella scribbled on her pad. "Got it. Be right back." She rushed to her customer near the door, dropped off his check, then handed my order to the cook through the pass-through window.

My gaze drifted outside. The bright light of an early Alaska morning bounced off the windshield of a beat-up Toyota 4Runner parked outside. If it hadn't been for the wind, this would've been a nice day to be out on the water. I checked my watch. Eight o'clock.

Still sticking to my schedule. At least after today I'd have some gold cashed in and some much needed money in the bank.

Stella finished with Rusty and returned with a full coffeepot in hand. She refilled my mug, leaned forward and said in a hushed voice. "Rumor has it that Lola's dealing meth. If you've seen Nate with Lola, that can't be good."

Although Nome was far from civilization, it didn't take long for illicit things to make their way here. "You think she's making the stuff? Or just selling?" I had a really hard time believing Nate would've fallen that far in such a short period of time. But without the rush of dredging, maybe he had to fill in his adrenaline needs with the high only a drug could bring.

Stella shrugged. "Officer Isaacs comes in here at least once a week. He's got a pretty big mouth. A few weeks ago he mentioned Lola, meth and a drug bust."

Isaacs was part of the small police force in Nome. With less than twenty people serving the area, they had a hard enough time keeping up with low-level crimes much less tackle the burgeoning drug problem.

"I remember seeing that in the paper, I think." *The Nome Nugget* usually covered the latest high school sports achievements, local business news, and goings on around town on a weekly basis. Every now and then, though, a shocking story would appear on the front page. "But I don't remember Lola."

Stella's eyes lit up. "Hold on. I've got my laptop in my backpack. We can look up the story on the *Nugget* Facebook page." She headed for the back room.

The short order cook placed a plate in the pass-through window and hit the bell with his fist. "Order up." His gaze trailed after Stella who'd disappeared into the storage room. He locked eyes with me and gestured at the plate with his spatula.

I got up, scooped up my breakfast plate, and carried it back to my table. Things were casual at the Polar Cafe. The Denver Omelet sizzled on the plain white plate and tempted me to take a bite. I'd scooped up a forkful when Stella returned with her beat-up laptop.

"Oh, great, Doug brought you your food. Nice."

I ate the chunk of omelet and let the truth slide.

Stella tapped on her keyboard and, in a few seconds, she turned her laptop sideways so I could see the result. She'd drilled down to *The Nome Nugget* Facebook Page and the story she remembered: *Drug*

Bust in Hoodoo Gulch.

We both skimmed the story. Stella, a faster reader than I, pointed to the name we'd been looking for: Lola Chang. She read aloud, "Nome police arrested four people and seized drugs including methamphetamine during a bust early Thursday morning. One woman tried to escape on an ATV, police say, which ended in a crash. The woman had moderate injuries and was taken to the emergency clinic for treatment, police say. According to police: The investigation began in May with tips from concerned citizens. Investigators say they discovered a steady flow of customers at the Glacier Bar on East 3rd Avenue and determined it was a drug distribution point. Leads from interviews conducted led officers to a small cabin in Hoodoo Gulch. Officers served a search warrant at the cabin just after 6 a.m. Inside, police say they found cocaine, methamphetamine, marijuana, prescription medication, handgun ammunition and more than $2,800 in cash. Police say those charged include: Edward Chang, Declan McTavitt, Sean Lewis and Lola Chang, all of whom face charges of possession with intent to deliver drugs, possession of a small amount of marijuana and possession of drug paraphernalia."

"Wow." I ate my breakfast and let that turn over in my brain.

"If Nate is hanging out with Lola…well, I'd say that's a bad sign. You should steer clear of him."

"Trust me, I'm not interested in getting into it with Nate. He's the one seeking me out. I'm not sure how to get him off my back. Whatever his problem is, it's with my dad, not with me."

"He seems to think you have some kind of control of things, so I don't know if that's gonna fly."

"Sort of wish I had somewhere to hide out until he cools off. Maybe I could patch things up with Kyle, sleep on his couch for a few weeks." Although my inner self cringed at the thought. His behavior the other day proved to me he didn't quite believe that our relationship had ended. I didn't want to risk Kyle getting the wrong idea.

"I wish you could stay with us."

Stella lived with her boyfriend, Matt Childress, and his sister who already slept on their couch.

"Don't beat yourself up, hon." I tempted her with a bit of my omelet. "This is my problem to figure out. I suppose my apartment is as safe a place as any." The words came out weakly. My mind turned to the wild look in Nate's eyes from last night. I shook off the fear.

"Sure. Sure." Stella patted my arm.

The cook dinged the bell. "Order up!"

"Give me a sec." She scooted off to pick up her customers' trio of breakfast plates.

Her laptop sat in front of me. I spun it around. Facebook hovered in my vision. I typed Nate's name in the search bar. He'd blocked both my father and me from his Facebook page—not as if he'd been an incredibly active poster, but I suppose it had been his way of disowning us after the big blow up last summer. Since Stella was logged in with her account, maybe I could find a clue about what he'd been up to.

I clicked on the link that appeared. His avatar had switched from a picture of our dredge to a close up of a new tattoo he'd gotten on his right forearm—a topless mermaid. Classy.

I quickly scrolled through his latest posts. But most everything he'd put up recently had been pictures of women, a tower of beer cans he'd created on his back balcony, and tattoos he found worthy of sharing. I didn't see anything connecting him to Lola, no pictures of drugs (as if anybody these days would be dumb enough to advertise), and nothing bizarre for a single man in his late 40s to post.

Stella returned.

For some reason the guilt sat in my throat like heartburn, and I quickly hit the back button on the browser to send it back to *The Nome Nugget* page where we'd begun.

"Doing some Facebook stalking?" Stella smirked.

Stella had a habit of using Facebook and other social media connections to dig into people's backgrounds. She'd hear about so-and-so's sister or that ex-boyfriend or this ex-husband or that former boss and would jump onto her trusty mini laptop that she kept in the back while she was working, tap a few keys, make a few clicks and tell me everything she could possibly find out. It never ceased to amaze me the tricks she used to dig up dirt. It was one of those powers I seriously hoped wasn't turned on me someday. Luckily, Stella and I were long-time friends. Plus, she wasn't a nasty person. Just curious.

I forced myself to swallow a bite of food. "Just re-reading the story about the drug bust."

Stella nodded. Her eyes lit up. "Let's check out your new diver!"

Before I could stop her, Stella clacked on the keys. "Benjamin Abel, right? A-B-E-L?"

My interest was piqued, I admit, but I didn't want Stella to know. Last night there'd been something between Ben and me. An unspeakable something. I didn't want to classify it. What if I'd read everything wrong? He'd rescued me from a dangerous situation. Every girl's 'knight in shining armor' dream. It was hard to pretend my mind hadn't gone there.

Stella's gaze flicked over the top of the screen and caught mine. "A bit of a mystery man, it seems." She picked up the laptop, crossed to my side of the table and forced me to scoot over to the next chair. "See?"

Like most men his age, his Facebook posts were light. His profile picture was an American flag, his background photo was a group of military men with their arms around each other out in the desert somewhere. I couldn't help it. My gaze slipped to the 'relationship' status.

Engaged.

CHAPTER ELEVEN

I let out a long breath of disappointment after seeing Ben's relationship status. I barely knew Ben, but the truth made things easier. He had only been a decent guy last night. A good guy who defended a woman from a monster. That was all. Nothing more to it. In fact, the information made things a lot easier now. I could turn off any tiny feelings that had been percolating and cut them off. I'm sure it had only been rebound stuff after breaking it off with Kyle.

Stella had already moved on to his photo album, clicking through pictures. There weren't many. Some old scanned ones from the 90s of old people and little kids at a barbecue, a school photo of a gap-toothed boy with wild dark hair, two huskies buried in a snowbank, an interior shot of a log cabin with an old man sitting in a recliner chair with several stuffed animal heads above him—a moose, a bear, a mule deer.

"Looks like Mr. America." Stella tired of the photos and clicked on his friends list.

At first I'd been curious about my diver, now I felt as if I were invading his personal life without permission. "That's enough for me."

"What?" Stella stilled her finger on the scroll pad and gave me a hard stare. "Don't make me into the snoop. I'm just trying to figure out if you're safe out alone on the open water with this guy. Former military. Lots of family pics. Seems normal enough."

"I gotta go." I looked at my watch for emphasis. Still fifteen minutes before my meet-up with Ben, but I'd rather not stick around any longer. My stomach flip flopped. Not sure why. I'd crossed a line somehow, and it made me uncomfortable. "Sorry, Stella." I handed her $20. "You keep the change."

My friend took the bill and stuffed it in the pocket of her apron. "You busy tonight?"

"Nah, can't go out on the water today, won't have any gold to clean, why?"

"Thought we could maybe stream some Netflix? Matt's gotta work."

Matt Childress worked varying shifts at the Bonanza Express gas station in the center of town. Odds were at least one night shift came his way every week. Saturday night was a bit of a bummer.

"Sure." Why not? All I had scheduled in my day was the visit to the assayers, so I could safely unload my pure gold into cash money and take a trip to the grocery store to refill my very empty refrigerator. Besides, after yesterday's encounter with Nate, it might be a good idea to lay low for a while. I could hide out at Matt and Stella's place until late. Then I could sneak home. If Nate was up to his drinking (or drugging, if I believed the rumors), he should be passed out somewhere.

Stella flashed her not-so-straight and not-so-white teeth at me. "Perfect. If you bring the soda, I'll grab a pizza."

"Want me to bring some popcorn? I can't stream without a steady supply."

"Not gonna turn it down. That's for sure."

I waved at Stella as I left the cafe. Everything seemed so normal. A regular Saturday in summer. Gold in my bag. Plans for the evening. If I could keep on that path of monotony, I'd be in good shape by the fall. No diversions. No changes. Mine when the weather is good, clean and count when the weather is bad. Deposit the checks. Limit my expenses. And everything should even itself out.

The only things that were not routine: my diver and Nate.

Alaska North Assayers was located only a few blocks over from The Polar Cafe. The gusty wind blew strands of hair across my face, and I wished I'd remembered to put on a hat to keep it under control.

Most of the buildings in Nome left something to be desired. Living so far from resources, building materials were expensive and in short supply. Beauty was not first on the list when building in Nome, and many structures used and reused materials when possible. The flat-roofed assayers office had been painted a mustard yellow and appeared tacked onto the end of a row of similar buildings. A bright yellow awning, which could use some scrubbing, identified the place as Alaska North. The sign in the window had been flipped to OPEN.

When I entered the shop, Ben stood waiting. A dark mountain of plaid flannel and bushy beard.

"Hey, Stu," I greeted the owner who sat behind the counter at his desk, which was covered in equipment. My dad had been taking me to Alaska North since my childhood.

Stu broke into a wide grin when he saw me. "Hey." Then he sobered. "How's your dad doing?"

The presence of Ben could be felt. Although Stu knew most of the details of my father's accident and had been a great friend through it all, I didn't want to cough up anything too personal. "It's going all right." But based on my phone call with Dr. Leskiv, I knew that wasn't true. Financially it was bad. Emotionally it was bad. And physically my father had been unconscious for ten days and was in need of life-saving surgery. But I swallowed my words. "I brought my new diver, Ben, with me so he could learn about this part of the process. Also, so he doesn't think I'm cheating him." I winked. "We've got a twenty-five percent cut going, so I'd appreciate it if you'd split the total that way for us."

"Check okay?" Stu gazed at Ben.

Ben grunted in the affirmative.

"Name?"

"Benjamin Abel."

"A-B-E-L," I said without thinking.

Stu scribbled it down on a piece of paper.

My heart thumped. Had I just let on that I'd been snooping? *Crap.*

"Here's our haul." I dropped the Tupperware container filled with gold on the counter.

Ben stepped closer and appeared oblivious to my gaffe.

Without my permission, my body wanted to lean toward him. Find comfort. Safety. I willed myself to stop. Such a strange and uncontrollable reaction to a man I barely knew. A man I'd found out had a fiancée somewhere.

Unavailable, Rory. Unavailable.

"So how does this work?" Ben asked.

Stu hefted the Tupperware container and removed the lid.

"Well, I check to make sure the gold is clean and dry." He poured the gold from our container onto a plate on his desk. "If it's under 10 ounces, I typically just buy it off you straight, with a fee tacked on—usually a few hundred bucks. Let's put it on the scales to see where we are. Not a bad clean-out, Aurora."

When he turned away Ben caught my gaze and mouthed "Aurora?" with a quizzical bent to one eyebrow.

I held back a laugh. Only old guys wanted to call me by my formal first name, oh, and my sister.

Stu set the plate on his scale. "Looks like about 6.5 ounces. Is that what you had?" He looked up and caught us in our silent fun.

I'd forgotten to weigh the gold myself. I nodded at his question, too embarrassed to admit my mistake. After cleaning the gold, one always weighed it out to ensure not only that your crew knew you were on the up and up, but so that you could make sure your assayer wasn't playing any games. But Stu was trustworthy. He'd been weighing out Darling gold for decades.

"Probably want to just sell it to me outright. I can cut you checks right now for an amount this small."

Ben checked out the rest of the strange equipment in Stu's office. "So if it was more than 10 ounces, would you use some of that stuff?" He pointed at the desk filled with gold bar molds, crucibles of various sizes, crucible tongs, jugs of acid, a spectrometer, and other things.

Stu smiled at the question. "Yes. We'd melt it down to get out the impurities. Typically, 10% of the weight are impurities. Then we'd make it into bars. We keep 2%, and you'd get 98% of the value. Pretty common percentage around here."

The bell over the door jingled.

"Oh, hey, Kyle." Stu's eyes crinkled at the corners when he smiled. With a big bushy white beard, his eyes were his most definitive feature. "I'll be with you in a minute."

Kyle.

My heart skipped a beat.

I turned to see if it was *my* Kyle…correction, Kyle the Ex.

"Hey Rory," Kyle said and nodded a greeting to Ben.

"Hey," I answered as casually as I could.

Ben grunted. "Hey." Ben either didn't remember the awkwardness between Kyle and me from the other day or he *did* and wanted to insert himself into it anyway.

Kyle focused his attention on me. "So how's your greenhorn working out, Rory? Finding the gold?"

The men's eyes locked for a brief moment.

I could sense the tension rising. Not sure why. Kyle had a new gig. Why did he care?

"He might be new to mining, but he's a quick learner." I glanced at Stu who was filling out our checks. "I think he's got it under control. Right Ben?"

Ben leaned against the counter. Cool as a cucumber. He never took his eyes off Kyle.

Seemed like a good time to change the subject. "How are your parents doing?"

His stance stiffened. "Fine."

I suppose I shouldn't have been surprised at the clipped response.

Kyle took a position to the right of me, a full ten feet away from Ben. "Hey Stu. Got my check ready? Jerry said I could pick it up today."

"Yeah, I got it here." Stu acknowledged Kyle's request while handing a check to me and a check to Ben. "Thanks for doing business. Hope to see you again soon. Give your dad my best."

"I will. Thanks." I tucked the check for a hefty chunk of cash into my bag. "See you around, Kyle."

Ben folded his, stuck it in his back pocket, and followed me to the door. As I turned the knob, he held the door open over my head. His height surprised me for some reason.

"Yeah, see ya." Kyle tossed at us. "Be careful out there."

Odd thing to say. Felt a bit like a warning.

We both left Kyle inside the assayers shop.

Ben kept pace with me as I headed toward my apartment.

"What was his problem?" Ben asked. "I thought you guys were over."

I scoffed. "We are." I couldn't believe he thought the tension was due to anything more than a competitive streak Kyle had when it came to mining. "He just wanted to show off. He started up with a new boat. Probably wanted to show us his check." I shrugged.

I wasn't going to let Kyle bother me. What did I care if he was doing better than I was? Although it was a bit of a jerk move, since he knew what my financial and personal situation was. Was this really the time to be competitive? He could've been a little less abrasive.

"Nah, he's still got it bad for you." Ben zipped up his jacket against the strong headwind coming off the ocean only blocks away. The sun could be shining in Nome saying 'summer,' but the wind could be howling 'winter.'

My thoughts muddied. I had the very distinct sensation of wanting to disappear. "We broke it off. You're wrong." What I didn't need to remind Ben is that I'd been at Kyle's a few days ago, and it had been clear to me then that Kyle still had feelings for me. That wouldn't really support my argument that the relationship was over. To get the attention off of me, I switched it around on Ben. "So, do you have a special someone in your life?"

Ben stiffened. "No."

Instantly, the friendliness between us evaporated. Cold settled around me.

Before I could muse about his strange answer, my phone buzzed in my pocket. I plucked it out and answered it. "Hey, Stella." I set aside my confusion and turned my attention to my friend. It had been good timing to break the awkward silence.

"You free?" Stella's voice was an anxious whisper. "You need to get back over here."

Stella's tone unnerved me. "What's going on?"

Ben treaded beside me, but he'd put distance between us.

"It's Ben. I don't know how to say this…"

I took a sidelong glance at Ben and slowed my steps ever so slightly. I didn't want him to think anything was off. "What? Tell me." My breathing slowed.

"He was arrested last year."

My stomach clenched. "For what?"

"Murder."

CHAPTER TWELVE

The Polar Cafe was right down the street. I picked up the pace, so I could find out more about the unexpected and scary news from Stella about my diver. And, to be honest, I wanted to put some distance between Ben and me.

Ben was oblivious to the internal shift in my perception of him. The sun disappeared behind a clump of gray clouds. I shivered. My insides were a mass of nerves. The silence continued until we reached his ATV.

Could Stella be right? Could Ben be a murderer?

I thought about the time we'd spent on the dredge, his heroism the other day when I'd needed his help under water. He'd been attentive, concerned. And yesterday, when Nate had been so threatening and out of control Ben had stepped in once again to help me.

I reviewed the events of last night in my head. Ben's emotionless visage. The robotic movements. As if he'd been on auto-pilot. He was capable of violence. I'd seen that for myself. But before I'd believe he was capable of murder, I'd have to find out more details. I couldn't square what Stella told me on the phone with the man who walked next to me.

"Tomorrow the weather should be better." I had to break the awkward silence somehow and separate from Ben so I could meet with Stella. Work was an easy fallback position for me. "The storm will blow through overnight. Let's meet on the dock tomorrow around 5."

I didn't know how I'd feel in the morning about being alone with Ben on my dredge, but I had to say something normal. I could deal with the aftermath once I knew the details from Stella.

"Sounds good." Ben stood for a moment staring at the gravel road beneath our feet.

"By the way, I really hate peanut butter," he confessed. "Why don't I bring the sandwiches tomorrow?" He gave a quick smile.

My pulse fluttered. Instinctually, I had a gut reaction to Ben—an attraction that I didn't want to have.

He must've taken my hesitancy as a question.

He whipped out his check and shook it. "I'm flush with cash."

"All right. But no mayo on mine." Although everything in my head said, *get away from this potential murderer*, my heart said to trust. "Mayonnaise is disgusting," I quipped, keeping the conversation light.

Ben rubbed a hand across his beard. "Got it. No mayo. 5 am. See you there." He waved briefly as we parted ways and climbed on his ATV.

"Yep, see you." I waved as he drove off.

*

Stella hunched over her laptop at the counter. She had a wrinkle between her thin brows. The room had emptied of patrons. Between breakfast and lunch the crowd had slowed considerably.

"What's this about a murder?" I said casually. I hoped she'd over-reacted, made a mistake. I smiled and set aside the fact that the wrinkle got deeper.

"Here. You read it. I can't." She turned her laptop around so I could see what had her looking so concerned.

The first thing I saw was a picture of Ben. Although he now had a heavy beard and much longer hair, the face in the newspaper article was undeniably his. Wearing his Navy uniform, his mouth a grim line. The headline screamed at me, "Local Veteran Charged With Fiancée's Murder."

November 20, 2018

The fiancé of the Boise woman who was found dead in her apartment three days ago has been charged with second-degree murder.

Benjamin John Abel, 28, of Eagle and a veteran of the U.S. Navy has been charged with second-degree murder in the death of 27-year-old Laura Snow. Snow was last seen by neighbors in her apartment complex the night of

November 17, 2018. Her body was discovered the next morning after a neighbor called about a disturbance in Abel's apartment.

Neighbors recall loud arguing and thumping in the early morning hours of November 17. One neighbor, Alicia Cortez, revealed she had considered calling the police about the noise earlier in the evening, but had changed her mind. She stated that she feared Abel as he had threatened her in the past when she complained about the couple fighting on previous occasions.

On Monday, police announced that they had issued a warrant for the arrest of a suspect in connection with Snow's death.

According to Snow's Facebook account, the pair were to be married on December 31, 2018.

A cause of death has not been released.

Abel has yet to be arrested, and anyone with information about his whereabouts or any other information about this incident, who has not already spoken with police, is asked to call the Idaho State Police.

My mind blanked. "How did you find this?"

Stella had a grim twist to her mouth. "You know me. I get curious. After we looked up that *Nugget* story, and we found his Facebook page with so little information, I went digging."

I knew. Stella had a curious mind and a knack for research.

Years ago, when we were girls and didn't have more than MySpace accounts with ridiculous puppy pictures and flashing graphics that would make your eyes burn, Stella had decided to be my personal private investigator. We were 13 or 14 at the time.

Although I'd handled my mother's sudden disappearance pretty well the year before, by my teens I had grown more curious. She had taken off and abandoned me. It didn't feel good to think she despised me so much that she'd rather cut out and disappear than stick around. I'd wanted to believe there had been a reason, something that would make sense. With the rabid curiosity only an 8th grade girl could have, I'd grown determined to find out more.

Stella knew my deepest darkest secrets. What middle school aged girl didn't confess all to her closest friend?

So Stella decided to take it upon herself to track down my mother. She'd asked me questions about my mom that most kids should know: Where was she born? What high school did she go to? What was her hometown? What was her maiden name?

Some I could answer. Some I could not. I mean, honestly, how many kids at that age know much about their parents? I had a vague understanding of who she was, but I had been more interested in what she was doing for me as a mother. What she represented. How that had affected me and my life. A mother was just supposed to be there. Through thick and thin. The kids were the ones who were supposed to have the tantrums. Not the parents.

Stella had found out pretty much nothing back then. My mother hadn't been very active online. Instead, I'd contacted my grandmother in Tucson and hoped she knew something. When I'd called her late one night, after screwing up my courage, she didn't even realize my mother had been missing. Henry had called me the next day and berated me over the phone for doing such a thing. He'd told me it had been his information to share, and that I'd broken a 'sacred connection' between husband and wife. Or something like that. At the time I'd felt terrible. I'd told Stella to drop it.

But looking back as an adult, I realize my stepfather had likely been embarrassed. I'd revealed a horrible secret he'd been keeping from his mother. His marriage was on the rocks. His wife had left him. Again.

The internet could be a vast place of personal information, and Stella knew how to take advantage. Did I want to go further? Did I want to find out more about Ben? If Ben had been guilty of murder would he really be free to come to Alaska with no restrictions?

I was curious and horrified at the same time.

"That was almost a year ago. Did you find anything else?" I clicked on the reporter's name hoping there might be additional stories on the topic. A page popped up blocking me from reading more without an account to the newspaper.

"And that's why I didn't get any further since I found the article about 15 minutes ago." Stella shrugged. "I mean, if you really want to know, we could cough up the $9.99 a month for unlimited digital access." She navigated to the page with subscription information.

I took a breath and thought about it. What would finding out the details tell me? Either Ben was a murderer or he wasn't. And, no matter the truth of the situation, I'd still need a diver. "If he's here in Alaska, I think it's a safe bet that he's innocent." I wanted to believe my own words, but I knew it hadn't come out very confidently.

"How can you be so sure?" Stella went back to his Facebook

page. "She's dead, Rory." Stella clicked on Ben's photo album and scrolled until she found an album labeled "Laura."

Laura Snow had been a beautiful woman. Thin, blonde, blue eyes, a perfect smile that was wide and full of white teeth. Laura skiing. Laura boating. Laura fishing. Laura being Laura in her car, in a restaurant, outside a movie theater, on a mountain surrounded by trees and sunlight.

"Could I get a glass of water?" I cleared my throat.

"Sure thing." Stella skipped over to the drinks station near the kitchen pass-through and filled a plastic drinking glass with ice and water.

I couldn't grasp all of this new information. Ben had been short with me only minutes ago when I asked about his personal life. Now maybe I had a concept as to why. But was that because he'd been grieving the loss of his fiancée? Or was it because he'd murdered her and was trying to keep it from me?

"Here you go." Stella set the glass of water on the counter.

"Thanks." I took massive gulps. I didn't realize my mouth had been so dry.

"So what are you going to do?" Stella blew a piece of her curly brown hair out of her eyes. "Fire him?"

"What? No." Ben was an excellent diver. He'd never done anything to harm me. I'd felt safe around him. I didn't quite know how to process the news article.

Stella looked at me aghast. "So you're totally fine being out on the water—alone—with a murderer?" Her voice rose.

I shushed her. I didn't need the whole world knowing Ben's secret. "A *suspected* murderer. There's a difference."

"Not to me."

"What about 'innocent until proven guilty?'" Even I didn't believe the words coming out of my mouth. I wanted to. I really did. But I'd seen the Beast in Ben last night. It existed. A scary, powerful, dark thing inside of him.

Stella bit her lip. "I don't know..."

I wrestled with my emotions. Ben had done nothing to make me distrust him when we were alone together. I could believe every word of the story in the news, freak out, fire him and then where would I be? I needed Ben. The summer dredging season was short. I didn't really have the luxury of dithering over whether or not Ben was a danger to me.

"I've got to trust that if he were dangerous, if he really did harm his fiancée, he wouldn't be here in Alaska. He'd be back in Idaho." I drank the last of the water.

Stella gave me a look. "Promise me you'll be careful." She fingered a thin gold chain around her neck.

"I promise."

"And if you ever need me or Matt, that you'll call right away?" She had an earnest smile on her face that wavered. "Not handle things by yourself?"

I knew she worried for me. I suppose I didn't blame her. She knew Ben even less than I did, and he was intimidating by appearance alone. To read that someone was accused of murder, well, I could certainly understand why Stella might be fearful.

"I'll call." I squeezed her hand. "And I'll make sure I always have my dad's pocket knife. How about that?"

That seemed to calm her down. "Yes, do that."

As I left the diner my thoughts drifted from Ben my rescuer to Ben the possible murderer. Was he only protective of me because he needed me? Maybe he was on the run from the law and need quick money. With his skills as a diver and Nome's reputation as a very fly-by-night sort of place with seasonal work paid in mostly cash, it'd be a good place to hide out while finding a way to fund your escape. Nome was miles from anywhere. Not easy to get to. No way to drive here from the lower half of the state. Everything was fly-in or float-in.

Would an innocent man choose to come to Nome, alone, in the middle of the summer mining season? I had no idea.

CHAPTER THIRTEEN

I shivered in my jeans and t-shirt on board the *Alaska Darling*. Five in the morning, even with the sun in the sky for almost a full 24 hours, did not equal 'warm.' But it did help me possibly avoid another uncomfortable encounter with Nate. My father usually lit out for the day around six, so I expected Nate would still be asleep or recovering from a hangover.

The water appeared incredibly calm, like glass. We might be able to get in more dredging before other boats appeared to interfere with our mojo. Although there were maritime rules about distance between dredges, most dredgers rarely adhered to it. If a less experienced dredger needed some help finding the gold, they learned right away which dredges knew what they were doing. The newbies would try to horn in on the pay streak. Not safe and not much tolerated either. However, instead of calling the authorities to deal with the infraction, the disagreement was settled with punches and foul language.

As I went through the motions of prepping the dredge, I couldn't help but circle back around to the news story Stella had found yesterday. I filled the tank of the generator with fuel. I sent a silent prayer skyward in thanks for the gold that kept us going. I'd also stocked the cooler with drinks and snacks. Today Ben would be treated a little bit better than before. When you were on the gold, it was a good idea to keep the help happy. And my help just happened to be an accused murderer.

The dredge dipped slightly.

"Ham and Swiss okay?"

I nearly jumped out of my skin at the sound of Ben's voice. "Jeez, you shouldn't sneak up on people like that." I gave him a hard glare.

"Sorry." He set his bag stuffed with his diving gear on the deck. "What do you want me to do?"

"Heads up." I tossed him a wrench. "Double check the fittings on the air hoses." Not that loose fittings was the cause of my problem the last time we were on the water, but I needed him to be doing something useful rather than standing there. I'd almost finished prepping the boat.

"Got it." Ben immediately tightened every fitting he could find.

His presence alone set me on edge, which annoyed me. The small amount of trust we'd built had been damaged by what Stella had discovered and, until I could find out exactly what his involvement was with the death of his fiancée, it would be hard for me to relax.

I left him busy on the deck while I checked on the systems inside the wheelhouse. I turned on the GPS to get us back to where we'd been before the weather turned. It had been a good patch of gold. Could be the *Goldfinger* and Kyle had sucked up the rest, but I had to go back to make sure before I spent time testing out new ground. No one had been out on the water yesterday, so a slight chance existed we could follow the streak and play it out without competition. I scanned the small boat harbor. Only two other dredges appeared manned for work this early in the day.

I switched on the comms systems. It crackled to life.

Good to go.

"Cast off. We're good." I hollered to Ben.

Ben untied the *Alaska Darling*.

I throttled us slowly out around the jetty and into the open water. The early morning glow of the sun lit up the horizon with a pink-white light. Above, wisps of white clouds dotted the expanse of a dark blue sky. Already the days were noticeably shorter than they'd been earlier in the summer. Each day past the summer solstice several minutes of precious sunlight slipped away until the ice came and the sun disappeared for most of the winter.

Ben joined me in the wheelhouse. "Nice morning to be out."

"Yes, you don't get many days like this on the Bering."

He stood to my left, a short distance away. We both stared out at the calm sea. His close warmth caused goosebumps on my arms.

I closed my eyes for a moment at the betrayal of my body. Was it the fact he was a possible murderer that gave me some kind of thrill?

"My grandpa used to love this place." Ben leaned against the doorway and crossed his arms.

"Oh, I didn't realize you'd been to Nome before." The new bit was a better explanation for why Ben had come to Nome—beyond the need for money or to hide out from the authorities.

"I haven't." He crossed his arms and tensed his shoulders.

His short, cryptic answer raised even more questions in my mind, but his demeanor indicated to me I should let the topic drop.

"I'll dive first." I craved the silence of the ocean today. Plus, I wanted to test the extent of my trust for Ben. Maybe I would pay the $9.99 when I got back to town to check out the rest of the news on Ben. "You go after lunch?" I could handle six hours under water. I think my max dive had been eight. Not typical for me, but possible. My dad had always limited my dives maybe out of some sort of protective gesture. But I didn't have that luxury anymore. Two divers. A full day of clear weather. Both Ben and I needed to be able to work our butts off to ensure a successful week.

I steered the dredge toward the marked spot on the GPS. The other two dredges I'd seen earlier swiftly headed away from our spot and toward the east. I wondered fleetingly if one of those dredges was the *Goldfinger*.

"Sounds like a plan." Ben coiled the dock line. The earlier tenseness gone. "I think I'm starting to get a feel for it."

I turned my gaze to the horizon. "Definitely. Our take was good last week. It helps when you're an experienced diver. You can focus on the material—too sandy, you aren't going to find anything. It's a certain kind of cobble that really holds the gold."

I powered down the throttle as we approached our spot. Not too far from shore. By some miracle this area hadn't been hit before except by the *Alaska Darling* and the *Goldfinger*. But it was a little deeper than most liked to dive. Some smaller dredges wouldn't even try this depth. With the public claims growing busier and busier each year, dredges that wanted a chance of making it had to take some risk, dive deeper, stay down longer.

I knew Ben could handle the depth, though. In fact, I thought he'd relish the challenge with his background. Half the time a new diver would quit because of the conditions—the cold water, the air hose getting tangled, working the suction hose. Not exactly reef diving. There were a lot of moving parts you needed to get right. Ben handled all with aplomb.

"I'll get us back on the gold," I said, "and then you can follow me."

My phone rang as I set anchor over our marked location.

The hospital.

"Change of plans." My phone vibrated and jumped across the surface of the plywood that served as a dashboard. "You suit up. I have to answer this."

Ben agreed and went to grab his dive gear.

"Hello?"

"Ms. Darling, sorry to call so early, but I thought you'd like to know: your father woke up a few hours ago. His doctor wanted me to get in touch with you right away."

Tears of relief pricked my eyes. "Can I talk to him?"

Ben brushed past me to hook himself up to the hot water line. I followed him out onto the deck to make sure the hoses didn't get in his way when he entered the water.

"Maybe in a few hours. He's being taken off the breathing machine. His voice might be a little hoarse. We need to assess his state of consciousness and then we'll go from there."

I knew a definite possibility existed he'd end up with some brain damage from his accident. He'd been without oxygen for a time after the heart attack. No one was sure exactly how long. "Okay. Can you call me after the assessment?"

Ben looked at me, but continued his dive preparations silently.

"Of course, Ms. Darling. I know it can be difficult when a loved one can't be here personally for a debrief."

Ben gave me a thumbs up with a quizzical look on his face.

I gave him a return thumbs up. What else could I do? Yes, it was good news my father came out of his coma, but so much unknown remained about his future and his health. He needed surgery, so the positive progress made that more likely, which also put more pressure on me to come up with the money he'd need for the procedure.

Ben smiled.

"I'll be reachable for the next six hours or so. Can you let the doctor know?"

"Yes, sure, I can do that."

"Thanks."

Ben jumped into the water and saluted me at the same time.

I hung up feeling hopeful for the first time in almost two weeks. I slipped my cell phone in my back pocket and started up the sluice.

The drone of its motor soothed me. So familiar a sound. It reminded me of all those summers I spent with Buck and Nate on the dredge. An odd place for a young girl to spend her summer, but it had been enjoyable. I had wanted to soak up every piece of knowledge my dad and his partner were willing to share with me. How to read the ocean floor. How to run the equipment. How to mark a good spot on the GPS. How to make a decent PB&J the way my dad liked. Butter on both pieces of bread, then jam, then a thick slab of peanut butter in between. Chunky, not creamy.

I checked the gauges to ensure Ben received good air and that the hot water line worked properly. Then, I went back to the wheelhouse to see if he'd located where we'd left off the other day.

"How's it going down there?"

Ben responded, "Just got to where we last worked. That big rock we turned over? I see a new path headed east, opposite direction."

"Great." I turned the volume all the way up on my phone, so I could hear it ring no matter where I happened to be on the dredge. I hoped the doctor would call me sooner rather than later. My whole body had become tense. So frustrating to be on the dredge rather than on a plane. But what good would that do me? I needed to be here, keeping the dredge operating.

After my dad and I had the falling out with Nate last summer, it had made it particularly hard to have a fully operational outfit for ice diving. Kyle, although he was a decent diver, flew to his parents' place in Texas for the winter months, so we'd been left to fend for ourselves with no back-up diver. It had been too much pressure for Buck, so we'd chosen to scrape by until the summer. That one decision put us further behind the eight ball when we started up this summer.

What I needed to find was one consistent source. One good spot where the gold was easy to find and quick to collect—like my dad's fabled nugget field. Finding a spot like that in the well-traveled open claims offshore had grown even harder over the last ten years as word had gotten out about the gold to be found beneath the Bering Sea waves. Every summer more and more 'outsiders' showed up. Serious miners had to work harder to make ends meet, dive deeper, explore further from shore.

"I think I found a new pay streak." Ben's garbled voice came across the comms.

"Fantastic!" Kyle might've played out the original track we'd been following, but sounded like we'd stumbled across something viable. I marked the spot with a new purple dot on the GPS map. "Good visibility down there?" If the weather would hold, we could keep on the gold all day.

"Not bad."

A dredge approached from the shore. It headed straight for us. The word had gotten out. A hot streak attracted a host of dredges who hoped to ride on the back of a more successful, knowledgeable dredger's work. "We got company coming."

"Gotcha."

I walked out on deck to check the sluice box, which would tell me if Ben had really found a new gold spot worth working.

Water rushed over the riffles. I dug through the deposited material in one of the tracks between the riffles. Specks of gold glinted on my finger. I also spotted a 'picker'—a larger chunk of gold that could be picked out from the junk. Ben had definitely found a new streak of pay.

Several dredges had arrived within 150 yards of where I'd anchored the *Alaska Darling*. I recognized one of the boats immediately—the *Rough & Ready*. I squinted in the brighter light of mid-morning. The waves had come alive with glints of summer sun. A tall, thinner man with scraggly hair appeared on the foredeck.

Nate Frazier.

CHAPTER FOURTEEN

Nate waved. An insincere smile on his face. I had an empty feeling in my stomach. He was the last person I wanted to see out on the water today. Couldn't he go dredge somewhere else?

I ducked my head and got back on the radio.

"You are definitely on the gold." The good news first. "I even found a couple of pickers."

Ben whistled. "Well, hot damn."

"But we've got about three or four boats setting up shop nearby." I hesitated to tell Ben about Nate. What good could possibly come of it? I needed Ben in a positive mindset, and Nate had clearly set him off the other night. "They might try horning in on our streak. Let me know if anyone gets too close."

"Aye-aye, captain." He paused and then grunted. "Oh, heck, yeah."

"What you got?" I looked out across the water at the *Rough & Ready* anchoring south of our position. The direction Ben had been headed. Those bastards. Nate could read the positioning of the *Alaska Darling* and the run of the air hose and water lines to make an educated guess as to where my diver would be. Plus, he knew my dad's methods. Easy enough to pick up on where the gold might be.

"Mega boulder. Just flipped it."

"Sweet." I did my best to keep my voice light, unaffected by the rivals about to suck up our gold. "I think you've got it, Ben. Can you keep it up for a few more hours?"

"No problemo."

The sight of Nate Frazier had set me off in a bad direction mentally. Old friendships had been ripped apart. Out here on the Bering it was every man for himself. Nate didn't care if he destroyed my father's business. He'd set course on a path of revenge for some unwritten promise I'd never heard of. He felt he deserved half the business but had nothing to back it up. All based on feelings and his own need for payback. My father chose me over his long-time business partner, and Nate had a very large chip on his shoulder about it. A dangerous chip, perhaps.

My phone rang. I pulled my gaze away from the *Rough & Ready* just as Nate was suiting up for a dive.

The hospital again.

"Hello?" My hand trembled.

"This is Dr. Leskiv. The nurse told me you'd only be available by phone for a few hours today. I hope I didn't call too late."

"You're fine. This is perfect. How's my father doing? Can you tell me anything?" I turned away from the *Rough & Ready* to focus on the conversation. "This morning the nurse implied that they'd need time to assess his consciousness."

"Although your father is currently unable to speak with you, I wouldn't be alarmed. He's slowly coming around. These things take time. He went through a major trauma."

Tears welled up and blinded me. "That such a relief to hear." I had trouble finding words. "Will he be fit for surgery?"

"We're going to do the work up later this afternoon. Once he's more lucid."

"Okay, okay, that's good news." God, I wish I could be there. See him. Talk to him.

"I know it's tricky being so far away. But we're used to this down here. Lots of patients get flown in to Anchorage during a crisis. If you'd like, we can hook you up with a patient care coordinator who can help you navigate what's going on with your father and help you understand the process going forward. Even after his surgery and release from the hospital, we don't recommend he return to Nome for at least two or three months so we can monitor his condition and help him learn about how to make effective changes in his daily living to give him the best outcome. That includes dietary changes, exercise, and even mental health counseling."

I sorted through the information the doctor had unloaded on me. So beyond the deductible I'd need to come up with, I'd have to prepare myself for finding my dad a place to live in Anchorage while he recovered. My shoulders sagged. "Thank you, Doctor. I'd love to get in touch with a coordinator. That would really help."

The crackle of the radio interrupted the conversation. "Rory, can you give me more hose? I can't move."

"Excuse me?" Dr. Leskiv asked.

"Oh, I'm sorry, doctor. I'm at work."

Ben tried again "Rory? Hose?"

"Can you text me the number of the coordinator? I'll get in touch as soon as I can."

"Of course."

"And could you let me know as soon as my dad is lucid enough for a phone call?"

"Sure."

"Rory!" Ben's voice went up an octave.

"Sorry, doc, gotta go." I hung up the phone and picked up the radio. "I got it! More hose. I'll see what I can do. I might have to move the dredge."

"For fuck's sake, what the hell took you so long?"

I dropped the radio and let the irritation at Ben's interruption roll off my back. Only a few feet of hose rested on the foredeck. Not enough to help. "Hold on, I'm gonna have to move the dredge." From the wheelhouse I could see the hose stretched quite taut and lead in the direction of rival dredges. Screw that. We were here first. "I'll take it slow. Keep an eye on your hoses." The last thing I wanted was to have the complex set up of air, hot water and suction hoses get tangled around my diver.

"Roger."

First, I headed out on deck to pull up our anchor. The current toward shore even during calm weather meant a dredge needed to be anchored well to ensure the boat didn't drift and the diver could work the ground with the least amount of interference. Then, I slowly throttled the *Alaska Darling* southeast, parallel to the shoreline, and closer and closer to the *Rough & Ready* and a few other dredges behind them. I took special care to keep the hoses to starboard so I wouldn't entangle any of the lines in my prop.

I sensed Nate's eyes on me. Watching, watching, watching. Ready to pounce at any moment. My failures, my mistakes were to his benefit. The *Alaska Darling* chugged along a little bit at a time until Ben's lines were behind the dredge.

I shut off the motor and set the anchor for a second time off the port side.

We were now settled in a spot that might be considered within the dredging area of the *Rough & Ready*. But I didn't care. This is how one established a presence on the water. Take your territory and make others shove you off. Like a game of King of the Mountain. We'd been dredging here for an hour before they'd showed up. Early bird gets the worm and all that.

I caught sight of Nate. He took a step and jumped into the water.

I calculated the distance Ben would cover in the next several hours. Most likely he would exhaust the lines again and be within range of Nate. I bit my lip. It would be my shift soon.

I had to knock the worries out of my head. I was making an assumption about what might happen under water, and I didn't even know if it would be true. I'd heard stories from my dad—and Nate—about underwater battles involving heavy suction hoses and twisted air lines. Even though everything slowed down under water, there were other ways to win a fight besides throwing a few punches.

While I waited for Ben to finish his dive, I searched through what I had in the wheelhouse to use as a defensive weapon—a wrench? A screwdriver? Maybe a hammer? I scrounged in the tool box in the back. Then I stopped myself with a laugh. What was I doing? Did I really think it would come to blows? Ben would be up top. He could handle the captain of the *Rough & Ready* if I needed help below. I dropped the hammer and shut the tool box.

*

The cool silence surrounded me. The current buffeted against my body as I set up the suction hose to continue where Ben left off. The trail of overturned rocks and missing cobble led me straight to unworked ground. Although I thought Ben could've created a wider path, he'd done a good job for a rookie.

Confidence underwater took time to build, but Ben had arrived with experience I could only dream of having. It made him an especially good dredger. Typical scuba diving took more training and skill. Using pressurized air tanks and keeping track of depth, time, and tank levels. As a diver in the military Ben's training most likely went beyond pure scuba training and involved other aspects of diving most civilians would never experience. To pick up on how to work the ground, the power of the suction hose, and being able to spy gold-containing cobble rather than previously worked areas or areas that held very little value was the biggest part of the job here in Nome.

When I'd begun learning to dive, I'd been around seventeen. My dad hadn't wanted to teach me. Too dangerous, he'd said. Too many things could go wrong down there, and Buck had seen his share of accidents and stupid moves. He didn't like the idea of me taking any risks. Until he caught me asking Nate for help one day when the water conditions were too choppy to dive. That's when my dad realized he'd better teach me, so he could keep an eye on me.

Nate used to be reliable. He'd be the one down at the docks prepping the equipment, checking the hoses and lines for any damage, topping off the tanks with fuel. He'd been an affable guy who'd make dumb jokes and tousle my hair. But as I got older, something shifted between us.

I drifted closer to the area of ground I'd wanted to work and turned my mind off to negative thoughts. They weighed on me up top. I didn't need them to follow me down here to my refuge. I straddled the suction hose, grabbed hold of the metal handles and directed the nozzle at the cobble. Back and forth. Back and forth. A pattern and rhythm I'd learned over the years working the ground. Each sweep of the hose gave me a sense of accomplishment. We'd managed to hit an ounce an hour in our old spot, I hoped for the same amount or better on this new one.

"Did you find it?" Ben's voice came through loud and clear over the comms.

The noise broke my concentration and peaceful mindset. "Yes. I'm on it."

The gold flake caught the light even fifteen feet down. A precious metal for which many had died or been injured, like my father, in the Bering. What did they call it? A harsh mistress. So true.

Every summer, if it had been a good summer for us financially, my father would say, "Let's go to Arizona. I'll sell the dredge, you could be a normal kid." We'd talk about it over the winter when the snow piled up and the thermometer dropped below zero, when the bank account grew lighter and lighter, when I needed dental work or he needed physical therapy on his arthritic knees. But it never lasted—the desire to escape. It never had been as strong as his desire to find that motherlode he believed existed. One more summer always turned into another one and another one.

And I never had any ideas of leaving. Where would I go? My friends, limited though they may be, were here. My best memories were here. I wanted nothing more than to stay with my father, please him, do what he wanted, because deep down I thought it was a way to make him stay. If I went along with his plans, no matter how crazy, he'd keep loving me.

In the murky distance another diver appeared. Straight ahead about 30 yards away. Right in the path of our find. Because of the distance, I couldn't tell who it was. Although my gut told me to be cautious, as it could be Nate, I kept on with my work. I sucked up a few nuggets the size of rice grains that I'd uncovered beneath a medium-sized rock. The day would end up being a good one by the looks of it. As much as I hated the idea of someone else using our work to make themselves some money, all of us dredgers had done it at one time or another.

The best situation would be to own my own piece of it. Have enough money someday to buy a claim. That had been one of my father's dreams. He'd had his eye on one or two, I think. Never really mentioned which ones, though. There were a few claims available, but hard for us small operators to scrape enough money together to buy one. But if my father and I had our own claim, the battling for every nugget, every ounce would be over. We could hunt undisturbed. A dream, for sure, but one we'd both shared, both obsessed over, both focused on. I and my father were of one mind on that topic. No matter what, I'd keep this dredge going for as long as it took until Buck could come back and be by my side again. Like old times. Buck and Rory Darling. An unbeatable team.

I ignored the diver coming toward me and did my job. Gold was what I needed to put in the box. And this was the way to do it— through hard work and effort. If this gold streak played out, we'd find another. And then another. And another. With about two or three weeks left until the season ended and ice began to form, I'd have to work extra hard to look for unworked ground.

CHAPTER FIFTEEN

We neared the breakwater. A heavy silence had settled between Ben and me. I'd pulled on my sweat pants and a ratty Budweiser t-shirt of my dad's. We both were tired, cold and ready to call it a day. Ben would climb on his ATV and head to who knew where. I'd go back to my apartment and make some macaroni and cheese and probably fall asleep while streaming old episodes of *The Office*.

I'd probably watched each episode a dozen times. Could quote lines by heart. Kyle used to roll his eyes when he walked in on me watching it.

"So predictable," he'd say. "You have a whole internet, and this is what you want to watch?"

I smiled at the stupid annoyances I caused him. I had to admit there were parts of Kyle I really missed.

Ben, on the other hand, was a whole different kind of man. Intense, fierce, and, even though he hardly knew me, loyal. He'd taken my side on several things in the few days we'd known each other. Not sure what I had done to deserve it, but I appreciated it nonetheless. To confuse things, the news story about his fiancée had been downright disturbing. I set these two things in my mind and could not match them up. Was Ben a killer or a man I could trust?

I went for it. "So why are you being nice to me?"

He gave me a quizzical smile. "What?"

"I mean it, why are you being nice to me? You barely know me."

"Do you want me to apologize for being nice?" He focused on

the water.

"No, it's not that…" I sighed. My words came out all wrong. "I appreciate you being nice and helpful and gentlemanly and whatever, but I want to know why. Why are you doing it?"

"Isn't that what a man's supposed to do?" He shrugged.

"But what if I'm a total bitch?" I crossed my arms and stood legs apart, so the ripple of the waves under the dredge wouldn't knock me over. "What if I take advantage of all of this politeness?"

"I know what a total bitch looks like, and you're not it." He guided the dredge around the tip of the breakwater and into the harbor. "Plus, you're paying me, right? I work for you. Why would I want to screw that up?"

He had a point. "I appreciate that. Not one person in Nome thinks I can run the *Alaska Darling*. If you haven't noticed, not many women captain dredges out here. They think I only ended up in charge because of my dad. Well, screw that." Even Kyle thought I'd only brought Ben on to run things. To be my protector.

He scanned my bedraggled figure. "You seem pretty capable to me."

That took me by surprise. "Thanks." I hadn't felt very capable as of late. Where was the independent girl Buck Darling had raised? I'd punched Nate in the nose, for heaven's sake. No one had helped me then. I took care of things myself. And when my mom had left I had taken care of things then, too.

"So, your dad gonna be all right?" Ben asked, deftly changing the subject.

His question set off a flurry of conflicting emotions: hope, fear, worry, sadness. "I think so."

"That's good. I'm glad." He steered toward the docks. "You want me to bring it in?" Ben worked the controls, slowing us down for the approach.

"Sure, go ahead." I willed my tired body to move. "I'll get ready with the line."

Ben slowed the dredge to a crawl and steered us toward a gap. I readied myself at the edge and waited until we were within a couple of feet of the dock. I jumped, rope in hand, and landed barefooted. As Ben shut down the engine, I tied the rope around the cleat, snugging the dredge up against the dock.

By the time I'd finished securely lashing the dredge, Ben had begun cleaning out the sluice. I joined him in the task. We hauled saturated mats full of heavy material from the bottom of the sound, which we both hoped was seeded with gold flake. A few smaller nuggets were visible to the naked eye.

"Looks good." I dumped a rolled up mat into one of the five gallon buckets. My exhausted limbs shook.

"Need my help with clean up again?" Ben put his mat alongside mine. "I got this." He waved me off as I went for the bucket handle.

After our discussion on the dredge about how capable I was, the fact Ben had to help me with the mats at the end of a long day didn't exactly prove his point. But a few other things needed my attention on the dredge before I left the dock for the day. "If you could get that out to the truck, I'm gonna check some of the equipment and refuel for tomorrow."

Ben agreed and carried the heavy, gold-and-gravel laden bucket to the edge of the dredge to lift it onto the dock. He set it on the well-weathered boards and took a step across the gap between the dredge and the dock. The dredge dipped. Out of the corner of my eye I caught a glimpse of Nate, just arrived on the *Rough & Ready*, taking a foot off the *Alaska Darling*. Ben lost his footing, grabbed for the edge, missed, and slipped between the dredge and the dock into the incredibly cold water in the harbor.

"Oh my God!" I leapt into action. I grabbed an extra boat fender and lashed it to the edge of the dredge so that Ben wouldn't be crushed as the waves pushed the dredge into the dock. It didn't give him much space. The water was treacherously cold. Someone could go into hypothermia with only a few minutes of exposure. "Does anyone see him?"

More dredgers had arrived and unloaded their crew and pay dirt, too. Confusion rippled through the men.

Nate had disappeared.

I spotted the top of Ben's head. He'd managed to move to the starboard side of the dredge and treaded water.

"Here." I dumped a rope ladder over the side.

The captain of the dredge next to me didn't even realize what was playing out in the water between our vessels. A few miners watched the spectacle from the docks. I didn't have time to criticize their non-action. I suppose they thought my diver was one hundred percent my responsibility.

Ben, although a strong swimmer, had trouble maneuvering to the ladder. The effects of the water temperature and shock had set in. He had a cut on his head that bled freely.

I whipped off my sweat pants and t-shirt and dove into the water. If no one else would help, I would do it myself. Show these boys a thing or two about how tough Aurora Darling was.

The water hit my body like a block of ice. As I surfaced, I sucked in air. My whole body shuddered from the shock of it. Ben floated a few feet from me. I turned off my mind to the cold and forced my numb hands and arms to paddle forward. I slid my arms underneath his and kicked backward with all the force I had. It seemed as if I went nowhere. I couldn't feel my legs. Ben relaxed and leaned back, letting me be the guide. He kicked, too, and together we made it back to the dredge.

At the base of the ladder I could barely grasp the ropes to pull myself up much less help Ben who outweighed me by at least fifty pounds. Ben put his whole arm through the ropes to hold himself up. Not quite sure of my next move, I climbed the ladder. The wind blew against my wet body. The cold was unbearable, but only half the work had been done.

"Hold on, Ben." I quickly made a knotted loop with a rope and tossed it down. "Put it on."

Ben slipped the loop over his head and under his arms. He gave me the thumbs up sign. He shivered.

"Can someone help?" I squawked.

Several miners who'd stood watching the scenario play out climbed aboard to add their weight to mine. As a team we hauled Ben up the ladder. At the top, he grabbed the last rung and heaved himself over the side onto the dredge.

Someone handed me a wool blanket from the wheelhouse, and I covered Ben with it. "Are you all right?"

He nodded. His lips pale.

A few miners clapped and cheered from the dock. I guess they didn't think I was such a neophyte after all. The recognition felt good. I smiled at my tiny fan base and waved.

"Here, Rory." I looked up and Kyle handed me a towel. He'd been one of the divers on the dock who'd helped.

I'd completely turned off my brain to the cold. With the crisis over, all I wanted was warmth: something hot to drink, a steamy shower, blankets, slippers, and a cozy couch to lay on. "Thanks." I took the towel and wrapped it around my midsection.

Ben shook the water out of his hair and beard, like a shaggy dog. Although he shivered violently, we'd both made it out of the water pretty much unscathed.

"Thanks, everyone. I appreciate the help." Kyle melted away into the crowd on the dock. I didn't really have much thought about his behavior. But maybe our break-up was still uncomfortable for him. A lot had transpired between us in a short period of time. Maybe the accident had been harder on him than I realized.

"What the hell happened?" Ben asked, teeth chattering.

"I was about to ask you the same thing." I had a sneaking suspicion Nate was to blame, but didn't want to get into it at the docks near all the other dredges and divers. "Let's get out of here. You're still at risk for hypothermia. We need to warm you up."

"So are you."

My hair dripped with icy seawater and my feet were numb. "That's a fair assessment."

"Shit, the bucket."

I followed Ben's gaze. When he'd slipped off the dock, the five gallon bucket had tipped over. Gold-laden concentrates lay spilled across the boards.

"Dammit." I dried off quickly, dressed and slipped on some flip-flops. I grabbed another towel and tossed it to Ben. "Take off your wet clothes. You'll freeze like that." On the dock I tipped the bucket upright and scooped concentrates into the bucket. My feet and hands were white with cold. But we needed the gold, so I had to recover what I could.

Ben joined me. His feet bare. He'd wrapped the wool blanket around his waist like a kilt and had draped the damp towel over his shoulders. He waited for me to add a last handful of concentrates to the bucket and then wordlessly carried it to my truck.

I didn't like leaving the dredge in such a state. I typically spent a little bit of time at the end of the day checking hoses, filling gas tanks, locking things up. But it was more important to get dry and warm. Ben loaded the bucket in the back of my truck.

I started up my dad's truck and rolled down the window. "Get in."

"What?"

"Get. In." I pulled on the door latch, and it popped open a few inches. "You're in no shape to go riding around on an ATV. You'll freeze. I've got some of my dad's stuff at my place. You can warm up there before you head back. I can put your wet things in the dryer." I had no idea how long a journey he had to get to wherever he was staying, but my apartment was only a five minute drive away.

He didn't argue. He slammed the door shut, and I drove us straight to my place.

"You think we lost much gold?" he asked.

I shrugged. "Not much we can do about it now." I turned up the truck's heat to full blast. I couldn't tell the difference between the gas and the brake, my feet were so frozen.

Ben put his hands up to a vent.

I was hyper aware Ben was practically naked in my truck. I had no idea what he wore underneath the blanket. I tried to keep my imagination on a low boil on the back burner. Would do no good to let my thoughts run wild.

"I've been on and off boats for years." He pulled the blanket more tightly around him. A violent shiver struck. "I don't do c-c-clumsy. What happened?"

Might as well 'fess up to what I saw. "Nate, I think." I pulled into a parking space outside my apartment building. "Looked like he stepped on the port side just as you were getting off the dredge."

"Bastard." Ben clenched his fists.

"I have no idea what his problem is. He seems to think I owe him something. Maybe with my dad laid up he sees me as an easy target, I don't know. And when you came to my rescue the other night, I suppose that didn't sit well with him."

"Next time I see him, I'll rearrange his f-f-face." Ben's shivering had gotten worse.

"Let's get inside. We need to warm you up. I'll get a tub running." Although I'd been in the water as well, my time had been limited, and I'd been prepared. I'd shucked off my clothes to make it easier to dry off and get warm. Plus, I'd had dry clothes to put on. "And we need to do something about that cut." I touched his forehead where blood oozed out of a cut above his eye.

He drew back. "Ouch."

"It's not that bad." I smiled. The big, bad military dude had said 'ouch.' "I actually do have a box of Band-Aids despite what you might've thought the other night."

"Well, wherever they are, they were not in a place that makes sense. B-b-bathroom medicine cabinet. That makes sense. Anywhere else? Just stupid."

"Come on. Let's get you inside before the neighbors start

talking."

Ben scanned the street. "Nobody's out there."

"It's just a figure of speech."

We headed up the stairs to my apartment. Ben's wool blanket dragged on the ground, threatening to tear loose with each step.

"My dad's stuff is in the bedroom closet." I unlocked the door. "I'm going to get the bucket out of the truck. I'll be right back."

Ben shuffled into the apartment. "Thanks."

The plastic handle of the five gallon bucket bit into my palm. Although I'd gotten the feeling back in my hands, every move I made felt awkward. A few more steps, and I could curl up under a blanket while I waited for some water to boil for tea. I set the bucket inside the door. It landed with a loud ka-thunk.

Ben came out of the bedroom dressed in my father's bathrobe. *Oh my.*

Since Ben stood much taller and had a build much broader than my father, the bathrobe gaped open down to mid-torso Although I'd seen Ben bare chested before, the combination of wet hair, muscled pecs, and those deep blue eyes made my heart skip.

"Your father and I aren't exactly the same size."

I'm sure my mouth hung open. "Noted." I quickly turned away and headed straight for the bathroom. "Let me start you a bath so you can warm up. Then I'll get the kettle on."

He stopped me. "Appreciate your help today."

Soft, quiet. In my ear. A breath of warmth against my skin. A shiver. Goosebumps. Why did I always find myself attracted to the wrong men? Stella would be bashing me over the head if she knew what was going on behind my apartment door.

"No problem. You would've done the same for me." I said the words, but they weren't just words. I knew that was true. Ben, more a stranger to me than a friend, had pulled my ass out of the fire twice already.

Ben let me go. I cranked on the hot water in the bathroom tub, knowing it would take a few minutes for the water to heat up. I opened the bathroom cabinet under the sink and grabbed the bandages and a tube of anti-bacterial cream.

I caught a look at myself in the mirror and was horrified to see I looked like a drowned rat. My damp shoulder-length hair was plastered across my forehead. My face looked thin and pale in the fluorescent light coming from the one fixture over the sink. I swept away the stray, tangled strands. Not much better. But at least I didn't look quite as unkempt.

I snapped off the bathroom light. "Let me fix you up."

Ben had stretched out on the couch and had covered himself with the comforter I slept under. "Not necessary."

The couch had been my bed for years. Although my dad had been in the hospital for over a week, I didn't feel right moving into his bedroom. If I kept everything as it was, that meant he would come back and we would go on as before. Nothing new. Nothing changed. Everything the same. Everything exactly as it has always been: Buck and Rory, two peas in a pod.

"I'll say if it's necessary." I set the First Aid items on the kitchen counter, grabbed the tea kettle and filled it.

"Really. It's fine." He rubbed at his forehead. "See?"

He had smeared blood across his face.

I gave him a look.

"Shit." He stared at his hand. "Toss me the stupid band-aids."

"I'll fix it." I turned the gas burner up high and plunked the tea kettle on it.

I sat on the armrest of the couch and dabbed at the cut with a Kleenex to clean up some of the blood. "The water in the harbor is so disgusting. We'd better make sure this is good and clean. Did you ever see the show 'Monsters Inside Me?'"

"No."

I smeared some anti-biotic cream on the wound—about an inch long, not very deep. But head wounds of this type always seemed to bleed more than one would think. "Well, there are nasty things that live in the water. Microorganisms, bacteria. It's disgusting actually."

He winced. "Hey. Careful."

"Baby," I chastised. I opened a bandage and carefully adhered it.

Ben looked up at me with his dark, dark gaze. I leaned forward. The deep darkness drew me in. Everything in me wanted to kiss him. I wanted those strong arms to pull me down, caress me, hold me. Sun had streaked his brown hair, and I wanted to run my fingers through it.

He touched my cheek.

I touched my lips to his.

The tea kettle whistled. I jumped back and shook my head.

"The water," Ben said.

CHAPTER SIXTEEN

Warmth flooded my cheeks. "Yeah, I got it." I headed to the kitchen to get the tea kettle. But then I heard water splashing in the bathroom "The tub!"

I left the tea kettle whistling on the stove and ran into the bathroom. The tub had been filled to the top, and the mirror had steamed up.

"I got the kettle." Ben said.

I turned off the faucet and grabbed a couple of towels off the rack to soak up the mess. "Damn."

What in the hell had I been thinking back there on the couch? I'd only just gotten out of a long-term relationship with Kyle. Was I now willing to dive right in with a possible murderer? Would it really be wise to start a relationship with someone who'd lost his fiancée under very suspicious circumstances less than a year ago?

The worst part was, he had no idea I knew about his complicated background. I had this heavy piece of information sitting in my head every time I looked at him. Was that really fair?

"Here you go. I found some tea in the cupboard. I think yours is lemon?" Ben handed me a Styrofoam cup. "Mine's maybe mint?" He sniffed the cup in his other hand and frowned. "Hm, maybe not. The print was sort of faded on the box."

I took the tea with surprise. He'd found something in my father's disorganized kitchen. More power to him. "The bath is ready."

He studied me.

I wanted to forget the kiss.

"So…" He opened the door to an uncomfortable discussion. "What was that back there? On the couch."

"A mistake?"

He scratched his jaw. "All right."

My heart beat as fast as a bird's. "The floor's a bit wet, but the water's hot." I scooped up the soaked towels. "I'll bring you some dry ones." I grabbed a stack of dry, folded towels sitting in a laundry basket near the couch. I stamped out that conversation. It just wasn't happening. Period.

"Great. Okay. Cool." Ben's words were clipped.

I handed him the towels and shut the door.

I leaned against it. My stomach in knots.

Water splashed. He'd climbed into the tub.

I entered my father's room and picked up Ben's wet clothes. Pants, shirt, socks. I knocked on the bathroom door. "I'm going down to the laundry room. Be right back."

All I heard was a contented groan on the other side of the door.

I threw on a parka, as I still hadn't recovered my body temperature. Might look like overkill for an August evening, but what did I care? I dumped out the mug that held spare change and counted out four quarters for the dryer. I put Ben's clothes in an empty hamper from the coat closet and headed down to the small laundry room at the back of the building.

Once I got outside into the real world, I let out a huge breath. Whatever emotions ran through me on the couch needed to be exorcised immediately. My mother had probably gotten into trouble for the same reason. No self-control. Instead of ignoring a visceral physical attraction to a handsome, virile man, she'd welcomed it.

Ben was not unattractive. He was built like a tank. On an evolutionary level, he fit the ideal: strong, tall, fit. But that wasn't an excuse for me to act stupid. I needed to straighten out my head before I went back upstairs.

I plunked down the basket and loaded Ben's clothes into the empty dryer. Thirty minutes should do it. I turned the dial and then took a seat on the folding chair someone had been kind enough to leave behind. A year ago, I used to sit on the washer and lean against the wall while waiting for my laundry to wash and dry. Someone must've gotten sick of that routine and sacrificed a chair for the public good.

My phone vibrated in my back pocket. Texts from Stella.

Can I come over? Matt at work. Lonely.

I knew it was more likely she was annoyed at the third wheel living in their apartment: Matt's sister, Alisha. Everything was so expensive in Nome—gas, heat, electricity, food. A lot of times friends and family shared the same cramped living quarters to make ends meet.

I thought about my guest upstairs. Not sure how I could explain that to Stella. I mulled over my answer. But then again, maybe Stella was exactly what I needed. I responded:

Sure. Bring pizza?

Stella answered:

You provide the beer?

I'd just purchased a couple of six packs yesterday so I could keep the dredge stocked for the end-of-the-day reward.

I texted a thumbs up symbol and typed:

See you in 30.

She could find out I had an extra guest when she got here. I had solved my uncomfortable situation in minutes.

*

The dryer shut off. I scooped up Ben's dry clothes, put them in the hamper, and headed back upstairs.

Unfortunately, Stella was already knocking on my door. Before I could shout out from below, the door opened, and Ben let her in. Not without a moment of hesitation, of course, and some conversation I couldn't hear from my position.

I hurried up the stairs. No one had noticed me. I bumped into the door with my body, my hands full. "Could you let me in?" I shouted.

The door opened.

"So it's a double date then?" Ben greeted me dressed in my

father's robe once more.

His cheeks were ruddy from the heat and steam of the bath.

"Glad to see you're doing better." I pushed my way in.

Stella rummaged in my fridge. A pizza box sat on the counter.

I held the laundry hamper out. "Here, why don't you put your clothes on?"

Ben felt the warm shirt and smiled. "Ah, thanks a million." As Ben headed into my father's bedroom to change, he said, "I hope you brought pepperoni."

Stella turned and gave me a sharp look. "Why didn't you tell me Ben was over here?" she hissed.

I opened the pizza box—garlic chicken. Hope Ben didn't mind. I picked up a slice, suddenly starving. "Because I knew you wouldn't come."

"How do *you* know? You didn't even give me a chance." She sipped a beer and grabbed her own slice. "Care to explain how your new diver…"

"…And suspected murderer," I whispered.

Stella nodded emphatically, "Yes, and *suspected murderer*, ended up half-naked in your apartment?"

"I wasn't half-naked." Ben reappeared dressed in his regular clothes.

For a split second I felt something like disappointment wash over me.

"I was *all* naked." He winked.

Stella blushed and gave me an even sharper look.

"He used my bathtub, Stel. For heaven's sake." I popped open a beer and handed it to Ben. "You have to be cautious around Stella, she will take your word for truth and, before you know it, Nome will be full of all kinds of scandalous gossip."

"I'll remember that." Ben took the beer and peered in the pizza box. "Chicken does not belong on a pizza." He pulled a face but took a slice anyway.

"So is anyone going to explain anything to me?" Stella's frustration was obvious. "Or I will make up something that you won't like?"

"I fell in the drink." Ben chomped down his first slice of pizza. "Actually, this isn't bad."

I picked up the story. "Ben fell off the dock, and I rescued him."

"Well, there was a little more to it than that." Ben gave me a sideways glance.

"Long story short, we both ended up in the water. Ben's got a long ride home, so I suggested he come here to warm up, get dry. That sort of thing."

Stella didn't seem too convinced. "Uh huh."

I wondered what Ben had told her at the door when he'd answered.

Although I knew Stella was likely erring on the side of caution when it came to Ben, he seemed to be winning her over with charm. I didn't even know this side of him existed until now. I liked it.

"And I'll be on my way shortly. Don't want to get in the way of a Girls' Night." He grabbed another slice. "I just need a ride back to my ATV at the docks…"

"I can take you," I offered. For some reason I didn't want Stella driving him back. Both of them in a car alone for a few minutes? She might slip up and say something. Why I was so afraid of him finding out what we knew, I don't know. But maybe deep down I wanted to keep our relationship drama free. Letting him know what we'd found online? Well, until I knew more, what would be the point? It could all be a mistake. It could be something less terrible than the story implied. Or it could be worse. My conscience kicked in that worry.

Stella wouldn't look at me. Her silent judgment settled on me like a heavy blanket. Smothering. Stella had only briefly met Ben. She didn't know him like I did. I didn't really need her to tell me how to view him. I could figure it out for myself. But her attitude stung a little bit, I had to admit. I wanted her approval, but I knew she wasn't going to give it to me so easily.

"Great." Ben plunked down on the couch with his drink and what remained of pizza slice number two.

My mind returned to a half an hour earlier when Ben had been prone on the couch, and I'd kissed him. I didn't want to think about it, but I couldn't help it.

Ben's gaze locked with mine. His blue eyes blazing.

I knew he was thinking about the same thing.

I shivered.

For a brief moment I wished Stella away. I could've had that. I could've turned her down earlier and told her I was tired, busy, whatever. But I didn't. I'd agreed to her idea because I knew what I was capable of, the mistakes I could make, the easy slide from one relationship into another. Kyle hadn't been my first and only boyfriend. There had been others. Stella knew. Stella had watched it all play out in real time, had been my shoulder to cry on when things had gone wrong, had scolded me—kindly—when I'd made the wrong move.

Part of me wanted Ben all to myself. I knew I'd stepped into dangerous waters. I ran the risk of destroying a good working relationship for my own carnal interests. But I needed to figure out how to live my life without Stella saving me. My choices. My life. My mistakes to make.

CHAPTER SEVENTEEN

Twenty minutes later Ben and I were in my dad's truck driving to the docks. My heart was a-flutter; my nerves were on edge.

"Look, I'm not stupid," Ben said.

I kept my eyes on the road. "Oh?"

"Stella didn't show up out of the blue. You asked her to come over." He tapped his fingers on the arm rest. "I didn't realize I made you so nervous."

"I wasn't nervous."

"Is that so?" He chuckled. "You practically shoved me into the tub fully clothed and then ran out of there after you kissed me."

"I did not." My hackles went up. He made me sound like a love sick school girl.

"That's okay. I get it," Ben admitted. "Hard enough to be Buck Darling's daughter around here, I've noticed; you don't need rumors running around town. I don't blame you. I've had my own experiences with ignorant people spreading stories."

I wanted to dig further on this topic, but didn't want to rock the boat. I stashed away his statement for later. "Nome is a strange place. Not only is it a small town, but it's a small town full of a lot of roughness. My dad knew it when I first moved up here. But you don't need to worry about me. I've dealt with these bozos for years. If they don't believe in my abilities now, they never will. Rumors or no." I took a deep breath and went for it. I could be an adult. "Look, I will admit, there is some odd attraction between us. But it's just the work. Nothing more." I needed to explain it away. Find a reason for it to be there. "It's a very intimate relationship between tender and diver. How do you think I ended up with Kyle? And that was a big mistake. It's really better if we keep things professional, don't you think?"

"I never wanted things to be anything else but professional." He cracked his knuckles. "You were the one that kissed me."

That got my pot boiling. But I needed to remain calm, the business owner with her head on straight. Not a messed up chick who needed a man to save her. "It was a mistake on my part. There, does that make you happy?"

"Sure. I never said what happened made me *un*happy."

I wanted to rant in frustration. Calm down, Rory, it wasn't worth the aggravation. He wanted to push my buttons and make the most of an embarrassing moment of weakness. "Right." I turned into the dock parking lot. "Here we are."

"Great. Thanks for the help."

"No problem. It's the least I could do." Before he got out of the truck I added, "Same time tomorrow?"

He nodded and then headed to his ATV.

Before I could return home and put this day behind me, my phone rang.

"Ms. Darling, I'm calling from the ICU at Alaska Regional Hospital," a nurse said. "Your father is alert and ready to talk to you, if you're available."

"Yes, yes, I am. Please put him on." I put the truck in park. My stomach filled with butterflies. "Dad? Is that you?" I briefly closed my eyes. I wanted so badly to hear his voice, to know that he was okay.

"Rory?" Buck's voice was raspy and quiet. Not the booming tenor I knew.

"Yes, it's Rory." I didn't know how much he remembered, how disoriented he would be. I knew the sedation plus the heart attack and its after effects might make him seem a bit muddled in his thoughts. "How are you, Dad?"

"Tired."

I smiled. "I'll bet." The sound of his voice steadied me.

"These nurses…" He coughed. "They'll be the devil of me. Never give me a moment's peace."

I imagined something like a Nurse Ratched from *One Flew Over the Cuckoo's Nest*. Stark white uniform. Stern. Coolly pretty. The unfeeling tyrant of the ICU, roaming the halls at night in her starched white uniform to make his life miserable. "You relax. They just want to make sure you're okay."

"Are you coming soon, Rory?"

My heart ached at the sadness I detected in the request. "Oh, I can't right now. You know it's dredging season." Who knew if he even had an idea what time of year it was or that he was in Anchorage, and I was in Nome.

"Right. Right." His voice rasped.

I watched as Ben's ATV disappeared. "I've got a great, new diver, though." Maybe that would settle his mind knowing I'd found good help in his absence.

"Oh? That's good." He drifted off for a moment. I could hear his breathing on the other end.

"Dad? Are you still there?"

"Don't let him take the map," Buck said, his voice sharp as a stainless steel pin.

"The map?" My mind blanked. "You mean the GPS?" He had been religious about keeping our GPS history a secret from anyone outside the 'circle.' The circle used to include Nate until last summer. Now the 'circle' was only Dad and me.

"The map, the map." Buck's voice grew insistent. "You don't want to lose it."

"I won't, Dad." I had no idea what he was talking about. It must be nonsense. The drugs talking. "No one's going to take the map," I placated him.

"That's good, Rory. Keep it locked up." His voice grew fainter and fainter. "Keep it locked."

My curiosity piqued. "Locked where?"

"In the box." He coughed. "We're gonna get that mother lode I promised you.

Before I could ask him anymore, a nurse got on the line. "I think your father needs some rest now. The doctor will call you to let you know more about when surgery can be scheduled."

"Oh, great. Okay, thanks." The voice on the other end of the line had already hung up.

I turned over in my mind the box my father had mentioned. What could he mean? I didn't remember any locked box he kept at the apartment. And there weren't a lot of places to hide things in the few rooms we had. No secret compartments. No space under the floorboards. No safety deposit boxes with secret keys stashed in bus lockers like they always had in the movies.

He'd sounded tired but lucid. My gut told me he wasn't making it up—the idea of a map to a big gold find in a locked box. Before I'd appeared in Nome, my father had worked on his dredge for years without a GPS system. In the 90s such a thing had been expensive and out of reach for two young guys scrambling to get together the cash for a dredge. A GPS would've been something only the big boats had. Men with investors and such.

So a map wouldn't be unusual for my father to have stashed somewhere. Maybe his heart attack had jumbled his memories around. Maybe he'd remembered a time long past. But he'd never mentioned a map before when we'd dreamed of finding gold nuggets as big as shotgun shells.

I drove back into town, mulling over my father's words. On a whim, I turned toward Kyle's place. Not only had he'd disappeared before I'd gotten a chance to thank him for helping save my diver, I wanted to ask him about the idea of a map.

The fact our relationship had frayed since our break up didn't sit well with me. And most of that was my fault for laying the blame for my father's accident at his feet. But, at the time, he hadn't defended his actions, so I assumed my thoughts about what had transpired on the dredge that day had been pretty accurate. Now that I'd had my experience with the air compressor conking out, I viewed the accident through new eyes.

I'd overslept that day. The three of us had been working the dredge with a routine like clockwork. Up at 5:30, on the dredge by six, back at the docks by five. Over and over and over. Sure, some days the weather kept us in, but without fail it was a threesome that went out and a threesome that returned.

The weather forecast had looked grim. Too windy. We hadn't planned to go out. But, for some reason, Buck woke up early and noticed the weather had shifted. The winds had stilled. He'd left me asleep in the apartment and had decided to head out with Kyle for reasons I might never know.

Kyle had tended, and my father had dived. While he worked below, the air line blew apart. A crack had formed in the tubing and gone unnoticed. Buck had been down pretty deep and, before he could make it to the surface, the strain had given him a massive heart attack.

As tender, it had been Kyle's job to check the equipment. So to me, that had been strike one against him. Strike two had been the delay in calling for help. Kyle didn't make the call for a good fifteen minutes. Fifteen precious minutes my father went without medical assistance.

I made the turn on Kyle's street. Flying the white truce flag might be the best solution to keep some of my personal dirt a secret. He'd reached out today. I might as well test the waters.

Luckily, the lights were on in his Quonset hut. I wanted to resolve the situation so the tension would go away. I needed to get past my negative feelings. I couldn't go back in time and change anything about the accident, but now I understood that sometimes things can go wrong, and no one is to blame.

Kyle answered his door after a couple of knocks. His automatic smile went stiff at the sight of me. "Oh. What're you doing here, Rory?"

"I wanted to stop by and thank you for helping out on the docks earlier. That was really nice of you."

He shrugged and shifted his weight from one foot to another. "It was the right thing to do."

"Well, half the guys there didn't bother." I paused and screwed up my courage. "Do you mind if I come in for a minute?" I thought briefly about Stella back at my apartment. But I doubted she'd mind a short delay.

"I guess." He opened the door more widely and tucked his hands in his pockets.

I followed him inside.

His place still felt like home. I'd spent the better part of a year living here. Although the lighting sucked and the place constantly smelled like motor oil and rotting seaweed, I missed it.

"Well?" Kyle sat in a kitchen chair with a ripped seat cushion and propped his feet on a plastic crate. "What's on your mind?"

It would've been easy for me to slip right back into our old roles. Kyle, the hard working yet quiet dredge tender and diver. Me, the dredge owner's daughter, mouthy and stubborn. We had made quite a pair. Some said we were mismatched. In public, we didn't seem very affectionate—that wasn't really Kyle's style. He also didn't express himself very much. Most of the time I had no idea where his mind was.

"I don't like the way things ended between us. I wanted to apologize for getting so upset with you after the accident." It took everything in me to say those words, but most of my anger had burned off in the last few days. "It could've happened to anyone." I wasn't so sure I believed that entirely, but if I wanted to make things right with Kyle, the words needed to be said.

He nodded. "How's your old man doing?"

"Not great, but the doc says he should pull through."

"Mm." He chewed his thumbnail.

A nervous habit of his I found irritating. I didn't feel any better about the situation between Kyle and me. I thought my forgiveness would clear the air and set things right. Instead, I felt as if I'd made things worse.

He wouldn't look at me. He jiggled his leg resting on the crate. "Is that it?"

"Yeah. I suppose so." I didn't know what else to say. I wanted to hear something more from Kyle, but he acted as a brick wall more than usual. "Oh, hey, my dad said something really weird when I talked to him a little while ago."

"Oh?"

Maybe Kyle knew what my dad had been rambling about. "He mentioned some kind of map. Do you know anything about that?"

"A map? What do you mean, like a road map?"

"No, a map of the Sound." I mulled over the conversation, thinking about how much I wanted to share with Kyle. "He seemed really anxious about it."

Kyle shrugged. "No, I don't remember anything like that." He popped up and walked me to the door. "Sorry I can't help."

"Oh well, thought it was worth a try." I scanned the junk-filled interior of the Quonset hut. "I wasn't sure if he was talking about something real or if it was the drugs or something."

"I get you."

We stood awkwardly at the door. Our relationship seemed a world away. Eons ago. By the end, we'd been more like 'friends with benefits.' More about needs than true feelings for each other.

He gave me an odd stare as I headed back to my dad's truck.

Maybe my father's accident had more of an impact on him than I'd originally thought.

*

Stella had moved from the kitchen to my father's well-worn easy chair when I returned. The pizza box had been relocated to the living room coffee table.

"What took you so long?" Stella asked the minute I stepped in the door.

"Oh, I stopped by Kyle's for a few." I went to get another beer from the fridge.

"Kyle's place." Stella raised her brows. "Interesting."

I sighed. "It's not what you think. I went there to thank him for helping out at the docks today, and we talked a little bit about my dad."

"Oh?" She moved from the easy chair to the couch to sit closer to me or maybe to borrow some of the ranch dressing I liked to dip my pizza crusts in.

I shrugged. "I'm tired of being angry, I guess. Accidents happen, right?"

"Right."

I spied the five-gallon bucket near the front door. "Crap. I forgot about the mats we brought home."

"Maybe you were distracted by Ben's pecs," Stella teased.

"Oh, Lord." I rolled my eyes. But in the back of my mind I knew she wasn't wrong. There had been a strong attraction between Ben and me. Or had it been one-sided? He'd appeared to find the whole thing quite humorous, to be honest. Maybe it had been all a big joke to him. The 'boss' hitting on him.

I set down my beer and got up to rinse the mats so we could use them tomorrow. I'd had to do it in the tub before. At times like these, I missed the ease of clean up at Kyle's. He had the space and a cement floor that could handle the mess.

"What's the deal with him?" Stella followed me to the bathroom. "Did you ask him about his fiancée? The murder accusation?"

"No. Are you crazy?" Ben had drained the tub, so I was able to set the bucket in it. I grabbed the removable shower head and washed concentrates from the mat into the bucket. "How would I bring that up in casual conversation exactly?"

"What about: Did you murder your fiancée?"

"You are crazy, Stel. I couldn't do that." I ran the shower head

137

between each groove in the mat, washing black sand and, hopefully, some gold, into the bottom of the bucket. As the bucket filled, the clean water ran over and emptied out into the tub. "Right now I'm relying on him to get me through the season. I don't really have time to piss him off or whatever. What if we're wrong? I need him to trust me."

"And you need to trust him. How can you do that if you don't know the truth?"

I set a clean mat in the tub and started on another. "Maybe we should pay the $9.99 and access the news site. Would that satisfy you?"

"That's a start." Stella played with one of her curls, stretching it out straight and then letting it spring back into position.

"All right. Well, let me finish here." I was about halfway through the second mat.

"Deal." Stella's face lit up. She loved internet sleuthing more than anything.

CHAPTER EIGHTEEN

I grabbed my laptop off the charger and opened it up.

The mats were clean and ready for tomorrow. The concentrates from today's gold hunt waited for a clean out, but the potential looked good. Doing a clean-up without all the crew present was atypical, but Ben was new to the game. He probably hadn't even thought of that when I dropped him off at his ATV. No worries. If he distrusted the result, I could use Stella as my witness. I set the thought aside and focused in on finding out more about Ben's mysterious past.

Stella took the laptop away from me and typed in the search terms she'd used last time. "I know what I'm looking for. I can do it faster."

She was right. I knew for a fact my typing skills weren't as good as hers.

"Here." She clicked from the news website's main page to the subscription page. "Give me your credit card." She held out a hand.

I dug into my purse and found my Visa. The one that still had credit left on it. "Want me to read the numbers?"

"Sure."

Ten dollars seemed a cheap price to dig into Ben's life some more. In the back of my mind, a pang of guilt lurked. Sneaking around behind his back didn't feel good. I already knew too much about him. I had been tempted to bring up the topic of his fiancée earlier. What if he got angry at me once he found out what I knew? What if the facts of the case were more than I could handle? If I screwed up our relationship, I'd be worse off than before.

Stella entered my billing ZIP Code and maneuvered the cursor to the purchase button.

"Wait." I had a thickness in my throat.

"Wait?" Stella's round, pink face glowed even pinker in the light of the laptop. I knew she was dying to push that button.

"I can't do it."

"Yes, you can."

I took the laptop out of her hands and snapped it shut. "I'm not sure if I'm ready to find out more just yet."

"What? You're making no sense. He could be a murderer. He could be dangerous. He could be on the run." Lines of concern etched the corners of her mouth. "And now you're wanting to stay in the dark?"

"It's not quite like that, Stel." I put the laptop back on its charger.

"I don't get you." Her curls vibrated with nervous energy. "Ben's a total stranger. For heaven's sake, he only showed up in Nome last week. Nobody's heard of him. Nobody knows where he came from. Who does that? Who just shows up in Nome all by himself and jumps right into everything?"

"Lots of people," I pointed out. "Every summer for dredging season."

"That's a load of baloney." Stella took her empty beer can to the sink. "It's August. Everyone has their teams together. Divers don't show up at the end of the summer to strike it rich. That's a man who has something to hide."

"If it were something I needed to know, he'd tell me." Tonight I'd felt enough of a connection I wanted to believe that. Maybe he wasn't attracted to me. Maybe he found me silly and goofy and nothing like the gorgeous beautiful Laura Snow. But I'd felt something. I hadn't made it up in my mind. My feelings had been real.

"Seriously, Rory? How can you be so naive?" Stella cleaned up pizza crusts and put away the Ranch dressing. "Why would Ben confide in you? Why would he feel any loyalty to you at all or any smidgen of guilt that he'd want to 'fess up to you? He could be dangerous."

"He's not dangerous." I picked up Ben's plate and set it in the sink.

"I don't understand you, Rory. This isn't like you at all." She wrapped up a leftover pizza slice in some tinfoil. "What would your dad say if he knew? I have half a mind to call him and tell him what you're up to. You're not making any sense."

Those words made my hackles stand up. "Don't you dare."

"What? Call Buck?" She opened the fridge and tossed in the tinfoil package. "Why not?"

"He's not in a stable condition." I thought of the strange conversation I'd had with him earlier. He hadn't made any sense. His mind was addled. I needed my father to rest and not worry. He didn't need to be dragged into my complicated life.

"Someone's gotta talk some sense into you." She wiped off her hands on a paper towel. "And if you won't listen to me, I know you'll listen to Buck. He'll set you straight."

"I'm not a child, Stella." My voice grew cold. "And I'd really prefer it if you'd stay out of it."

Stella crossed her arms. "Really." Her usual jovial expression had hardened. Her sunny, bubbly personality squashed by my harshness. "Hey, I thought I was being helpful here. If you don't want my help, then I'll get out of your way."

Stella grabbed her jacket and slipped on her shoes. I didn't stop her.

"You know where to find the information. Up to you whether you care to find out more." She shrugged. "Don't blame me if something happens. I warned you."

The door shut behind her.

*

I'd driven Ben away by inviting Stella over. I'd driven Stella away by not going along with her need to dig for information. And Kyle, although he accepted my apology, had given me the cold shoulder. Not the best night I'd ever had. I wished I had the luxury of taking a sick day tomorrow, so I could linger in my negative emotional state while I ate a carton of ice cream and streamed corny romance flicks with only saccharine sweet happy endings.

I picked up my cell phone, scrolled to my sister, Zoe's number, and dialed.

"Hey, Rory. Kinda late isn't it?"

I looked at the clock. 10 pm. Washington State was an hour ahead. Whoops. "Sorry, Zoe."

"Everything okay? I haven't heard from you since, well…"

We'd ended our last conversation on a bad note, and I supposed she hadn't expected me to reach out so soon. "I had a pretty crappy day and needed someone to talk to." She was my sister after all. We weren't big on heart-to-hearts, but she'd been a decent sounding board in the past for girl-type topics that Buck couldn't even begin to understand. I hoped I could draw on that past to get rid of the negative feelings that lingered.

"Okay," she sighed. "What happened?"

Zoe might not enjoy listening to my freak-outs, but she'd had to play the role of 'mom' many times over the last twelve years. When my mother had run off oldest daughter, Zoe, had borne the full brunt of the responsibilities she'd left behind.

"I broke it off with Kyle, and now he's mad at me." Days of stress and worry flooded out of me. "Stella and I had a fight over something stupid. I don't know if I can do this by myself anymore." The tears welled up. I didn't like to admit any kind of weakness, especially not to my older and thinks-she-wiser sister.

"Hey, hey, hey," Zoe soothed. "This doesn't sound like the girl from last week who told me to shove off when I suggested you sell the dredge." She paused for a moment. "Are you changing your mind about my idea?"

"No." Annoyance pricked at me. "I'm just frustrated is all."

"Oh. Okay. I thought maybe this was a call about coming back home." Zoe had fantasies for years about reassembling our destroyed family. "You know dad's door is always open."

"I'm not changing my mind about anything. I wanted to blow off some steam." The last thing I wanted to do was go back in time and re-live a similar conversation we'd had years ago when I decided to stay in Nome.

"I thought you wanted a solution or something." Her voice lowered. "I'm sorry."

I could've let my emotions get the better of me. I could've hung up on her and continued sulking that Zoe and Henry didn't see my life the way I did. But where would that get me? I would only wall off more people and dig myself a deeper, lonelier hole. "It's okay, Zoe. I appreciate your ideas, even if they might not be ones I'd agree with." I took a deep breath to dial it back a notch. "It's good to know I've got a back-up if everything did blow up in my face."

"Have you heard from John or the hospital?"

Her change of subject surprised me. Her stance had been as long as I could remember that I'd abandoned my 'real' father—Henry—for a Disneyland Dad scenario. To Zoe, DNA did not a dad make. "I spoke with his doctor and got a chance to talk to him on the phone. He sounded good." I lied. He had sounded lost and confused, but she didn't need to know everything.

"That's great. I'm sure you'll figure out a way, Rory." She added with feeling, "You always do."

And Zoe was right. After my mother had disappeared, most twelve-year-old girls would be in a state of shock, devastated. Not me, I'd shrugged it off and made a batch of very burned chocolate chip cookies. My mother had never really shown me a lot of affection, so what exactly was I missing with her being gone? I decided not much. Sure, maybe inside I felt unlovable and unwanted by my own mother, but I didn't let it show. I never let it show. And when I'd arrived in Nome, a motherless girl in the wrong clothes, I leapt into my new life with vigor. I'd gone from suburbanite middle schooler Aurora to hard as nails Rory who could shoot a .22 as well as the boys and even dive for gold, when no other girls my age went anywhere near the cold Bering Sea.

"Maybe after all of this is over, I'll fly down for a visit." I could barely believe the words came out of my mouth. I hadn't been back to Seattle for years.

"Dad and I would really like that." Zoe's voice, usually practical and snappy, came across as warm and sincere.

Her words soothed, which surprised me. Somehow the chip I'd carried on my shoulder had gotten smaller. I'd carried around a lot of resentment toward my stepfather. For what, I had a hard time defining. The feeling just existed. A wall of emotion that I couldn't seem to break through. I guess my stepfather represented everything I'd felt about my mother. I no longer had my mother around to make her into a target of my hurt, so I'd turned it on Henry. I reflected back on my whiny request for financial help last week. As if Henry owed me anything—or Buck.

Henry had never even met the man. My stepfather had put me on the plane when I was twelve, and in his mind I was his daughter. He'd raised me as his child since I was born. It dawned on me how much my stepfather had already sacrificed for me, and I'd wanted to take even more from him. How much that must have pained him.

Zoe and I said our goodbyes and, even though she hadn't really helped me figure out any of my problems, the weight of my life had lightened. She was right. I'd find a way to make it all work out. I wasn't about to give up. Even if I'd ticked off my best friend, my ex and my very much needed diver, I had no choice but to plow forward. I couldn't give up.

I made up my bed on the couch, and as I laid my head down to sleep I caught the familiar aroma of peppermint and gasoline. Even after his dunking from the docks, Ben had left his mark. I breathed it in as I drifted off and dreamed of finding a wide river of gold beneath the waves, Ben at my side, his blue-eyed gaze burning into me.

CHAPTER NINETEEN

Ben knocked on the driver's side window, startling me. "Everything all right?"

I'd pulled into the parking lot at the docks with butterflies in my stomach. Last night had ended badly. The lingering feeling of my lips on Ben's put me in a very awkward place.

Our gazes met.

My face heated.

He smiled a different smile than he had before. A knowing smile.

My heart thudded.

"Yep. Just checking the weather." I showed him the open weather app on my phone.

"We good?" He'd tied back his mass of brown hair and trimmed his beard. The defined edges of his face stood out. Angled jaw line. A bit of a crooked nose. Very masculine. And very, very sexy.

I opened the door. "Looks like the wind's going to behave for now."

He held out a hand to help me down.

I wore an old sweatshirt, my favorite pair of camo shorts and probably had sleep marks on my face.

Perfect.

I placed my hand in his. I imagined the warmth of his palm sliding over my body. Finding dips and valleys.

"I'm glad," Ben said, his voice a low rumble.

We danced around the conversation I'd wanted to have. It was all body language talking now. The words were meaningless.

A blaze of heat erupted in my core. I'd never felt attraction quite like this before.

Lord, help me, I wanted this man.

No matter how attracted I was, it didn't change the fact I'd hired Ben to do a job, and I didn't need to mess that up. If I wanted to prove to the rest of Nome that Aurora Darling could hack it out on the water with the rest of the dredgers, then I needed to keep a distance between Ben and me.

Shut it down, Rory.

The whole of the dredging community had their eyes on me. More trucks and ATVs pulled in. Other miners suited up for the day, prepared equipment and watched the drama play out between Buck Darling's daughter and her hired hand.

"Let's get moving. Daylight's burning." My voice shifted to a colder tone. I squared my shoulders and removed buckets and a cooler from the truck bed.

"Here," Ben offered. "Let me get that."

"I got it." My words clipped and remote. "Why don't you get the engine warmed up and check the lines? I'll be there in a minute."

"All right," Ben said. His blue eyes hardened to black.

The window had closed. A twinge of guilt. I took a deep, painful breath and closed my eyes as he walked away.

*

The next few hours were brutal. Ben did the early shift beneath the rippling water. I tended up top and spent too much time alone with my own head. I needed to keep my priorities straight. My main purpose was to keep the business afloat and take care of my father.

As if on schedule my phone rang—the hospital.

"Ms. Darling? This is Dr. Leskiv. I wanted to talk to you about scheduling your father's surgery. We did some tests this morning, he's doing quite well. The medication seems to be working. We think he's strong enough for the rigors of the double bypass operation."

"I'm so glad to hear that. I've been working with the Patient Care Coordinator to arrange for a temporary living situation in Anchorage. I should be able to get down there in a few weeks once the season has ended up here."

"Ah, yes, your father mentioned that he owns a dredging

operation. I couldn't quite believe it when he told me his daughter was running the show in his absence. Can't imagine that's very easy."

My gaze shifted to the scene in front of me. Several dredges had followed my lead and anchored within 100 feet. Including the *Rough & Ready*, which I'd ignored as best I could. In the back of my mind I kept fuel levels, air pressure, the angle of the sluice and umpteen other facts stored away for use at a moment's notice. I never realized how complex the whole operation could be until I had to take the entire load on my shoulders.

"Well, he's been prepping me for years." My irritation rose over the doctor's assumption I couldn't handle the dredging on my own. What did it matter if I was a daughter or a son? But I let it pass. "So when will he be scheduled for the surgery?"

"Thursday."

I looked at the wall calendar pinned to the plywood wall of the wheelhouse. In two days. "Oh, wow. Okay." I thought about how much money I had in the bank and when the hospital might bill me for my father's portion of the very expensive surgery. A knot formed in my stomach. "And after that how long will he be in the hospital?"

"Probably four or five days. Your father arrived in pretty bad shape, but he's a very strong man. There shouldn't be any delays in his recovery."

"Okay, I'm not sure if I'll be able to fly down there to pick him up once he's discharged." I thought about setting up a flight. I didn't have any back-up plan for my absence. No one else to pick up the slack if I couldn't run the dredge.

"He'll need someone to stay with him for two to three weeks. Getting back his strength will take time, and he'll need to take it easy. But you can discuss that with the Patient Care Coordinator. In-Home Health does a great job when family members can't be there."

I made a mental note to find out the cost of in-home care and whether or not his limited health insurance would cover any of it. I took a deep breath to calm down. "Oh, great. Thanks so much. I'll make sure to call the Coordinator this week to get it all figured out."

"If you'd like, I can have the switchboard connect you to your father's room."

"Oh, yes, thanks." I hadn't prepared to talk to my father again. My palms grew sweaty.

"Not a problem. It was good speaking to you, Ms. Darling. Everything should be just fine."

Before I could say anything else the line clicked several times.

"Rory?" My father's voice came across strong and clear. "Is that you?"

"Dad, how's it going?" I wanted to sound chipper and confident. Not worried at all. Especially didn't want to bring up the topic of money. "I hear you're going to have some surgery soon."

"Yeah, the doc just left about an hour ago. Looks like my ticker is strong enough to handle it."

"Great. Great." Cool and relaxed, Rory. Cool and relaxed. "Hey, he told you about the recovery and all that?"

"Yeah, yeah."

"You're sounding a lot stronger than last night."

"A lot less drugged up, too." My dad chuckled.

I smiled. This was the father I knew, not the weak, confused man on the phone yesterday. "I found you a month-to-month studio arrangement. Furnished. It'll only be for a few months, and then you can fly back home."

"You sure we can handle that?" His voice tightened with worry. "You doing all right with the dredge?"

"We'll be fine, Dad. Everything's fine." I didn't want to confide in him the actual truth of the matter. I had had enough to pay a deposit and first months' rent on the studio I'd found, but it had bottomed me out. Now I had to worry about possibly paying a nurse to stay with him for two weeks. The numbers kept climbing.

"Good, good."

"I'm not sure I'm going to be able to get down there once you're discharged. I wanted to help you get settled, but with the season winding down…"

"Oh, you don't need to do that, Rory. I'll be fine."

The doctor had described his post-surgical care and what would be required. I really need to find that in-home care quickly. "But I want to be there, Dad. It's bad enough you're there by yourself after what happened."

"Rory, the dredge is what matters. You need to keep that going. That's what's important right now."

"I don't know." It didn't seem fair I had to choose between gold mining and my own father. "I think your health is more important than any dredge."

"Don't you say that." His sharp tone surprised me. "I've put everything into the business. Everything. You can't let that slip away."

"I just meant that…" I'd offended him. I had to fix it. "To me your health will always be more important. Sorry if you don't agree. But I love you, Dad. You know that, right?"

"I love you too, honey." He sighed. "You're right, Rory. You're right. I shouldn't get so worked up."

"No, you shouldn't. You can trust me. I got this. Everything's going to be fine." The pressure never seemed to let up. My dad had taken responsibility for me and found his way through financial hardships in the past. This time, it was my turn.

"Thanks for all you're doing. I'm really proud of you."

Those words filled me up and took away some of the worry. "I appreciate that, Dad. I'll call you after the surgery, but know that you can call me any time if you need to talk. Your surgeon sounds very confident. I'm sure everything will be just fine."

As I hung up, I noticed the *Rough & Ready* had pulled anchor and was headed right for us. They'd moved too close and continued to close the gap even further.

I picked up the handset. "Keep an eye out, Ben. We've got company coming."

"Roger."

I pointed my binoculars at the person standing at the wheel.

Nate Frazier.

"Shit."

CHAPTER TWENTY

I'd experienced my fair share of testosterone-laden miners act like two bull caribou clashing antlers over a herd of cows. Fist fights on the docks, spraying ice cold water, dredge crashes, wrestling over gold spots under the water. Most disagreements went no further than a lot of swearing and middle fingers. But a gal needed to be prepared for anything.

The *Rough & Ready* quickly closed the distance between us.

I picked up a Super Soaker water gun my dad had on hand for such encounters. Nobody liked getting doused with 42 degree water straight from the Bering Sea. With a range of about thirty feet, it was a close distance weapon.

Nate turned Jerry's dredge at the last minute, missing my hull by about three yards.

I fired my weapon too early and missed. My stream of cold water landed too far aft.

One of the divers in back yelled, "Go back to the kitchen."

Another pelted me with eggs and laughed.

One hit me in the head. Raw egg white slid down my face. Another hit me in the stomach like a brick and then exploded on the deck.

I corrected my aim, but egg dripped into my eyes, making it difficult.

Ben appeared out of nowhere, grabbed the fire extinguisher we kept on deck, and let it rip.

A white stream of chemical agent burst from the extinguisher

and created a white cloud, which enveloped the divers. The *Rough &*
Ready was too far away for a direct hit, but the cloud obstructed their
view so that the egg bombing came to a halt.

"Screw you," Ben yelled. He dropped the empty extinguisher,
picked up a sun-bleached flipper and chucked it at the fleeing
watercraft.

I wiped egg out of my eyes.

Half a dozen eggs had landed on the deck.

"You okay?" Ben asked. He picked a chunk of shell out of my
hair.

"I was going to handle it," I snapped. "Why did you surface? I
wanted you on the gold." I moved the empty fire extinguisher out
of the way.

"Excuse me for wanting to help you out." Ben picked up the
bigger eggshell pieces from the deck and chucked them into the
water.

"It was nothing. Just some eggs." I spooled out a few paper
towels from a roll in the wheelhouse and wiped my face.

"You've been pissed at me since I showed up this morning.
What the hell is your problem?" he asked.

I couldn't face up to my feelings, so I ignored his question.
"Time to head in. Wind's picking up." It wasn't, but I couldn't stand
to be trapped on the dredge for one more minute. I needed to get
away. Squash down any emotions I had and get things done. I owed
it to my father. The egg attack had been humiliating. Nate knew me
well. He'd never been comfortable with me on the dredge or my
father's interest in bringing me into the business. Since he didn't
succeed in scaring me away with physical intimidation, he'd hoped
demeaning taunts would demoralize me and drive me away.

"Sometimes, Rory, you need to trust someone and let them
help. This idea that it's you against the rest of the world? I've been
there." Ben cleaned up the decks, shut down the machines, and
prepped for a clean out. "And it won't get you anywhere but further
away from what you really want."

I took a bottle of water and rinsed my egg-coated hair. I used
my scratched reflection in the wheelhouse plexiglass window to pick
out pieces of shell. I knew Ben watched me, and I worked hard to
keep the tears at bay.

I knew how to do this. I was a good diver. I'd tended other
divers for years. It got my dander up that none of my fellow dredgers

believed I could do the work without Buck here to help.

*

I headed toward the gas station to fill up the truck before I headed home. The sluice box had been quite empty, so we left the clean out for another day. I hoped I'd made it clear to Ben last night had been a fleeting mistake. I could take care of myself. I didn't need him or anyone else solving my problems. I was 100% capable of taking over all the responsibility while my dad was recuperating. He'd done it alone for years, why couldn't I?

Mindlessly, I turned into the Bonanza Express and pulled next to an empty pump. An ATV took the opposite side.

I picked up the pump handle and selected the gas grade. Then, I looked straight into the eyes of Benjamin Abel.

Of all the goddamn luck.

"So now you're following me?" I scoffed. Annoyed I couldn't put the day's events behind me.

Ben filled his ATV's gas tank. "You wish."

The credit card processor wouldn't accept my card. "Just go home wherever home is and let me do my own thing." I pulled out a different one. "Is that too much to ask?"

"I didn't know I wasn't allowed to fill up at this particular gas station." Ben grabbed some paper towels and wiped at some gas that had dribbled on the front fender. "Excuse me."

"There are other gas stations." The machine beeped again. I snorted in frustration and grabbed a twenty of out my wallet.

I passed between the pumps to pay inside.

He grabbed my arm. "So why did you back off the other night?"

I wanted to run away. "Because."

"Because isn't an answer." He loosened his grip. His fingers ran up my arm. "I know you felt something."

I willed myself to ignore his touch and the goosebumps he caused. "Because I knew it wouldn't work." I looked him straight in the eye. "You and me. You're not my type." Although I knew after other failed relationships, he was exactly the type I needed. Rugged, strong, a risk taker and gentle when he needed to be.

"What have I done to make you think it wouldn't work?" His ego damaged, his eyes shifted from blue to black.

I couldn't bring myself to tell him what I knew. I didn't want to look like the bad guy. The Internet stalker who had dug up dirt online. It sounded so high school, so stupid. So I lied. "I still have feelings for Kyle."

"Bullshit."

I took a step back. His definitive comment had caught me off guard. "It's true." I could hear the weakness in my own voice. Weak and pathetic. I needed to squash any feelings I had for Ben. It would be insanity to move things further and expect anything but a disaster. I had enough going on in my life without making a bad romantic decision and ending up a pathetic repeat of Cindy Pomeroy. No way.

"All right. If that's how you want to play it. Fine. I'll chalk it up to mixed signals. But you, lady, need to get your head examined. You've got some bigger problems than your daddy issues."

"Excuse me?" I cocked my head.

"Look, I'm sorry your dad's in the hospital. That sucks, but you are letting your whole life revolve around him. Have you ever thought about what *you* want? Where *your* life is going? If your father were gone tomorrow, would you still be on that rickety dredge pushing yourself so hard? Putting up with all the crap they give you? Is this really where you want to be? Just scraping by? Living hand to mouth? Hoping for the big discovery that never comes? Putting your heart and soul and life into something for someone else is insanity."

Tears pricked at the corner of my eyes. "You might not believe it, but, yes, I would choose this life. I would if my father weren't around anymore. It's what I'm good at. It's all I know. Do you think a woman can't dredge? That I don't have what it takes to succeed out on the water? Cause I'll tell you what, Benjamin Abel, I sure as shit have what it takes. I know these waters as well as any other diver out there. You go ahead and ask." I gestured at other trucks and drivers who had pulled into the station. I didn't care who in Nome heard what I said. "They thought once I turned eighteen I'd go back to the Lower 48. Move back in with my sister. That I wouldn't want to stick around this back water place. That I'd want malls and shopping and boyfriends. Well, I'm not my mother. I'm not. I'm Buck Darling's daughter through and through. So shove that up your ass." I pushed him back and headed inside to pay.

A few gawking spectators stepped back to let me by.

The tears flowed. I was sick of it all. Sick of Nome, sick of the people who surrounded me every day making me feel as if I couldn't succeed, sick of the stress of not knowing how much money I'd have by the end of the week, month, year. Add Ben onto the pile. I was mad at myself for letting him in so easily. Why did I flit from Kyle right into Ben's arms? Was I really that needy? Did I need a man to save me from myself, my bad choices, my life? Is that what I'd turned into? A carbon copy of my mother? A desperately needy woman who'd run off and disappeared without a word twelve years ago. Who left her family hurting and alone. Was that my destiny?

"Rory, come back." Ben shouted at me. He didn't chase after me, I noticed. No, that wouldn't be like him. "I'm sorry. Let's talk."

I'd had enough talk for one night. Enough reflecting on my weaknesses. I pushed through the glass doors and stepped up to the counter to pay for my gas.

I heard Ben's ATV drive away, and a heaviness filled my chest.

I wanted to make the dredging operation work. I'd been at my father's side learning, watching, waiting for my chance to prove myself worthy. And when my father truly needed me, I doubted it all. My skills, my feelings, the very core of who I thought I was. Rory Darling, daughter of Buck Darling, the best female dredger operator to ever work the Sound. I sighed. The *only* female dredge operator to ever work the Sound. What was I trying to prove?

Ben had tapped into my deepest doubts and insecurities. I didn't remember any man ever pegging me like he had. And it scared me. How was it that he saw through me so easily? My first instinct was to build a higher wall, not take it down.

Maybe I needed to call off the dredging tomorrow. Get a break from Ben and get my head on straight.

CHAPTER TWENTY-ONE

I parked my car in the usual spot near my apartment building. I didn't want to fight with Ben. That had been the last thing on my mind. But he had a way of getting under my skin. Possibly because I cared what he thought about me. I'd been dismissed by people in Nome who thought of me as a 'Daddy's Girl' who'd been spoiled by her father. Operating a dredge and commanding a team was physically draining, dangerous, and required a toughness that not many women cared to build in themselves. The few women out on the water typically tended boats for divers who were their boyfriends, husbands, fathers. They took the caregiver role rather than the risk taking role.

When my father had put me on the dredge with his small crew, I'd been the entertainment. A go-fer who poured coffee and handed out sandwiches. The men saw me as plucky and a bit of an ugly duckling. My father had no idea what to do with a 12-year-old girl. He'd dressed me in army surplus gear and church bazaar rejects. But I didn't care. I'd wanted to be close to my real father, the only real person I had left in my life.

So I'd made it my mission at that tender age to make myself into the best damned girl dredger Nome had ever seen. I absorbed everything. I swallowed my fears when I'd first dived alone in the cold, dark waters. I'd wrestled the suction hose and not let my dad or anyone know how close I'd come to a breakdown at fifteen feet. I'd made it happen by sheer force of will. Even though Buck and Nate and other men who'd worked on his crew knew my capabilities, the truth didn't get out past the dredge. I'd been okay with that for a while. I knew my dad believed in me, was proud of me, and that's all I'd needed for a long time.

Now, however, without him here, I felt the full weight of what I was up against. The aggressive tactics of my competitors, the blatant jealousy and violence that lurked under the surface, waiting for the right moment to burst out and swallow me down whole. Nate was a manifestation of that world. A world my father had done a pretty decent job sheltering me from.

Ben, however, was a whole different animal. He'd started out as my employee. Another tough-as-nails manly man who thought he could eat me up for breakfast if necessary. I'd sensed that in him from day one. The raw animal power he had. He'd been 'The Beast.' A compilation of everything I was up against here in Nome. I'd entered Ernie's Pub as an alien in my own town. I'd never really fit in the way I'd wanted to. I'd assumed it had been all about learning the ropes, putting in the time, showing I could do the work. But it had been more than that.

Ben had shown me it was about teamwork, about trusting your partners, about setting aside differences and making something really great happen. It never had been about me as the only female dredge captain. I'd learned in the short time Ben had been my diver, it had always been about showing I could lead, that I could move forward even in the worst moments and keep the trust of my team. No matter how small my team was.

I headed up to my apartment. I took the stairs two at a time, ready to shower, eat and get a good night's sleep. When I got to the landing, I noticed the lights were on inside. I never left the lights on. Everyone in Nome learned from a young age that electricity wasn't cheap and wasting it was a crime worse than most. Had I been in a rush this morning? It didn't make sense.

I approached, key in hand. The door stood open a crack.

Someone was in my apartment.

My pulse raced. I heard a boom-boom-boom in my ears. The rush of blood. My nerves on edge.

I opened the door.

A dark shadow appeared.

CHAPTER TWENTY-TWO

The morning light shone into my eyes, and I squinted at the brightness. A throb of pain exploded at the back of my head. Reflexively, I touched the sore spot. My fingers smoothed over a bulk of bandage and medical tape right behind my ear.

What had happened to my head?

I dug through my memories. What was the last thing I remembered?

A shout of surprise. Sharp, terrible pain.

And a face. A blurry face I couldn't remember.

"You're awake." Stella held a Styrofoam cup full of a hot, steaming drink. "Thank God, you're okay."

I was in the hospital.

My mouth felt dry. "Water." I pointed at the pitcher on the stand next to my bed. My voice sounded raspy and thin.

Stella poured water into a plastic cup and handed it to me.

I drank greedily. My head pounded.

"The police want to talk to you." Stella fiddled with her cup and picked bits of Styrofoam off the edge. A habit she'd had since our middle school days. "I already gave them a statement."

"Were you there?" I couldn't remember. Everything was hazy, fuzzy. "What happened?"

Stella's brows came together. "You don't remember anything?" She rubbed the ridges of the cup. "I didn't realize."

"Stella, what happened to me?" I felt for the bed remote so I could sit more upright.

My friend sighed, "Someone attacked you in your apartment."

"Who?" The fuzzy face. I wish I could remember.

"That's why the police want to talk to you. They've taken some evidence out of your apartment, fingerprinted things, that kind of stuff. But they need a rundown of who might've had access, who might've been inside." Stella's eyes became red-rimmed. "I was so worried when the police showed up at the diner this morning. I didn't know. I'm sorry, Rory, I should've been there for you." She touched my arm.

"Yes, my apartment." I remembered arriving, but nothing else.

"The police asked me if I had any idea who might want to hurt you." She picked more chunks out of the cup's rim. "I remembered what you told me about Nate."

I nodded.

Had it been his face I'd seen?

"And then I told them about Ben."

"Ben?" My thoughts scrambled. "What did you tell them about Ben?"

"That he was a murder suspect." She glanced at me. "And I saw you two arguing yesterday. I mean, was that wrong? I thought it would be something the police would be interested in. We don't really know much about him, do we?"

I remembered being at the gas station. The argument we'd had. I knew people had witnessed it, but I didn't know Stella had seen me.

I said quietly, "Ben's never done anything to hurt me." I'd read the same news article as Stella. How well did I really know Ben? In fact, maybe I'd pushed aside any negative thoughts about him because I'd needed to. My gold operation depended on him. Without Ben, what would I have? And maybe that desperation had clouded my judgment a little too much—and my growing attraction to him.

"You did say that he attacked Nate," Stella reminded me.

"Yes, but that was to protect me."

"Was it really? Or is he an unstable man who is out of control?" Stella set her cup on my tray and folded her arms. "They asked me what I thought of Ben and what I knew about him. So I told them. I'm not going to lie to the police."

"I didn't ask you to lie." The conversation was going nowhere fast. I didn't want her visit to turn into an argument.

"I had to give them my fingerprints, too. *Elimination prints* they called them." She let out a loud breath. "Somebody had ransacked your apartment, apparently."

I didn't know what to think when Stella said that. It seemed more likely Nate would've been the one who broke in and then attacked me. But would he really have had time to get to my apartment before me? We'd left him on the water, I thought.

I wished I could remember more about what happened last night.

"Look, I can see you're tired. Me throwing all of this at you is probably pretty exhausting." Stella picked up her destroyed cup and its bits and pieces and threw them in the trash. "Plus, I have to get back to work. It's the breakfast rush."

"That's fine, Stel. I'll be fine." I turned over these facts in my muddled mind. I wanted to piece them together, but my memories were fuzzy and broken. I didn't know what was real and what was drug-induced haze.

She gave me a kiss on the cheek and a gentle squeeze. Then waved goodbye and left.

Someone had attacked me in my own apartment. Goosebumps rose on my arms. Somebody in Nome wanted to hurt me, and I had no idea who it was. Having this piled on top of what I already had on my plate made my life even more stressful and complicated. It also revealed how much my father had been protecting me. Without it, I'd become a sheep fed to the jackals.

A nurse, short, dark and with Inuit features, slipped inside the curtained off area that served as privacy in the room. "Your friend told me you woke up. I'm Kathy, your nurse. The doctor should be here shortly to do some tests. I'm here to check your bandage, though, and replace the dressing."

"Should I just sit here or...?" I made motion to swing my legs over the side of the bed so it would be easier for her to get at my wound.

She held up her hands. "Whoa, take it slow. With a head wound like that, you really should stay in bed until the doctor clears you. You lost consciousness, so you could have a concussion. I can check your wound right where you are." Nurse Kathy set gauze, medical tape, and some other supplies on the tray table and rolled it over the bed. "If you could turn your head to the left, please." She put on some disposable gloves.

I complied and cringed as she peeled back the tape.

"So who was that hunk who brought you in last night?"

"Huh?" I winced as she touched the tender skin above my right ear. I hadn't really thought about how I'd gotten to the clinic's emergency room.

"Tall. Buff. Beard. And those eyes." Nurse Kathy whistled. "Haven't seen him around Nome before."

Ben. She must mean Ben.

"I don't remember anything about last night." Although I'd had a few fleeting memories, nothing came together in a chronological way that made any sense.

Nurse Kathy mused, "Hmmm. Well, he looked pretty worried about you. Stuck around for a couple of hours to make sure you were okay and then, I don't know, he disappeared somewhere. Was right near the beginning of my shift so I was a little busy."

"Ouch." Whatever cream or salve she touched to my wound stung. "By your description, I'd say it was my diver, Ben. But I have no idea why he'd be the one to bring me in." I'd left Ben at the gas station. He'd taken off on his ATV before I'd paid.

Although that gave Ben time to get to my place before I'd arrived...

I mulled over the timeline.

Ben had had opportunity. I hadn't seen what direction he'd gone in after our dust up.

Was it really feasible, though, that the perpetrator would attack me and then take me to the ER himself? That made zero sense.

Although Stella had her reasons for being wary of Ben, the new bit of news let me scratch off Ben from the list of suspects. To me that left only one: Nate.

Nurse Kathy cut several long strips of medical tape and stuck them to the tray. "Ben, huh? You know if he's single?"

"I think so." I said without thinking. "You said he left?"

"Yeah. I remember the police showed up a little while after you were brought in and wanted to talk to him. He'd already skedaddled out of there."

"Do you know who called the police?"

"I assumed your friend, Ben, had."

I knew that couldn't be true. Ben had likely taken off because the police had arrived. The other day he'd looked wary of me contacting them and seemed relieved when I'd decided against reporting Nate's behavior.

A few hours later the doctor cleared me to be released. My head wound and my response to his questions indicated I wouldn't have any lasting effects after my attack. The only bad thing was I wouldn't be allowed to dive for ten days while my stitches remained. I'd be 100% dependent on Ben for any diving. Money would be even further out of reach, if all I could do was tend the dredge. I wanted the nurse to pump me full of meds and let me go back to sleep.

Before I could find the motivation to get up and change into my clothes, two officers entered. I recognized one, Mr. Isaacs. The other was younger and not familiar to me. Maybe a transfer from down state.

"Hey, Rory," Officer Isaacs said. "I heard about your dad. I'm sorry. How's he doing?" He touched my arm in a caring gesture.

"He's doing better thanks."

"I'm sure he'll be up on his feet and back to his old self in no time." He took a step back. "This is my new partner, Brandon Garber. I'm letting him take the lead on your case. Hope that's okay."

Garber nodded.

I smiled at the younger officer. I trusted Mr. Isaacs. "Sure. But I'm not sure if I can help you very much."

Officer Garber went right to work, changing the tone of the conversation from friendly to serious. "Ms. Darling, this should only take a few minutes." He took out a notepad. "We need to ask you a few questions about your attack and what you remember."

"I'll do my best." After my conversations with both Stella and Nurse Kathy my head had cleared some. I hoped with pointed questions, I might get closer to exactly what had happened last night.

"That's all we ask," Officer Isaacs replied. "And if at any time you remember something new, you can contact us for another interview." He handed me a business card with his name and number on it.

"Sure. Thanks." I set it on the nightstand next to my bed. "And you can call me Rory."

"Rory. Okay." He blushed. "Do you remember what time you came home last night?"

"Around three or four o'clock. I'd finished dredging for the day and was headed back to my apartment to get cleaned up, eat and relax."

"Did you notice anything unusual when you arrived at your apartment? A car? Someone hanging around the building? Anything different?"

My mind was a blank. I dug deeper. "I remember getting in my dad's truck and driving home from the docks. Took the usual route home down Seppala Drive. Stopped at the Bonanza for some gas. Made a right on Bering. Left on 3rd. And then home." I scanned some more for a memory of the street. Did I notice anything or anyone unusual? "I don't remember paying attention to who was parked there. No neighbors were out. Don't remember seeing anyone lingering around."

"And then what do you remember? After you parked your truck?" Officer Garber jotted down a few things.

"I grabbed some things out of the back..." The gold! I'd completely forgotten. "Oh, my God. Is my bucket of concentrates still in my apartment? We had a half day of dredging in that."

"So you grabbed some things..." Officer Isaacs prompted.

"Oh, yes, I grabbed some stuff from the truck and headed up the stairs to my apartment. I remember the light was on inside, and I didn't remember leaving it on when I left that morning. Then I noticed the door was ajar." That hollow feeling in my stomach returned. The feeling that told me something was not right, to be careful, to watch out. But I'd reached for the door anyway. Instead of taking out my cell phone and calling the police, I'd touched the doorknob. Stupid mistake. "And I don't really remember anything after that."

"Did you see anyone inside your apartment?" Garber asked.

"I don't remember."

"Can you recall if you'd told anyone to meet you there or were you expecting anyone that evening?"

"No."

"Do you have anyone you can think of that might want to hurt you or may have wanted to break in to your apartment?" Garber added.

My mind grabbed onto the obvious suspect. "Nate. Nate Frazier."

Garber wrote down the name. "Anyone else?"

I remembered what Stella said she'd told the police. That Ben could've done this. But I knew that wasn't right. He wouldn't hurt me. Our argument at the gas station had been personal, not business.

I shook my head.

"What about Benjamin Abel, your diver?"

"I don't have any reason to believe he'd want to hurt me. Plus, the nurse this morning told me he was the one that brought me in."

The officers exchanged glances. Garber wrote in his notebook.

"Your friend, Ms. Hansen, gave us the impression he had a suspect background and was someone we should look into."

"Ben has never done anything I'd consider suspicious or harmful. I don't know why Stella would say those things."

The officer took a few more notes. "You mentioned Nathan Frazier. Why?"

"He used to work for my father. We fired him last summer. After my father's accident he's been very aggressive toward me. One night he followed my truck back to town, flashing his lights. Last week he showed up at my apartment complex and wanted to make trouble. He attacked me."

"Did you report this behavior to the police?" Officer Isaacs asked.

"No."

"Why not?" Garber shot back.

"You know, Mr. Isaacs," directing my answer at the man who understood the dynamics in Nome. "He's got a temper, but I've never seen him do anything radical. I thought maybe he was in some kind of financial bind and was taking it out on me. He seems to think my father owes him money. I really didn't think it warranted a call to the police. I thought he'd cool off and come to a right frame of mind."

Isaacs nodded. "For now, your apartment is a crime scene. Do you have somewhere else you can stay for a day or two?"

My mind scanned through the possibilities. I could stay with Stella, but she didn't really have the space. I could ask Kyle for a favor, but it would put me in a really awkward position, as I'd just moved out and our relationship seemed finally back on an even keel.

At that moment my cell phone beeped. Ben texted me. I felt a rush of warmth. I blurted out, "Yes, I have a place to stay." Before I even asked him. Before I even knew where Ben stayed.

I glanced at his text:

R U OK?

He'd have to wait.

"Good." The officer wrapped up the interview. "We also need you to find a time to walk through your apartment when one of our officers can accompany you and see if anything is missing, such as that bucket you mentioned."

I thought about the bucket of gold concentrates in my bathroom. I assumed it'd be gone. Especially if the perpetrator was Nate. His whole problem seemed to be money-related. "Okay, I can arrange that."

"We are waiting the results of the fingerprint analysis, but we need some elimination prints from you and anyone else who has been at your apartment in the last week or so."

I scanned through the list of possibilities. "Stella, Ben and me. I think that's it." For a split second I worried about Ben needing to give fingerprints.

"Do you have contact info for Mr. Abel?"

Although Ben had just texted me, I shook my head.

Isaacs gave me a penetrating look. I don't think he believed me.

"When you come into contact with him, please let me know we need him to come in to the station."

I nodded.

The police left.

I picked up my phone and texted back:

Can U come get me?

CHAPTER TWENTY-THREE

I sat in the waiting room at the clinic ER. I held a plastic bag full of supplies to dress my wound for the next several days, plus a pain prescription and instructions for bathing and several warnings about symptoms to look for after a head injury.

Ben had offered up his place as a refuge until my apartment was cleared. Luckily, he'd been in town to check his mail and said he'd come pick me up. The idea of spending a few days alone with Ben wherever he lived didn't bother me.

The receptionist sitting behind the check-in desk kept glancing up. I should've been gone an hour ago.

As the clock ticked closer to noon, I crossed and uncrossed my legs. I would've paced in the small waiting area, but Nurse Kathy had warned me to take it easy. Rest up. Not do too much.

I picked up my phone to text Stella as a back-up plan.

Ben drove up on his ATV.

I looked heavenward and let out a sigh of relief. Finally. I wanted to get out of here and leave the attack behind me.

He climbed off, removed his helmet and his shook out his shaggy head of hair.

My stomach fluttered.

With masculine grace he entered the building.

"You ready?" Ben asked.

"Let's go."

Ben took my bag. "Do you have a jacket?"

I shook my head.

"You can wear mine."

When we exited the building, he stuffed my bag of supplies into one of the compartments over the back wheels and shrugged out of his leather jacket.

"Thanks." I put it on. It was warm from his body heat and smelled of peppermint and sweat.

He handed me an extra helmet, which I put on gingerly over my bandaged head.

"Get on." Ben revved the engine of his ATV.

Even though his Polaris had been built for one, there was enough room on the seat for two in a pinch.

I hesitated. Not that I was afraid of riding on an ATV. I'd done it for half of my life. No self-respecting Alaskan would balk at getting on an ATV and riding off into the wilderness. I hesitated because everything in my soul told me to get on that machine. It scared me how much I wanted to be close to Ben. The Beast. A potential murderer. What was wrong with me? Was I as psycho as my mother? Seeking out difficult, impossible men in order to destroy any chance I had at a normal relationship?

I exed the thought out of my mind.

I am not my mother. I am not my mother. I am not my mother.

I zipped up the jacket and climbed on behind Ben. I snaked my arms around his taut midsection and found I liked it. Liked it too much. I leaned my head into his back and turned off the flashing red warning signs popping up in my brain. I didn't care anymore.

Wasn't this why I asked him to take me in rather than my best friend? Didn't I want this deep down? The closeness? The excuse to be alone with him? Where no one could find me?

Ben drove us out of town, turned off the main road, and headed out into the tundra. My hair whipped around the edges of my helmet, and the sound of the engine filled my ears, blocking out any other sounds. The drone soothed me. Let me drift off into another place. I'd almost died last night. I had the stitches to prove it. How ironic I sought out the help of one possibly violent man to save me from another.

The bleak tundra landscape whizzed past. Mile after mile of empty, rolling hills of brownish green vegetation dotted with mushy spots and mud puddles. Taller mountains, the Kigluiak range, sat on the horizon. Distant. Mysterious. Daunting.

Ben kicked into a lower gear and turned us toward a slope

sprinkled with low shrubs. The ground was more solid here. Rockier. The ATV's engine churned hard to carry two bodies up and over the ridge. As we came down on the other side, my torso melded into Ben's back, and I gripped him even more tightly. And I liked it. The feeling of closeness. The warmth. The hardness of him.

We were far away from town. No one could see me. No one could judge me. Kyle could go to hell, as far as I was concerned. So could my sister. Stella may have thought Ben was attractive the first time she'd met him, but the news she'd discovered had turned her off. She would've been the first to scold me over my choices. My best friend in the world, and I didn't want to hear it.

We were about twenty miles from town when Ben turned off the barely maintained trail into the brush. Although there were ATV tracks ahead, I knew Ben was likely the only ATV which had come this way. My stomach dropped. Reality set in. I'd chosen to come out in the middle of nowhere, where no one could find me, with spotty cell service on the back of an ATV. The only way out was the way in: with Ben's help. I'd put my safety in his hands. I hoped that choice wouldn't come back to haunt me.

A few tundra-stunted pines appeared. With the harshness of the weather in Nome, trees were a rarity. Most couldn't survive the brutal winter weather nor thrive in the odd, tundra soil, which froze in winter to a solid, ice-threaded mass many feet below the surface and turned into a swampy mush in the spring. However, further out from town, I knew some spots existed where trees managed to flourish. Pilgrim Hot Springs, likely a good 30 or 40 miles from where we were, thrived as a subarctic oasis with pine trees, cottonwood, and balsam poplars. Completely out of place in the bleak northern Alaska landscape. The hot springs had created a warm spot that defied the bitter cold and allowed for a lush landscape. I'd never been to the hot springs, but my father had described them to me.

Ben veered left down a narrow trail into a grove of stubby pines. The edges of a man-made structure appeared through the branches, small and dark.

"We're here." Ben announced. He turned the key.

The silence surrounded us.

In front of me stood an old miner's cabin. Stacks of logs made up the main walls. The roof appeared to be tin. The windows were old single pane glass in wood frames with chipped white paint.

"You come way out here every night?" I stayed on the ATV, uncertain. I imagined the 5 am mornings at the dock when I'd been frustrated when Ben had been ten minutes late. My earlier annoyance embarrassed me. I hadn't had a full understanding of Ben's situation. I'd assumed he stayed in town or at least close to town. Out here a whole different world existed. Rugged. Isolated.

"Yep." Ben unloaded my bag and slung it over one shoulder. "Come on inside. It's getting cold out here."

I shivered in the leather jacket and my Levi's. Although the sun hovered well above the horizon in a cloudless sky, a definite cold wind blew through the trees. A change of weather would arrive in the next twelve hours or so. "How did you find this place?" For some reason the cabin seemed familiar.

"It belonged to my grandpa. He used to be a bush pilot up here—years ago now."

The pictures on Ben's Facebook page. This was the cabin. For some reason the recognition calmed me.

I mined my brain for any old codger I remembered from my childhood. I didn't know if 'years ago' was before my time. There'd been a few off-the-grid 'mountain men' who'd show up in town come spring. But my memories were so cloudy, I wouldn't be able to recall if I'd met Ben's grandpa or not.

"Did he build this himself?" I took in the hand-hewn logs. They were small in diameter for a log cabin, but I supposed raw logs were hard to come by up here. A homesteader made do with what he could get his hands on in this part of the world.

Ben held open the door. "Yep. Before I was born. My dad barely remembered this place. He and my grandma moved to Idaho when he was still in grade school."

My heart raced. I don't know why. Ben only wanted to give me a safe place to stay while I waited out the police tracking down Nate.

I stepped inside. The small space had been filled with animal heads, furs, a beat-up leather couch and arm chair and a gun rack. Of course. Standard issue in Nome—well, in any home in Alaska, to be honest. To the left a long plank of wood acted as the kitchen countertop with a small, propane-fueled refrigerator, a gas stove with two burners, and a sink with a hand pump serving as the faucet. Despite the lack of space, a dish drying rack held a few dishes and pieces of silverware, and the counter was spotless and uncluttered. Two doorways on the back wall revealed a bathroom and a bedroom.

My gaze traveled back to the arm chair. The same chair pictured on Facebook with the older man sitting in it—Ben's grandpa. "So you never visited before this summer?"

Ben set my bag next to the couch. I supposed I had been absentmindedly assigned to it for tonight's sleeping arrangements. "I'd always wanted to visit. But I didn't make it before..." His blue-eyed gaze grew dark.

I wasn't sure how he did that. Brightest blue one moment, dark as night the next.

"I'm sorry." A lump appeared in my throat. "I didn't mean to pry."

"It's okay. You want some coffee?" Ben approached the small stove and a pot that sat on it. "All I've got is instant."

I nodded.

He worked the pump handle at the sink until a slow trickle of water ran out. It grew stronger the more he pumped. He filled the pot and then lit the stove. Flames heated it. While we waited for the water to boil, Ben leaned against the counter. "My grandpa died last summer. Parkinson's. Wasn't pretty. He hadn't been able to live out here in over ten years. Hit him pretty hard being in the nursing home in Nampa."

"That's in Idaho, right?" I played stupid. He didn't need to know I'd already looked up Nampa on the map online, even zoomed in at the street level to see the apartment listed as Ben's last known address.

"Yeah. Near Boise."

"Parkinson's. That's rough."

His gaze remained black. "Especially for a man like Grandpa. Capable. Independent. Stubborn as hell." He ran a hand through his recently trimmed beard.

Ben filled the cabin with his presence. All muscles and wild hair. His shoulders almost too broad to fit through the handmade doorframe. Intimidating at first. But in the moment, remembering his grandfather, a gentleness appeared I hadn't seen before. Maybe the boy within the man shining through.

"Sounds like someone else I know," I said softly.

His eyes locked onto mine. The heat in his gaze caught me off guard.

"The water's ready," I said. Steam rose from the small pan.

He turned to tend to the boiling water.

I breathed a small sigh of relief. What were we playing at here? Why did I feel the need to push it with Ben? The police had told me to stay with a friend for a few days. That was it. Until they could locate Nate, that was the safest thing to do. Ben had only obliged me because I had nowhere else to go.

I could've asked Kyle. He probably would've let me stay at his place. But I knew why I didn't ask him. I also knew why I didn't beg Stella to let me cram into her already crammed apartment. I could have. She would've let me do it. But instead, I had wanted this to happen. I had wanted Ben to step up. I had thrown myself on the tracks in front of a speeding train. Maybe because I liked the risk of it all. Maybe because I wanted to know more about the mysterious Ben. What woman in her right mind would've gotten on an ATV and ridden out in the middle of nowhere with Benjamin Abel, suspected murderer?

Only a woman with a serious lack of self-preservation.

Ben dug into a wooden crate that served as a cabinet on a shelf above the sink. "You like it black, right?" He spooned crystals of instant coffee into two chipped mugs.

"Yes, black."

"You want a shot of whiskey in it? I'm sure my grandpa kept a steady supply around here." Ben scrounged in the crate. Nothing. He tipped up the armchair. Nothing. His head just about hit the ceiling near the outside walls as he patrolled the room. He reached inside the mouth of a mounted bear head. "Ah ha!" He pulled out a bottle of Kentucky Bourbon.

Nurse Kathy had warned me away from alcohol. Not a good combo with the pain meds I'd been given.

I nodded.

He poured.

I drank.

After a few minutes the alcohol helped loosen tightly held questions from my mind. "They told me at the hospital that you were the one who dropped me off."

"You don't remember?" He frowned.

"I remember coming home, but that's about it." My body floated comfortably. The whiskey had done the trick and taken the edge off my nerves. I repeated over and over again in my head the path I took from the truck, up the stairs, to the door. A spike of fear and then blackness.

"Well," he began slowly. "I wanted to apologize—about the argument we had. I'd headed out to my cabin, and something told me to set things right. I have trouble sleeping sometimes. And I've learned not to let things fester. Festering only makes things worse." His brows drew together as if the words had triggered a bad memory. "When I got to your place I could see from the street your door was wide open, the lights on bright. Could sense right away something was off."

"Someone broke into my apartment."

He nodded. "I saw your truck there on the street, but didn't see you. My first thought was Nate had come back, done something worse."

"Did you see anyone?"

"No. Whoever had broken in was long gone. When I got to the top of the stairs you were lying in a heap. The blood…" His face grew ashen.

For a tough military guy he sure got freaked out pretty easily over a little bit of blood. My mind whispered, *murderer*. I banished the thought to the back of my brain.

"Hey, I'm okay. See?" I showed him my bandaged head.

"When I saw you there on the ground…" He shook his head. "I just acted. Your truck keys were on the doormat. I scooped you up and took you to the hospital."

For a fleeting moment I wished I'd been wide awake for that moment. "I suppose I should thank you. Who knows how long I would've been lying there if you hadn't come along."

"Anyone would've done the same."

I thought about my neighbors. "Not so sure about that." I shared the second story with an elderly woman who lived in the apartment next to me. She'd never said one word to my dad or me in all the time we'd lived there.

"I'm glad you're all right." Ben's blue gaze burned with intensity.

I kept eye contact with him, though I felt exposed and vulnerable. I wanted to stop talking, to put a finger over his lips, climb into his lap and kiss him. Pick up where we left off the other night. I was ready to set aside my worries and act on instinct alone. Raw, animal instinct. "Why didn't you stick around to make sure for yourself?"

He looked away. The moment cooled.

I set my mug of spiked coffee on side table. I'd had enough. My self-control had been weakened. Not good.

"Let's just say me and the cops don't exactly get along." Ben's voice grew brittle.

That was a pretty casual way of telling someone you'd had a few brushes with the law. Not something an upstanding veteran of the U.S. Armed Forces would say. "Well, you're going to have to talk to them. They need your fingerprints. And they'll want your story. It might help them figure out who did this."

"You know as well as I do it was Nate."

"We might know that, but the police need to prove it." I kicked myself for not reporting the incident with Nate behind the apartments the other night. I might have avoided the mess altogether. "Giving your side of the story and your fingerprints will help with that. Until then, Nate roams free."

"I'll think about it." He'd picked up a small chunk of wood from the same table where I'd set my mug and took out a pocket knife. He absentmindedly shaved off bits and pieces, which fell on the rough-hewn floorboards.

"What do you mean, you'll think about it?" Maybe what I felt for Ben was only one-sided. I'd thought at the gas station he'd indicated otherwise, but perhaps my negative reaction had turned him off. "You need to help me on this, Ben. What do you think is going to happen when you won't talk to them? Don't you think that will look a little suspicious?"

He let go of a breath of air he'd been holding. "Look, I'm the one that brought you in. Why would the police think I'd be the one that hurt you?" He sliced off a perfect three-inch curl of wood. An owl took shape in his hands.

"I don't know. I'm just saying, why avoid talking to them and draw more attention to yourself? They want to ask you a few questions and get your fingerprints. Unless there's a reason you don't want to give them your fingerprints." I pushed it a little too far with that comment. Surely he'd guess what I'd found out about him. It wasn't as if he was unaware of the Internet or the news story written about him. He had to know that with a little bit of curiosity and digging I, or someone else, might find out more about him.

"I got it. I hear you." His voice went up a notch or two. He dug into the owl's face to carve out a beak.

"Ben, why won't you talk to me?" I curled my legs under me.

"I know there's something you're not telling me." I might as well go for it. I knew too much, it was sure to slip out at the wrong time.

"Just drop it, please."

"How am I supposed to do that when we're stuck out here in this itsy bitsy cabin?" The alcohol had loosened more than my mouth, my emotions were raw and exposed. "Why won't you explain it to me?"

"I'm not sure why my life is any business of yours." He dug harder into the owl, making tiny little cuts all over its body. Feathers. "I didn't ask you about your mother. Seems you've got a story you don't want to share either."

I shot him a look. My mother was a topic I avoided, but if that's what it took to get to the truth, I could give him the short-and-sweet version. "She abandoned me, if you need to know. Pretended for twelve years that Henry was my dad, until she told me the truth. Then she split. Haven't seen her since. There, happy?"

"I'm sorry," he said quietly. "I didn't know. That's awful."

I wanted the sympathy to roll off my back. I'd never wanted it or needed it, but hearing those words soothed me. I feigned interest in my coffee mug. "If there's something you don't want the police finding out about you, don't you think I have a right to know at this point?" I couldn't stop the freight train now. It had already left the station. "You're my employee. You're tangled up in the mess I found myself in. When you chose to keep working for me, saving my life, making me fall for you…"

He looked at me. "What?"

CHAPTER TWENTY-FOUR

I choked on my own words. My face heated. A confession I didn't know I even had inside escaped out in a rush.

Goddamn my stupid, stupid mouth.

I turned away.

He wouldn't let me get away from it. "I care about you, too, Aurora."

My name was like a caress.

"I've been in this place before, though, and I don't know if I'm ready to do it again." He looked down at the half-completed owl carving in his hands. "And when I found you outside your apartment, I felt as if I was reliving the worst moment of my life."

"What do you mean?" Even though I very well thought I knew what he meant, I played innocent.

"It's a long story."

"I've got time, remember?" I gestured at the empty, isolated cabin we were sitting in. "I'm stuck here for the night, and you don't have a tv."

He gave me a smile, but it was a pained one. "A couple of years ago I lost someone close to me." He set down his half-finished carving.

"Oh?" A plaid blanket had been strewn across the back of the couch. I sunk my fingers into the scratchy wool. It would be nice to cuddle up under a blanket like this, get a fire going in the wood stove in the corner.

"Here." Ben helped me swath myself in plaid wool. He touched his fingers to the bandaged wound above my ear. "That bastard better hope I don't find him before the police." His voice lowered to a growl.

Although his touch was gentle, I winced. "Ow." The area had become sensitive. The pain meds they gave me must've worn off.

"Sorry." His gaze sharpened to blue. Instead of returning to the arm chair, he settled next to me. "She was the exact opposite of you. All about shopping and clothes, makeup and hair. A real girly-girl type."

I suddenly felt very self-conscious about my appearance. I'd spent the night in the hospital. I had taken a quick shower before I'd left, but had braided my boring brown hair and wore the same clothes I'd worn the night of my attack.

"We'd met in Florida. When I was going through some more advanced dive training. At a bar. Not the best place to meet a girl, I know." He looked down at his feet. "I thought it was going to be a fling. She was beautiful and seemed to be really into me. After a deployment to Iraq, I was ready to forget about the bad stuff. Put it behind me. Laura—that was her name—there was nothing unhappy with her, it was all fun, fun, fun, party, party, party."

My mind shifted back to the picture of Laura Snow on Facebook. Her angelic looks, her perfect smile. I was nothing like Laura.

"We got serious too quickly."

"Serious?"

"I guess you'd call it engaged."

"Oh." I knew this, yet hearing the words was like a punch to the gut. I didn't want to hear about his gorgeous blonde fiancée who probably was a million times more interesting and accomplished than I was. I had been a throwaway to my mother, a messed up, misguided, and unlovely girl who'd always felt awkward in her own skin. Who'd cried and cried when my brown hair just got darker and uglier and more boring. With my too-skinny legs and tomboy approach to everything. I was used to being covered in dirt and sand and smelling like rotting fish and seaweed. I didn't know what it must be like to be Laura Snow. Perfect, smiling Laura.

He gave me a quick glance, his blue eyes penetrating. "It was a mistake. I realized that eventually."

I had the words bottled up inside me. I knew what happened to her. Laura had been murdered. Someone had taken away her life.

Kind of an awful way for me to realize my competition was no longer around. To be pleased inside that this woman could no longer step in and take Ben away. But I kept silent. I waited for Ben to tell me. I wanted him to tell me. Confess everything. Let me be his one and only confidant. And I would keep his secrets. I would listen and nod and not say a thing. I just wanted to keep him near me. Keep him with me. Not lose another person. Not see someone else walk away whom I loved.

Yes, loved.

I surprised myself when I thought this. Was I in love with Ben Abel?

"I deployed again. She waited for me. Nine months. We'd Skype and email and all that, but it was obvious she'd moved on." He sighed. "But I stuck with it. I kept believing it would work out. Every guy deployed wants to believe he's got a girl back home, someone he's fighting for that makes it all worth it. Laura had made me care again."

"So where is she now?" I had to keep up my end of the game. Pretend I knew nothing and that I believed the gorgeous, perfect Laura Snow still roamed the earth ready to snatch Ben out of my grasp.

His expression clouded. "She died."

"Oh, I'm so sorry." I touched his hand. I willed him to tell me the rest of the story. To tell me about her murder and why there was a news story that said he had killed her.

"Nothing to be sorry about."

"Well, I mean, breaking off a relationship is one thing, but ending it that way…so abruptly."

He nodded. Then he looked away. He said nothing else. What did that mean? Why did he turn from me?

My emotions had become numb after my father's accident. I'd felt adrift. Just like I had felt after my mother ran off. The same gnawing empty hole in my core that needed to be filled with something. Or someone.

"I couldn't imagine losing someone so close to you." Even though I knew exactly what he was feeling. The loss, the pain, the confusion, the emptiness. I couldn't help but push it further. "Was it an accident?" I wanted to know, did he end it or did someone else? Did he end up doing something regrettable or did he merely get caught up in the whirlwind such an investigation would bring? I wanted him to confess to me, unload it all. Because at least then I knew I had his trust. And if that is all I could have, I would take it.

"I'd rather not get into the details."

I couldn't stop myself. The words poured out. "Does it have something to do with you not wanting to talk to the police?" I studied him carefully looking for something, anything, that would help me understand what was going on inside his head.

"Please don't ask me anymore tonight. I'm tired. I'm hungry." He got up from the couch. "We'll figure this all out in the morning. Can I make you some eggs?" He took a carton of eggs out of the fridge and plucked a frying pan from the drying rack next to the sink.

"Sure. That'll be fine." I curled up on the couch with the blanket across my legs. When Ben turned his back to me to cook the eggs, I studied him. He stood legs apart, his back straight, muscled shoulders strong. He had the physique of a man who could do someone great damage if he'd wanted to. In my head, I could see a fight between lovers, first a slap, then anger, then grabbing by the shoulders, maybe large hands around a narrow, soft neck. I exed the thought out of my mind. That wasn't the Ben I knew. No way. Or he shoved her too hard and she slipped and fell, hitting her head on the edge of a bathtub or fireplace. My imagination ran away with me. Why did I choose to believe Ben could kill someone? Why was I attracted to such a person?

*

The couch wasn't as comfortable for sleeping as it was for sitting. I tossed and turned on the worn leather. Although the cabin had curtains made from burlap sacks, the late night sun filtered through enough to keep me awake. And, after all that whiskey, my injured head throbbed.

I touched the bandaged bump. Strange how it would bother me more now than it did when I had been attacked.

Adrenaline rushed through me at the memory of it.

The sensing of a presence behind me in the dark.

The quick turn and then the explosion of pain.

I thought I hadn't seen his face. But as I laid in the dark of the cabin, Nate's face marred with a hideous grimace filled my mind. My breathing quickened as if I were back in my apartment and at his mercy. My heart raced.

"No!" I sat up.

"Are you all right?" Ben appeared in the doorway of his bedroom with a battery-powered lantern.

I held a hand to my forehead. "I thought I was awake, but it must've been a dream."

Ben wore only a pair of boxer shorts. His muscular torso appeared even more defined with the harsh light of the lantern. I turned away, embarrassed. I was a grown woman, not a child. Only children had nightmares. It had been years since I'd last had one. Mostly about my mother—me searching for and never finding her.

"Let me get you a glass of water."

I had enough light to read my watch: 3 am. "I'm sorry I woke you."

He handed me a plastic cup. "Drink."

I took a sip and pulled my feet up under me. "I was dreaming about the attack." Tears welled up in my eyes. I didn't know why. Maybe because my dream made it feel so real, so recent. I didn't want to be so afraid.

"Hey, hey, hey." Ben saw my tears, and his demeanor changed. He sat beside me. "Shhh…" He put a finger to my lips. "Don't cry, Rory. Let me fix it." He took the cup out of my hands and kissed me.

My heart thudded. From fear to desire in seconds. His lips was warm and soft on mine. Without thinking I darted my tongue into his mouth. I tasted peppermint and a hint of the whiskey he'd drunk earlier.

The kiss intensified. He pressed me into the sofa. I clutched his arms as he held himself above me. Hard ropes of muscle. Kyle had been lithe and lean. Ben was a giant in comparison. I liked it.

"Don't cry, please." Ben whisked a single tear off my cheek. "No more." He nibbled at the corner of my mouth. I took in his natural scent, pine and musk.

His gentle kisses stoked a deeper fire within. All the pent up fears and feelings I'd had since my father's accident were pushed aside. I wanted to be in the moment, not thinking or analyzing. Just do what my body wanted. Without guilt, without embarrassment, without expectations. We were so far away from everything in my normal life. The dredge, my bills, the attack, the worries—all far, far away. Ben was here, I was frightened, and he wanted to comfort me. I took it all in without caring what it meant. No one would see me. No one would know.

Hungry for more, I slid my hands down to the waistband of his boxers. He sucked in his breath as I worked them off. Naked in the lantern light. I marveled at the size of him. His legs like tree trunks. His shoulders broad as a beam. When I'd first met him, his bulk had frightened me. Tonight, I drew comfort from it. Protection, safety, security. I kissed across his collarbone.

"Jesus," he groaned.

He pulled at the t-shirt I wore. I helped him take it off.

Then, he pushed me back against the sofa. His thighs captured my legs. I brought his head down to mine again. All thoughts left me. I didn't care a bit about who Ben really was, where he came from, what he was hiding from. In this crazy place I'd found myself, I had very few people I could trust. Stella was one, and Ben had become the other. Steady, strong and dependable. The fact that he might be a murderer far from my mind.

"Are you sure you want to do this?" Ben asked poised inches from my face.

His eyes were a beautiful, ocean blue. That amazing, deep blue that only appeared in the Bering Sea certain times of year. "Yes. Yes, I'm sure." I dove down deep into those eyes and let everything else go.

CHAPTER TWENTY-FIVE

I woke up the next morning in the bedroom, the plaid blanket twisted around my legs. Ben had an arm around my waist, my back against his front. His naked front.

I squirmed. I should never drink whiskey when taking opioids. Ben awoke.

He skimmed his hand along my side. "Good morning, gorgeous."

I flinched and twisted away.

What had I done?

"Hey, no reason to get squirrelly." He laughed a deep rumble of a laugh.

I quickly pulled on my clothes, grateful for the poor lighting. "I'm gonna go make us some toast, m'kay?" I dashed out of the bedroom into the larger living area. I really wanted to streak out the front door and run deep into the tundra, miles and miles and miles.

I just had sex with Ben Abel. Possible murderer.

"I don't have a toaster." Ben called from the bedroom.

"I'll fry up some eggs." I pretended all was normal. That I didn't mind I'd hopped into bed with a man I'd only known for a week. Totally normal behavior for Old Rory. Totally normal.

My nerves jangled.

I spied my cell phone on the coffee table where I'd left it last night. Only twenty-five percent battery life. How did one charge a cell phone in the middle of nowhere?

"I've got some cheese in the fridge."

"Great." Several text messages had come in earlier. I also had a few voicemails. I never even heard it ring. I checked the signal strength. This far out in the tundra barely a bar.

I read the texts first.

Stella from late last night:

Where are you staying? Hospital said you checked out. Worried.

Then another a couple of hours ago:

Rumor has it police are looking for Ben. CALL ME!

Then another an hour later:

Matt heard Ben's fingerprints on weapon. I'm scared. Where are you?

The hackles went up on the back of my neck. Could my instincts have been so wrong? How could I have been so stupid? Had Ben been pretending all this time about his feelings for me? Was last night just a game for him? Get stupid Rory to sleep with her attacker?

My gut clenched and nausea set in. I had to get out of here.

I wasn't safe with the Beast.

Quietly, I slipped on my shoes.

"Do you know how to work the burners?" Ben appeared in the doorway of the bedroom one-hundred percent naked. "You going somewhere?"

"I, uh, wanted to get some fresh air." I looked away. My face grew hot. I worried he would know I'd lied.

Relax, Rory. He doesn't know that you know.

"I'm gonna hop in the shower. You have to take quick ones out here. I only have a small hot water tank."

I slipped my phone in my front pants pocket so he wouldn't notice. "I'll be right back and get on those eggs and coffee."

"Thanks, darlin'." Then he laughed. "I almost forgot that's your last name."

I had a tightness in my chest.

Ben closed the bathroom door, and I made a break for it. I

dashed out the door. He'd left the keys to the ATV in the machine. I hopped on, turned the key, and gravel flew as I sped out of there.

My heart hurt so much I could barely breathe. I really was as stupid and sex-crazed as my mother had been. I'd made a horrible, horrible mistake. My instincts were terrible. I knew that now. I had been flailing through life like a fish caught in a net. Not even aware my flapping was useless. I was trapped. I had nowhere to go. The way forward was impossible.

My hair streamed out behind me like a horse's mane. I hadn't had time to put on a helmet. As I rounded a bend, I was surprised to see a Nome Police UTV headed my way. I pulled over into a shallow ditch to make room for them to pass.

I knew where they were going.

Ben.

Officer Isaacs gave me an incredulous stare as he passed.

*

The rest of the ride to town was much longer than I remembered. I dreaded hitting the city limits. If Matt and Stella knew about the fingerprints, then everyone else in town did, too. It wouldn't be long before every man, woman and child in Nome found out I'd spent the night at Ben's place. I wanted to keep on driving Ben's ATV and take the Beltz Highway all the way north to Teller, never to be heard from again. But what would my father think if I abandoned our dredge and our livelihood? It was a crazy thought.

When I arrived on the outskirts of town, I thought about my options. I was exhausted. My apartment was off limits until the police finished their investigation. Kyle's place was a no-go as I'd burned that bridge already. No going back. I could try Stella and her over-stuffed place, but I already knew she'd bombard me with questions, and I'd have to survive the Spanish Inquisition from not only her, but Matt and his sister, Alisha. The last place left was the *Alaska Darling*. I could sleep on the couch for now while I licked my wounds and figured out what to do next.

With the engine rumbling, I took out my cell phone to listen to my voicemail messages.

Two from Stella, one from the Nome Police and one from the hospital in Anchorage.

My hand trembled. I pressed play on the message from the hospital.

Ms. Darling, it's Janie from the Patient Care Coordinator office. I wanted to let you know that your father has his surgery scheduled for tomorrow at 7 am. He will likely be in the hospital for about a week before you need to arrange for his transport to the temporary living situation you worked out here in Anchorage. The surgeon should call you tomorrow after his surgery to let you know how everything went. Please let me know if you have any concerns or questions about your father's care.

A normal person might call her father the night before he has major surgery. I felt my state of mind would drag me down, trip me up, make me say the wrong thing. I knew he'd ask about the dredge, the gold, the bank account. And I had no answer for him. All I had were more worries piled on top of worries. How would talking to him help any of it? With my stitches I couldn't dive, my diver had turned out to be everything I pretended he wasn't, and I had absolutely no way to get back to dredging. I'd come to the end of my rope. There were no more choices to make. The night in Ernie's Pub when I'd found Ben had been my final attempt to save everything.

I wished I'd never tried. I wanted to ex Ben out of my head forever. The worst mistake of my life.

I deleted both of Stella's messages without listening. I didn't need to hear more of my friend's panicked voice as she'd tried to track me down and save me from myself. I didn't deserve her friendship. She'd warned me. And I'd ignored every red flag Ben threw up—because I'd wanted to.

I was sick in the head. I needed help. What was wrong with me? Any other woman would've gone back to Kyle and begged for forgiveness. He'd been steady. He'd been a bit of normalcy in my life for a year-and-a-half. Why couldn't I just forget about my father's accident and go back to how things were? Kyle and I had been a good team.

I suppose I was hopeless and messed up. Just like my mother. The apple didn't fall far from the tree after all.

I gunned it and headed toward the docks. I hoped I could sneak onto the *Alaska Darling* without anyone noticing.

In a daze I parked Ben's ATV in the gravel at the docks. Too much had happened in less than 24 hours for me to keep up. My head was a muddle of thoughts and feelings. The worst was my body's betrayal. I couldn't get rid of the memory of Ben's hands on my body, the sweat, the heat, the hardness. The intensity of the sex pervaded everything. God help me, but I wanted him.

I made it to the wheelhouse, grabbed a wool blanket from the back of the dilapidated love seat, and curled up. I wanted to be deep asleep, dreaming and not doing any thinking. But I couldn't help looking at the message from the Nome Police that had been left yesterday evening. It waited there like a shark lurking in the deep, circling its prey, ready to strike.

I pressed play.

Ms. Darling, this is Officer Garber. We have some more questions for you about your employee, Benjamin Abel. If you could please come to the station at your convenience. Thank you.

I played the message a few more times, wishing it said something different. But I already knew what they'd ask: *Did you know Benjamin Abel is a murderer? That he is wanted by the police? That he has a history of violence?*

Isaacs had seen me on the dirt trail to Ben's place. Did he think I had just ignored his message? Or maybe he thought I was a stupid woman who had no more sense than a jack rabbit.

I pulled the blanket over my head and wept silently.

CHAPTER TWENTY-SIX

I entered the police station and asked for Officer Garber. The person on duty pointed to a couple of uncomfortable-looking plastic chairs and told me to wait. After hiding on the dredge for a few hours I'd worked through enough emotions to feel capable of confronting the truth.

While I waited, I played Candy Crush on my phone. It kept my mind from dwelling on my impossible situation.

Ten minutes ticked by.

Officer Garber finally appeared. "Ms. Darling, will you come with me please?"

He strode off toward a security door, waved a pass in front of it, and let me through into a larger office space in back.

"Please, have a seat." He sat me down on a padded chair near the back of the space and behind several cubes filled with officers— one in uniform, others in shirts and ties. "Thanks so much for coming in."

"No problem." I supposed Garber knew where I'd been last night, but I didn't care. I played innocent. Anything else was too embarrassing. "I'm sorry I didn't get your message until today. Bad signal, I guess." I shrugged.

Garber stared blankly at me for a few seconds.

I squirmed in my seat.

"We arrested Benjamin Abel earlier today."

"Yes." I kept quiet about how I knew.

"Not only did his fingerprints match those at the scene, he had an old warrant out of Idaho." He leaned back in his chair, never taking his gaze off of me. "Second degree murder."

A sick feeling settled in the pit of my stomach. "I see."

"Did you know he was wanted for murder?"

I didn't know how to answer that. "I didn't know he had an outstanding warrant, if that's what you're asking."

He frowned. "What is the nature of your relationship with Mr. Abel?"

"He's my employee—my diver."

"Nothing more to it?"

I clenched my jaw. "He's my employee, Officer Garber. Nothing more." It really was none of his business what I'd been up to last night. I wasn't the one who committed a crime.

He formed his hands into a steeple. "Can you think of any reason Mr. Abel might want to hurt you?"

"No."

"Did you ever have any altercations or arguments with Mr. Abel before your attack?"

"No."

"Your friend, Stella Hansen, says you did—the night of the incident at your apartment."

"That wasn't an argument. It was more of a disagreement about personal matters."

Garber changed his line of questioning. "We've spoken with a few people down at the docks. Told me Abel didn't seem like the type to get riled up easily. Seemed like a steady fellow. Is that how you would describe him?"

I thought over the short time I'd known Ben. "He's been a good diver, even saved my butt a couple of times. I'm having a really hard time understanding why he would've wanted to hurt me. Are you sure you got the right fingerprints?"

"We're still analyzing the evidence. There were latent, fresh prints on the doorknob of your apartment as well as several others throughout the living room and kitchen area. We ran all the fingerprints we picked up at the scene through CODIS. Then Abel's warrant popped up. His arrest had nothing to do with the current investigation."

"But you have him in jail?"

"That's how it works when you have a warrant in the system." Garber clicked with his mouse a few times and then spun around his computer screen. "These are pictures we took at your apartment the night of the attack. Do you notice anything missing?"

So maybe Stella's information had been wrong. Garber didn't say Ben's fingerprints had been on any weapon used on me. Only that his fingerprints were at the scene. But a warrant for second degree murder was a lot scarier to me than some fingerprints.

I scanned the photos, digging through my head for what had been in my apartment and where. My laundry basket of folded laundry had been dumped on the floor, the drawers in the kitchen had all been pulled out—some even dumped upside-down on the counters. Couch cushions had been strewn about, my dad's small closet torn apart, but the bucket of gold concentrates—the thing I assumed Nate would've been after—sat right where I'd left it just to the left of the tub.

"It's hard to tell from the photos. It's such a mess."

Garber hesitated a long time after showing me each photo. Letting me take my time to review carefully. "I know it's difficult. Do you have any items of value in the apartment?"

"The gold we dredged." I pointed at the bucket that had been left untouched. "But beyond that, not really."

"Perhaps you returned before the perpetrator could take anything." Garber clicked out of the photo array and turned the screen back toward him.

"Seems strange someone would make such a mess with the bucket right there in plain sight."

Garber shrugged. "Maybe he wanted to cover up the real reason he'd broken into your apartment."

"Maybe." That didn't make much sense to me either. If I'd walked into my apartment, the first thing I would've noticed was a missing bucket of gold concentrates. "When can I get back in?"

"Probably tonight. We got all the evidence logged." He refocused his gaze on me. "One more question before you go, who else has a key to your apartment?"

My mind blanked. "What? Wait. I thought someone broke in to my place. You're saying someone used a key?"

"Either that or he was incredibly skilled at picking locks." Garber smirked.

I'd only moved back into my dad's place a few weeks ago, after the accident. "No one. I've got a key and my dad..." I scanned my memory for the day of my father's accident. He'd been taken to the

ER, stabilized and then flown to Anchorage as soon as I could arrange it. Were his keys in his pants' pocket? "My dad has the other key."

"So no boyfriends with keys?"

"No."

At that very moment, Kyle entered the room with Officer Isaacs. His shoulders were slumped, his hands were shoved in his pockets. We locked eyes for a moment. He quickly looked away.

"What about Kyle Stroup?" Garber focused an intense brown gaze on me. "What is the nature of your relationship?"

"We broke up after my father's accident." My mind raced. "Why are you asking about Kyle? And why is he here?"

Isaacs and Kyle had disappeared through a door at the other end of the room.

"We are bringing in everyone with fingerprints at the scene."

"Kyle's never been to my dad's apartment." I was bewildered. Shortly after Kyle and I started dating, I'd pretty much moved in with him. There'd been no need for him to be at my father's place. We did all our clean up in his Quonset hut as soon as we'd been forced to relocate from the house to the less expensive apartment. "You must've made a mistake."

"No. His prints were found..." Garber clicked again with his mouse and read off the screen. "On the front doorknob as well as some areas in the kitchen. We were able to identify him because we had his prints in our local fingerprint database from an altercation last March at the Iditarod."

The Iditarod Sled Dog race ended in Nome, and every year a number of parties and events took advantage of the crowds. Kyle had been picked up for getting in some stupid fight at the Airport Pizza and Beer Tasting Extravaganza. I'd had to pick him up the next morning from the drunk tank.

"I'm telling you, Kyle's never been to my dad's place." The news didn't give me much faith in our local police department. Besides, Kyle wouldn't have any reason to break in or attack me. If he needed anything, he'd just ask me. The whole thing made no sense. "You must have it wrong. What about Nate Frazier? Have you spoken to him?"

"We spoke with Mr. Frazier yesterday after the details you provided to us at the hospital."

"And...?" They'd gotten this all wrong. Arresting Ben, bringing in Kyle for questioning, when the real perpetrator was so obvious.

"He provided us with an alibi, which we are checking into. As I said, this investigation is still ongoing."

I made it out of the Nome Police station fifteen minutes later more confused than ever.

CHAPTER TWENTY-SEVEN

Stella pulled up to the Nome Police station in her boyfriend's beat-up GMC Jimmy. "Where have you been? Why didn't you answer any of my phone calls? I was worried sick."

I secured the seatbelt. We drove past Ben's ATV, which I'd left in the parking lot. I'd given the keys to Officer Garber and told him to give them to Ben. "I spent the night on the dredge." I shifted in my seat and wished I had a Tums to settle my stomach. I was a terrible liar.

"I know you're lying to me. It's all over town."

Of course it was.

My shoulders slumped.

"You stayed at Ben's place. All I want to know is why, Rory? Why would you do that?"

"I don't know. Because I love self-destruction? Because I love picking out men who disappoint me? Maybe I'm just permanently screwed up in the head like my mother."

"You aren't your mother, Rory. Please stop it with that nonsense. She left when you were a kid. You barely even remember her."

I remembered.

"But why would you run off with Ben after everything we found out about him?" Her eyebrows squished together. "I don't get it. He's dangerous."

I couldn't say the words—Ben had saved me in more ways than I could count. He'd helped me when no one else would. He'd stood

190

up for me and took care of me. "He's not dangerous. Ben didn't attack me. You got your information wrong."

"What?" Stella drove down Bering Street toward the diner. My plan had been to hang out there until I could get back into my apartment.

"Ben had a warrant. That's why he was arrested. They identified his prints or something."

"You just said he wasn't dangerous," Stella scolded. "A warrant for what?"

My throat tightened. "Second degree murder."

"Holy crap." Stella pushed hard on the brake and brought us to a complete halt in the middle to the road. Luckily, Nome wasn't known for its traffic. "Are you serious? He *was* on the run, then. And you thought he wasn't dangerous. Are you kidding me?"

I shrugged. I didn't know what else to say. There'd be hell to pay if Stella found out I'd spent slept with Ben, accused murderer.

"What if he blames you for the arrest and comes after you?"

"He's not going to come after me, Stel." I couldn't think through everything at once. So much had happened since I woke up in Ben's bed. I needed a shower. I needed to change my bandage. My head hurt. Where was that pain med prescription? I pawed through my purse looking for the bottle. "Isn't second degree murder the one where you did it by accident?"

"That's manslaughter, I think." Stella got the truck moving again. "Look, does it really matter? He killed someone. I can't believe I even have to explain this to you."

"You don't. That's enough. Really. I get it. Ben's a crazed murderer. I was lucky to escape from his dungeon. Yadda yadda yadda." I ran my fingers through dirty hair. "Do you think I could get a shower at your place?"

Stella scanned my figure as if she'd just noticed how awful I looked. "Oh my God, hon. Of course." Instead of continuing down Bering, she made a left on 4th at the Eagle grocery store toward her and Matt's place.

"Thanks." Not only was I looking forward to cleaning up, I wanted to eradicate the smell of Ben from my skin. I couldn't escape the memory. Torso to torso, kisses across my collarbone, sweat and heat and all sensations wrapped up into one. And the last feel of him—my naked back against him. The hardness of his erection. He'd wanted me again. My face flushed at the memory. I changed the subject, "My dad's having his surgery tomorrow."

"I'm sure everything will be fine." She squeezed my hand. "And then before you know it, he'll be back in Nome acting like his old self again."

"Yeah." Her desire to lighten my mood made my heart full. But I knew the truth—there wouldn't be a dredge to come back to. I was sunk. My only course of action would be to sell it before the season ended. Without a diver and with my injury preventing me from diving, I had no way to keep the operation going. I would tell my father after his surgery when he was on his way to recovery.

I had no idea what I would do after that point, but at least I'd have the money I needed.

Out of nowhere Ben roared up next to us on his ATV. "Rory," he yelled, a muffled voice through closed windows. "I need to talk to you."

My skin flashed hot and cold.

Stella rolled down her window. "I think you've done enough damage. Why aren't you in jail?"

Ben ignored her and stared right at me. "Rory, please. I want to explain."

"Forget it," Stella answered for me. "Do you want me to call the police? Stop harassing my friend."

I could feel his eyes on me. The hot weight of his stare knocked the wind out of me. I used every shred of willpower I had to keep from getting out of Stella's truck and climbing on the back of that ATV. The wind in my hair. The dust and grime of Nome long behind me. To go back to that magic cabin in the woods where I'd forgotten where I came from, the worries I had, the decisions that needed to be made and got to be just Aurora Darling, lover of Ben.

Love.

The word popped into my head. My muscles tensed. Adrenaline pumped. Somehow I'd fallen in love with Ben, and I hardly knew anything about him. I was working 100% on instinct and not using my head. This is what had gotten me in trouble every single time. I made rash choices and gut decisions, rather than look at the facts and make a studied, carefully thought out choice.

I had to fight to stay in Stella's truck. My hand clutched the door release. I wanted to pull it and be free. But every other time I'd acted on impulse, I'd been wrong. Today was the day I'd start making rational decisions.

Listen to Stella, for God's sake.

She'd been lecturing me for years. And now I wondered where I'd be if I'd listened to her.

"Rory," Ben pleaded.

"Get me out of here," I whispered to Stella.

She punched the gas, and we left Ben behind in a swirl of dust.

*

A couple hours later I sat on Stella's futon in a pair of Alisha's yoga pants and an old t-shirt of Stella's that said *Keep Calm You Live in Nome Alaska*. Someone's idea of a joke, I guess.

"Thanks for letting me use your shower."

"No problem." Stella handed me a cup of green tea.

I didn't like green tea, but I did like the gesture. I took a sip and tried not to make a face.

Stella fussed about the room. She was a stickler for neatness and, with three people sharing a one-bedroom place, the clutter drove her a bit mad. "When are you going to be able to get back into your apartment?" She asked with a bit of a fake smile.

I suppose she viewed me as another piece of clutter.

"Tonight." I gently rubbed a towel across the hair around my wound. I'd washed it as best I could without wetting the stitches. "Officer Garber said he'd call me."

"I printed out that application you asked for." Stella handed me a one-page application for the Polar Cafe. "I'm not sure what shifts are available, so I'd just mark all of them."

"Thanks." I set it next to my purse. "I've got a few people in mind who might be interested in buying the *Alaska Darling*. And if that doesn't work out, I could probably part it out no problem. The air compressor is practically new." I took a drink of the awful tea to clear the sour taste from my mouth.

"I know how hard it was for you to come to that decision, Rory." Stella picked a butter cookie from the tin on the coffee table and dipped it in her tea. "But what other options did you have?"

I thought talking about selling the dredge would help me work through the emotions of failure and defeat. Instead, each word out of Stella's mouth dug a deeper wound. I wanted to be in a better frame of mind. With the dredge sold, I could forget about Nate Frazier's crazy fixation on the business, I wouldn't have to run into Kyle on the docks anymore, and Ben would be a tiny blip in my checkered past of failed relationships. Maybe it would even turn into an interesting story someday: 'I slept with a murderer.' Could make for good bar conversation.

"It might be kinda fun if we can work together." I imagined Stella and me at the Polar Cafe, filling coffee mugs and slinging reindeer sausage around. I'd have to get used to making small talk and maybe putting on some lipstick once in a while.

Stella gushed. "That would be awesome. Sometimes it can get a little monotonous. You and me?" She picked up her phone and started up one of her playlists. "We could liven it up a bit."

She was in her Pitbull phase. A rhythmic beat filled the room.

I didn't feel much like celebrating, but rocked to the music a little.

Stella got up and danced her empty tea cup to the kitchen sink. Then she trotted back to where I was sitting. I handed her my cup, and she slinked her way back.

I couldn't help but laugh.

Stella lip synced the lyrics and did the two step, swinging her arms in rhythm to the beat.

My phone vibrated in my pocket. "It's the police station!"

Stella fumbled with her phone and shut off the music. She suppressed a giggle.

"Hello?"

"Ms. Darling, it's Officer Garber."

"Can I get back into my apartment?" I wanted my life to move forward. Part of that began with retrieving the paper work for the equipment out of the top drawer in my dad's bedroom and figuring out exactly what I had to sell.

"Yes, that shouldn't be a problem. We've wrapped everything up and have made an arrest."

"Oh, wow." From the questions I was asked earlier today, I didn't get a feeling they were any closer to pinning my attack on anyone.

"Kyle Stroup confessed this afternoon."

CHAPTER TWENTY-EIGHT

"Kyle?" I sat in the same chair I'd been in earlier at Officer Garber's desk, overwhelmed with confusion. "That doesn't make any sense. Kyle has no reason to break into my apartment. He would never hurt me."

Officer Isaacs was also in attendance. He breezed past my objections. "After speaking to Mr. Stroup, we were able to get a confession almost immediately. We've arrested him and have him detained her for the time being."

"He confessed?" I felt lightheaded. "I don't understand. Why would he confess to something he didn't do?"

"We found some of your father's property at his residence." Officer Garber dragged a cardboard box out from under his desk. "A toolbox labeled with JOHN DARLING. That is your father's name, correct?"

I recognized the tool box. It had been in my living room under a pile of other things I'd brought home from Kyle's place. "But why would he want my father's tool box? I don't understand. And why would he hit me instead of just asking me for it, if it was really that important to him?"

"I know this has come as a shock to you. Kyle told us about your relationship," Garber said. "I know it can be hard to understand when someone you loved and trusted does something like this, but people in desperate circumstances do terrible things sometimes."

"Desperate circumstances?" I shook my head. It didn't compute. I don't remember Kyle once telling me about anything in his life that would be close to desperation. In fact, at the assayers he'd picked up a hefty dredging check. He seemed to be doing better without my father and me, not worse.

"After Kyle's name came up we found out some interesting things about his background. Apparently, his parents filed for bankruptcy a few years ago, and he took on the responsibility of setting them up in a new place in Texas," Isaacs detailed. "And the place he rents, he's going to be evicted in a few weeks' time. He's several months' behind on the rent. As I said, 'desperate circumstances.' Sometimes people can't see a way out."

"But there's nothing of any value in the toolbox, just some old tools." I could see Kyle stealing gold or valuable things he could resell, but my father's old toolbox had nothing of any real value inside. "Did he take anything else? Like some extra diving equipment?"

Isaacs shrugged. "Maybe he thought there was something in there worth hocking. I don't know. Maybe he thought you'd be an easy mark. He knew your routines, knew your neighbors wouldn't think anything out of the ordinary if he showed up, that kind of thing. He thought he could get in and out, and no one would remember he was there. But guess he didn't plan on you coming home so soon."

Garber offered me the toolbox. The weight of it was heavier than I remembered. Or maybe my whole body had weakened from the shock of the news. "Thanks." As I stood up I asked one more question, "Am I allowed to talk to him myself?"

"To Mr. Stroup?"

"Yes," I said.

"You do know that even if you don't want to press charges for the theft, the assault charge is going to stick, right?" Isaacs warned me.

I nodded. "Will I need to testify?"

"You'll likely be subpoenaed. So expect that in the future," Garber said. "Not for a few months' though. Takes time to get a hearing date."

"I'd like to talk to Kyle if I may." I couldn't leave the station without more of an answer. The two officers maybe solved the case from their standpoint, but I had more questions.

"I wouldn't recommend it," said Isaacs.

"Why?" I was the victim here. If I wanted to talk to my attacker,

I should goddamn be able to.

"Sometimes after a traumatic event like you experienced, it can trigger a lot of stress and anxiety," Garber explained. "I could set you up with a victim's advocate." He dug through a desk drawer and handed me a business card. "They can walk you through the next steps in the process. Confronting the perpetrator is probably not the best first step."

"I want to see him." I uncrossed my legs and sat up straighter in the chair. "Please."

Isaacs eyeballed me. I knew he was reading my level of stubbornness. Likely drawing on what he remembered of me from the days I went to school with his kids. "Wait here. I'll see what I can do."

I briefly closed my eyes. "Thank you."

They moved me to a lumpy couch in the back of the office. The police department buzzed quietly with the regular work of the day. I wished I could be one of them. With a regular job. Regular hours. Steady paycheck. Benefits, even. The last thing I'd needed was another hospital bill. Tears threatened to spill.

Why on earth would Kyle break into my apartment to steal my father's toolbox and possibly other things? Even the officers' explanation didn't make sense to me. Kyle knew my financial problems, why would he target me over anyone else he knew in Nome? His parents had both been teachers, as I recalled—his mother at an elementary school, his father at a middle school somewhere near Houston, I think. I didn't know they'd had financial problems. Not sure when that all happened. Kyle didn't really share those sorts of details about his family life with me. In fact, Kyle and I had never had what someone would call a heart-to-heart talk. But from what Kyle had told me, his parents were two responsible people, and my dad, in comparison, lived the life of a free spirit—a bit of a modern day pirate. If anyone was going to succeed in life, it would've been Kyle. He had a great family, with a stable home life and pretty much whatever he'd needed. I'd never thought to delve into his relationship with them. Now I wished I had. What kind of girlfriend had I been, if I didn't know these things?

*

Kyle sat on a mattress in the holding cell. His head hung down. Despite what had happened to me, I felt sorry for him. The whole scene made no sense.

"Hey, Kyle," I said gently. I didn't know what to expect. Was he angry, sorrowful, distant?

His dirty blond hair appeared unwashed. When he tilted his head, his brown eyes were bloodshot. I didn't know if that was from lack of sleep or something else. "Why are you here, Rory?" He had a pained expression. "I fucked up. I really fucked up."

"Why, Kyle? Why did you do it?" A small bench sat opposite the cell. "I don't have anything to steal. I don't understand."

"I didn't mean to hurt you. This isn't about you at all." He held his head in his hands. "Why did you have to get in the way?"

"In the way of what? You aren't making any sense." The Kyle in front of me was a completely different Kyle than the one we'd run into at the assayers. What happened to the confident, almost arrogant, man I'd seen?

He sighed and chewed on a thumbnail. "I wanted the map back. That was all."

"What map?" In the back of my mind my thoughts went to my father's strange conversation with me about a map. And when I'd asked Kyle about it, he'd denied knowing anything.

A lie.

"My great uncle." His tone deepened. "Your dad stole it from him."

"What?" A sudden coldness hit my core. "My dad is no thief."

Kyle's brow came together in a tight knot. His face flushed. "This is why I never said anything. I *knew* you would defend him. You'd always take his word against mine. *Always.* Do you ever wonder why things never worked out between us?"

I frowned.

"Because no matter how many times, no matter how many arguments, you always believed your father." He pounded a fist on the mattress for emphasis.

"What are you talking about, Kyle? What arguments?" I scanned my memory trying to think of anything that matched up to what he was saying.

"Who got the most gold? Buck. Who knew where the hot spots were? Buck. Who was a better diver, tender, mechanic, prospector? Buck." His eyes grew hard as flint. "Never once could I do or say anything that was better than Buck. Nobody can compete with that kind of loyalty."

I bit my lip. The memories came back in fits and starts. Times I would stand up for my father's opinion and would reject Kyle's. I suppose most of it was Buck's experience and maturity over Kyle's that would convince me to go along with my father 99% of the time. But I could see how that could've gotten to Kyle. He wasn't one to express his feelings openly. He'd harbor a grief until he couldn't hold onto any more. "I want to know, Kyle. I'm here to listen. Tell me about the map."

"I'm sorry, Rory." His eyes got redder and wetter.

I'd never seen Kyle cry, but he was awfully close. "I know." I touched the bandage over my stitches. "Tell me about your Great Uncle."

He paced his cell and chewed more intently on his thumbnail.

"My father had an Uncle…Uncle Arthur." Kyle sighed. "Uncle Art, he called him. He used to live around these parts. He'd been a prospector his whole adult life. Started out on the beach running sand. Worked really hard for everything he had, but he managed to scrape together enough gold to buy himself a little claim about twenty or thirty miles outside of town. That was right around the time the dredgers really got going out in the Sound."

I remembered my father telling me the same story about when dredging took off in the Bering and the desperate scramble by locals to get an operation together.

Kyle darted a glance at me. "Uncle Art was having a rough go of it out at the claim. He couldn't get the right equipment, much less truck it out there. The land had potential, but he didn't have a way to work it. So he decided to dredge. He was pretty handy. He slapped together an outfit with a friend of his—pieces and parts they'd bartered for. This was way back before GPS or any of that tech stuff. People just went for it out there. Like the Wild West."

I nodded.

"You found a spot, you did whatever you could to map it, keep track of it, get back to it the next good day. Knots, bearings, all that shit. Mark it on a map. Get back to it the next day and the next and the next." Kyle's gaze became unfocused. "Uncle Art had a gift, my dad told me. A gift for knowing the right kind of cobble to look for, knowing when the ground had already been worked, sniffing out the gold under water like a goddamn blood hound. Over time, his map held the notes for every good spot, every potential good spot and every overworked spot out there. When the other dredgers were in drinking and waiting for calmer seas, Uncle Art got out there and added more detail to his map."

Kyle tightly wrapped his arms around his middle, head down, pacing, pacing, pacing. "Some thought he was nuts. But his mapping skills became legendary. He turned a quick summer scheme to finance his claim into a successful operation. Everyone would've killed for an opportunity to get a look at his map. Some say he found a spot with gold nuggets bigger than anyone dreamed possible."

The mother lode.

Kyle was a stranger to me. All of this information, and he'd never brought it up once. Here I thought he'd been some random guy from Louisiana only to find out he'd had family in Nome. "So where does my dad come into all this?"

"I'm getting there." He held up a hand to silence me. "Eventually Uncle Art couldn't really dive much anymore. He'd developed rheumatoid arthritis. Really bad. His knees locked up, his hands couldn't work right. He had a few friends who helped him out. Maybe Buck had been particularly kind to Uncle Art. Maybe he got to trust Buck enough that he showed him that map, told him about his big find. Eager to share with someone who had the same passion, maybe. A couple of years after his diagnosis, Uncle Art moved to the Lower 48 where he had an ex-wife and a couple of step kids. He handed over everything he'd owned to my dad. But not the map. He'd lost the map. Uncle Art was torn up over it. His life's work, all of his notes, his drawings, everything. The massive nugget field. Gone. My dad actually came up here to look for it. He poked around in every nook and cranny of Uncle Art's old place. My dad never found it. Not too long after that Uncle Art passed away, and the map became a mystery."

I fidgeted on the bench.

"But it had always been Uncle Art's suspicion that someone close to him had taken the map. He never could quite point a finger at who, and after a while, he got too sick to care so much about it anymore. My dad told me the story, though. I got the gold bug like Uncle Art. I learned to dive, so I could come up here and carry on his legacy."

I remembered the day my dad had hired Kyle. Tall, lean, and confident. I think that's what my dad liked best about him—his supreme confidence. For someone that young, it had been unusual.

"When I got that job on your dad's dredge, I didn't know

anything then, I swear, Rory. I'd heard he'd needed a diver, and I thought you were pretty cool. Seemed like a good gig. Saw Buck as kind of a second father to me. He'd been patient, kind, showed me the ropes. I had a little bit of knowledge, but Buck had been willing to really explain things."

My heart ached hearing that. I missed my father's guidance.

"But the day you didn't show—it had been only Buck and me out there. He'd sent me to get a tool from the wheelhouse. It wasn't where he said it was. A hammer, a screwdriver, I don't even remember what he'd asked for. I saw that old toolbox of his under a pile of hoses in the corner. A toolbox that I'd overlooked before, because I'd never really needed to look for anything. But for some reason I was drawn to it. I opened it and inside was Uncle Art's map."

I gasped. "I don't believe you." My father wouldn't steal from someone. Never. He'd been the best father a girl could ask for. Honest, hard-working, loving. It couldn't be possible.

"It was Uncle Art's map, Rory."

"How do you know the map didn't belong to my father?" My stomach fluttered.

"It had my Great Uncle's initials on it at the top: AHS. Arthur Hiram Stroup. Plus, besides the coordinates and details for spots to dredge, he had drawn his claim on it."

All the air escaped my lungs. My father. The one parent I'd come to depend on had built his life on a lie. "Did you try to kill my father?"

"No, Rory. No." His face paled. "I'd never—not intentionally…"

"So you found your Uncle's map and said nothing to Buck?" A sudden coldness hit me. "I find that hard to believe. If you had such a great relationship as you say, why didn't you ask him why he had it in the first place?"

His expression soured. "And you wonder why we fell apart after the accident?"

"You knocked me out, Kyle." I turned my head so he could see the bandage. "You hurt me over a map. Clearly, there was more that ruined our relationship than my attitude toward my father's accident."

"You found the toolbox at my place, and I'd hidden it pretty well." He pointed a finger of blame. "You were looking for it. I know you were. I'll bet you knew about the map the whole time."

I gasped.

"Don't play innocent with me, Rory." He came up close to the cell bars. His usual mild expression replaced with one I didn't recognize. "I'm not buying it anymore."

My stomach churned. I backed away and banged on the door that led out of the holding area. "I want to leave."

"You knew about it. You and your father." Kyle's voice echoed in the concrete space. "He's a thief and you're just as much responsible as he is."

My mouth ran dry. "I want out of here." I banged with both fists.

An officer unlocked the door with a frown.

I raced outside, taking in breath after breath of cool air. I couldn't comprehend what Kyle had told me. I needed to talk to my father. He'd straighten this out. He'd tell me the truth. My father was no thief. Kyle had to be crazy.

CHAPTER TWENTY-NINE

My father's apartment had been turned upside-down. Fingerprint dust dappled the door knob, door frame, tables, counters and every surface imaginable. I scanned the living area for a place to begin the clean-up. I wanted to lose myself in cleaning and straightening and reorganizing. Everything I'd built my life around had crumbled into a flaming heap. I was beginning to wonder if I had no ability to detect a liar from a truth teller. Had I been this naive my whole life? Or had I developed my naivete after I'd arrived in Nome?

I started with the silverware drawer. Putting each knife, spoon and fork into its proper place soothed me. I suppose I needed to begin with what I knew was real—and the stainless steel, mismatched set of utensils from the resale shop in town was very real. The cool metal in my hand. The tines and blades were something I could touch and see and categorize.

When I finished one drawer, I moved to the next. Spatulas, pancake flipper, bottle opener, whisk, ladle. Real. Real. Real.

I'd finished up the last kitchen drawer when someone knocked at my door.

Nate Frazier stood on my door step.

I held back a gasp. "What are you doing here, Nate?"

His eyes were red-rimmed. "I need that map." His words came out quiet and calm.

How did he know about the map?

The hairs raised on the back of my neck.

"Right now's not a good time, Nate." I moved to shut the door.

Nate put his foot in between the door and the jam. "You're gonna give me that map."

My cell phone sat on my couch. If I let him in, I could maybe grab my phone and call the cops.

Nate could be unpredictable. Confirming the map had been in my possession would do nothing but enflame him. "I don't know what you're talking about."

Nate entered. "Your old man. He has it. I know he does." He had a slight sway to his body. "He showed it to me."

"He did?"

He snorted. "A long time before you ever were in the picture, honey." He took a few steps closer. "You think you and your dad are so buddy-buddy? That he tells you everything?"

"I just spoke with Kyle at the police station, and he told me the truth, Nate." I maintained eye contact and stood my ground. Nate didn't scare me anymore. "My dad stole that map from Kyle's uncle. Buck found most of the gold using someone else's hard work."

Nate's eyes sharpened. "Kyle's uncle?"

"Arthur." Sounded as if he had no clue about Kyle's relationship to the map. "Yes. The map belonged to Arthur."

"I didn't know—I couldn't have known…" Nate's expression collapsed from harsh to soft in a moment. "I wouldn't have gone along with it if I knew it was stolen and that the kid was involved."

"Looks like my father lied to more people than just me." 'The Kid' had been Nate's nickname for Kyle. In fact, Nate had been more broken up about losing Kyle's companionship on the *Alaska Darling* last summer than being fired from his job.

"That's fucked up. I knew Buck could be underhanded—but shit." Unexpectedly, Nate sat on the lamp table next to the couch. "That ain't right."

"I'm sorry, Nate. My father isn't the man I thought he was." Sure, Nate had his problems—the drinking, the anger issues, and now the drugs—but that didn't mean he didn't have feelings. "Look, I don't know what the arrangement was between you and him. And now that I've found out the whole map story, I'm more inclined to give you the benefit of the doubt about your business relationship."

Nate stared off into nothing. "All that time on the dredge. The hours I worked for free to get that thing running, repairs over the winter to make sure it was ready for the summer season, the time we spent ice diving and I almost lost fingers because of his damned stupidity."

I'd never really paid attention to Nate before. He'd been my dad's partner, sure, and he lived with us for a while, but I'd been a kid and more focused on myself and my own internal problems to really see what went on between Buck and him. As I reviewed the years of working on the dredge, the duties had been quite skewed. My dad had been the one to make the decisions, decide where we were dredging, how long we were dredging, who would be doing what. For someone who'd considered himself my dad's equal, it must've been humiliating to put up with it for so long.

"He brought me on when I was a nobody with nothing," Nate reflected. "But I helped him put the *Alaska Darling* together, one piece at a time. I was the brains behind it all, and he was the one with the means to get it built. You think what he did was more valuable than what I did to get his operation up and running?"

"No."

He pulled a face. "Then he brought this twelve-year-old kid on board one summer—outta nowhere."

"Me."

"Yes, you." At that moment he actually cracked a bit of a smile and met my gaze. "And everything changed."

"I never meant to get between you and my father," I said.

"I know. But how could you prevent it? You're his kid."

We both sat there in silence for a few moments.

"I'm selling the dredge." The words slipped out. "I want you to have half."

Nate raised his brows.

"But only if you'll use some of the money to get some help."

His eyes welled up with tears. "I'm into some serious bad shit, Rory."

I touched his hand. "I know. Let me do this for you." We may have had our moments, but I couldn't stand to see Nate in such a mess. It would be what my father would want. "I'm sure there's a place down in Anchorage. And my dad's going to be down there recuperating for a while. He'd like to know there's a friend nearby." Maybe they'd find a way to fix their relationship.

"Thanks."

*

I finished cleaning up the apartment after Nate left. He'd stuck around for an hour or so while we talked about the best price for the dredge as a whole and each piece of equipment, if I had to part it out for sale. Although he'd been sad to hear about my father's financial picture being so dire, he agreed that selling was the best avenue. Before he left he asked me to let Buck know he wished him the best.

With surgery scheduled for tomorrow, I had wanted to call my dad one last time, but the day had gotten away from me. And now, with the evening setting in I was emotionally and physically exhausted.

My phone rang.

Zoe.

A good distraction from a phone call I dreaded making. I plopped into the recliner chair and answered, "Hey, sister."

"Aurora, how are you doing? How is Buck? Did he have his surgery yet?"

"It's scheduled for tomorrow. And then he'll be down in Anchorage for a couple of months before he can come back home."

"Sound rough." Zoe's tone sounded truly sympathetic. "I know things are tight financially."

"Well, I did some thinking since we last talked." I didn't have the energy to explain to her all the drama I'd experienced over the last few days. Sometimes simple was best. "I took your advice to heart."

"You did?" The shock in Zoe's voice was evident. Her little sister *never* listened to her advice.

"You were right, Zoe," I said. "I'm selling the dredge."

"Wow. I'm surprised. That's very mature of you. I know how hard a decision that must've been."

"You know, until I decided to sell it, I didn't realize how much worry I carried around. My dad didn't leave us in a very good position when he had his accident." I thought about the stack of unpaid bills on the kitchen table I'd been avoiding for the last week. "I had no idea the kind of financial juggling he'd been doing. I'd just relied on him to take care of everything."

"You're making the right move," Zoe said. "Now the next step is figuring out where you're headed."

I had barely made it through today much less thought about what I was going to do going forward. "I hadn't even thought about it." On the coffee table I spied the blank application for the Polar

Cafe that Stella had given me earlier. "I'm kind of thinking short-term here. How to keep going through the winter."

"So not much leftover after the medical bills and such?"

"I won't know about the exact billing for a couple of months, according to the Patient Care Coordinator I've been working with. They'll bill his insurance first and then they'll come after me for the deductible and any other costs that weren't covered by insurance. At least I have a clue what the deductible will be. This health insurance junk is a nightmare."

"Welcome to the real world."

"Yeah. Thanks a lot." I smiled to myself. Although I wasn't pleased with the responsibilities that had been tossed in my lap in the last few weeks, I'd somehow muddled through it and came out the other end as a more informed person. "For right now I'm more concerned with the recovery costs—rent, in-home nursing care, food—that kind of thing."

"Are you going to be okay? You know you're always more than welcome to come stay with us for the winter, if things get too tough up there. Nobody says you have to do this alone."

I thought about the idea for a moment. I could get away from the mess I'd made of my life in Nome—the humiliation of failure, the embarrassment of my one-night stand with Ben that everyone in Nome probably knew about, the knowledge my father had stolen from a local. I could take the easy route, the escape hatch offered. Let someone else be responsible for me and my life again. Let Zoe and Henry dictate the best course for me after my 'crazy period' in Alaska.

"I want to do it alone," I said. If I'd learned anything about myself, it was that I was capable of a lot more than I'd given myself credit for. And a lot more than my fellow dredgers cared to give me credit for. "I need to figure out what I want to do with my life. Where I want to go in the future. What I want to be doing and who I want to be doing it with."

"That sounds like relationship talk. Are you not telling me something, Aurora?"

Weird, but I hadn't even thought about Ben since I'd made up my mind about the dredge. "I don't know if I'm ready to really have a serious relationship, Zoe. I think I've made a few pretty awful mistakes lately, and I'm probably better off figuring myself out first, you know?"

"Yeah, I totally know where you are coming from, Aurora." My almost-30 unmarried sister hadn't quite figured out the dating scene herself.

The specter of my mother and how she'd torn apart our family hovered over both my sister and me. I was half Cindy Pomeroy. Half of that distant, but beautiful woman who'd made her way through life in the messiest way possible. Interested only in her own happiness, her own desires. Leaving a path of destruction in her wake. She'd abandoned two daughters and a husband. I'm not even sure why I thought about her at all. But how can a girl avoid thinking about her mother or desiring her love and approval? I'd only found disappointment in another parent—my father. Buck Darling was supposed to be my savior. The dad who loved me unconditionally and would do anything for me. But then I discovered the truth. He had his own ambitions, too. His own desires. He'd wanted me to believe he was Super Dad. Because without that, what was he? An aging dredger using someone else's information to get ahead. A cheater and a liar. He really had accomplished very little on his own. He'd gotten my mother pregnant and then had run off to keep searching for his fortune—and instead had stolen someone else's.

Both my parents had pretty bad faults.

Then my mind turned to Zoe and Henry, my stepfather. They had always been there for me. They'd worried about me, sure, and wished I'd chosen to stay with them rather than move in with a father I barely knew, but they'd never forced me to live my life any way but mine. And how hard that must have been to watch me navigate life from a thousand miles away.

"Look, once you figure out what you're doing, call me back," Zoe insisted.

I never thought a few weeks ago I'd be having a chummy conversation with my older sister. But, somehow, without even trying, we'd repaired the rift in our relationship.

*

The next day I selected Alaska Regional Hospital's number on my cell phone and asked the operator to put me through to my father's post-surgical room. I'd found out his surgery had gone well from a message left on my phone while I had been asleep.

I bit my lip while the phone rang.

"Rory." My dad's voice sounded stronger than it had the last time I'd talked to him. More confident. The deep timbre had returned.

"Dad." Without wanting to, I burst into tears. The last few days, what I'd found out about Kyle, and the financial and emotional burdens I carried around caught up to me.

"Hey, hey, hey," my father soothed. "Don't cry. Everything's okay. The doc said the surgery went well. I'll be out of here in two shakes. I promise."

Where to begin? How would I even broach the topic I'd been dreading? "I'm glad you're okay." I sniffed and willed myself to get my emotions in check. "A lot's been going on since your accident, dad."

"The dredge okay?"

Always the dredge. Constant worrying about the dredge. Dredge first. Daughter second. "The dredge is fine." I didn't have the guts to tell him the truth yet. I hadn't yet put the *Alaska Darling* up for sale. I took a breath. "This is about the map."

"What map?"

"Dad, I know about Arthur Stroup's map." My heart filled my throat. "Everything. Kyle told me. But I need to hear from you: is it true?"

Buck paused. I could hear his heavy breathing on the other end. "Goddamn it."

His tone of voice surprised me. "Dad?"

"Rory, Kyle is a goddamn liar. Whatever he told you. It's not true."

"But how can you say that when you don't even know…"

"Arthur couldn't tell the difference between his ass and his elbow by the time I knew him. His mind was going—and that map? He was gonna burn it." He repeated the last words slowly, "Burn it."

"What?" This didn't sound remotely like the story Kyle had relayed to me.

"I saved that map from being destroyed. The motherlode was on there somewhere."

"But it didn't belong to you," I pointed out. "It belongs to Kyle, his family."

"So I was supposed to let Art throw it away? When he was so senile he couldn't remember where to piss much less where to park a dredge to get the best gold?"

"Everything you taught me. It was all a lie." I could feel the tears coming on, the thickness in my throat. "You made me think you knew everything about finding gold. I believed in you. I looked up to you. I even *bragged* about you to my friends. And all along you were cheating using stolen information."

"If I didn't use that map, you know where you'd be right now? Back in Seattle with Henry. Is that what you wanted, Rory? I did whatever I could to keep you with me. *Whatever I could.* And if that meant using that map then, goddamn it, I was gonna use it. And I don't feel bad about it one bit. Not. One. Bit."

"I never asked you to steal for me." I spoke the words quietly. My mind raced to understand who the man was on the other end of the phone. This was not my father. This was not Buck Darling. I had hoped for some kind of explanation that made sense. For a way out of the idea my father lied and stole. But he fully admitted it.

He sucked air through his teeth. "I'm not going to apologize for doing what I had to do."

The phone clicked. He'd hung up on me.

CHAPTER THIRTY

I parked at the docks and carried a couple of cardboard boxes to the dredge so that I could box up the few personal items still on board. I needed to wipe the GPS clean of data points, sort through the odds and ends that had collected over the years, and make sure equipment was in working order before I could show it to a couple of interested parties. The vultures always came around this time of year when they smelled a failed operation. Rumors brought buyers to my doorstep before I'd truly made up my mind.

My heart had been numbed by the truth. Although half my life had been built around the *Alaska Darling*, to think most of my father's success had been stolen wouldn't leave my mind.

Maybe I truly wasn't cut out for dredging. Maybe I'd fooled myself into believing my dad knew what he was talking about when he dreamed of me being the first female dredge operator in Nome. A dream built on deception and lies. He knew I couldn't live up to the expectation without cheating. Without using ill-gotten information from a poor, old man who'd died without knowing the truth behind the disappearance of his map.

Nome had looked up to my dad. Seen him as a success, a good businessman, a risk-taker who had been rewarded for his efforts. And I was to be his successor. Buck Darling had been the 'local' who made good. A consistent presence on the water even when other operations failed.

I'd thought it had been smarts and tenacity.

My whole life in Nome had been a lie, and I'd bought it hook, line and sinker.

I stepped onto the dredge, and it dipped in the water as I added my weight. I'd miss that feeling of free floating and drifting with the tide and the waves. The wind in my face, the sun in my eyes, my body shivering after peeling off my wetsuit, the joy of discovery, my gut telling me to push, push, push for one more hour of dredging rather than giving in to my body's weaknesses. A woman who set out every day to make her father proud had been reduced to the daughter of a thief. Everyone in Nome knew it. After the attack and the truth came out, I'd felt their eyes on me.

"Bobby at Ernie's told me I might find you out here." Ben appeared on the dock. "Need some help?"

Heart beating. Breath stuck in my lungs. He'd caught me off guard. I'd written him off. Assumed he'd disappeared or gotten shuttled back to Boise. I hoped I'd never see him again, but then I hoped I *would* see him again. Mixed emotions. Confused thoughts. Easier to avoid them than confront them.

I hadn't seen Ben since he'd tried to run Stella and me down on the way to her place. I'd texted him one last time to let him know his final payout check would be with Stu at Alaska North. He'd tried contacting me a few times after that, but I didn't answer hoping he'd get the hint.

I shoved my expanding emotions into a box. Sealed it shut.

I grimaced and shook my head. "I can handle it." I worked the wrench with trembling hands. I couldn't loosen the nuts on the sluice. My hands were cold and trembled.

"Here," Ben took the wrench. "Let me." In a few swift cranks, the first nut came loose. He worked through the next one. "Seems kind of early to be shutting it down for the season."

Out on the Bering a few larger dredges worked the grounds despite the chop.

I unfolded a tarp from the bin on the deck. "I'm selling the dredge." I wanted no pity. I only wanted him to know he was no longer needed. Whatever our relationship had been, the diver-tender relationship had ended. Kaput. Done.

Ben paused. His back was to me. "Oh." Then, he again worked the wrench. Barely skipping a beat. "I see."

"To be honest, I thought you'd find another outfit by now. Sorry I didn't make it clearer that I'd shut everything down." I made note of a few other bodies on the docks in case something went awry. He'd murdered someone. No matter the circumstances, I couldn't put that thought out of my mind. "I can give you some recommendations. Good captains. Fair treatment."

"Guess I'm glad I came by."

"I was going to tell you." I couldn't be honest with Ben or I'd have to admit he scared me. I wanted to forget we'd ever slept together. Huge mistake. Reminded me how desperate I'd been for male attention. Pathetic, really.

"I'm sure you would've eventually. Or maybe you were going to wait until I noticed your dredge had disappeared." He smiled tentatively. Testing me out. Looking for something I didn't know I could give.

"I sort of came to this decision suddenly."

Ben set down the wrench. "Rory, you can let me in. You don't have to do everything by yourself."

I avoided his gaze. "The dredge is my responsibility. My family's business is my responsibility." I shook out the tarp and refolded it. "Yes, I kind of have to do everything by myself."

Ben caught me by the shoulders. "Stop it, Aurora. Stop it."

My stomach fluttered.

"I didn't come to Nome looking for this." His thumbs brushed my collarbone. "I actually came here to get away from thinking too much, feeling too much. I wanted to get away from people staring, asking, wondering. And now I see it in your eyes, too. I see the fear." His face tightened. "I'm sorry I didn't tell you everything, but I didn't know how to bring it up. And then when I knew I had to tell you— that night in the cabin—I couldn't. I chickened out. After everything that had happened I wanted to hold onto something good for once, you know?" He traveled from my shoulders to my face, caressing my cheeks. "And now that I found it—you—us, I don't want to let it go." He drew closer. "It feels too damned good, too damned right."

He kissed me hard.

It took my breath away.

Deep down inside the sadness that had crept into me over time melted away. That feeling of aloneness drifted. I leaned into him. I wanted Ben to stay. I didn't want him to leave.

He enveloped me in his arms and whispered in my hair, "Don't push me away. I need this. I need you."

My shell cracked. "I need you, too."

CHAPTER THIRTY-ONE

We sat on the love seat in the wheelhouse and looked out at a perfect day for mining: no wind, blue skies, clear water.

"Have you ever felt betrayed?" I asked, not really intending for Ben to answer. I wanted to understand how I could love and hate my father all at the same time. How I could find myself in the same exact place I'd been twelve years ago when my mother had left. Alone. Confused. A victim of someone else's lies.

"Yes." Ben spoke the word bitterly.

"Was it her? Laura?" I didn't even mean to ask. The words slipped out without me thinking. The whole murder thing hung between us like a dank, dark cloud. "Tell me about her. Tell me what happened."

I needed to hear the story, no matter how ugly, no matter how terrible. I'd been screwed over before by people I loved—or thought I loved. I couldn't handle one more person turning on me. Lying to me. Leaving me. I needed to trust Ben one hundred percent. My belief in my ability to judge character had been ravaged. I wanted to know it all. Because if I couldn't handle those facts now, they would only destroy our relationship later down the road.

"When I came back from my deployment to Afghanistan, I realized I'd made a terrible mistake—the engagement." Ben threaded his hand with mine and squeezed. "The fun loving, happy person I thought I'd gotten engaged to didn't exist. She was a drug addict. I'd been stupid not to see it before. She met me at the base, and I could see it in her eyes. Even though she'd been sending me emails,

Skyping with me, making me think we were together, she'd been shacking up with random guys she met. Out partying."

"Oh my God. That's terrible," I said.

"But I was too much of a coward to confront her. I hoped she'd come back to me somehow. Be the girl I remember from before. And I felt guilty, as if I had caused some of what had happened because I was overseas and out of touch, I let things spin out of control. We fought more and more. I waited for her to be something she'd never been. And I paid the price for that."

"You were in love." I leaned my head on his shoulder. "You were trying to help her."

"The addiction got worse and worse. I mean really bad. She begged me to stay." He gritted his teeth. "I thought if I left she'd have no one but these creeps she'd been hanging out with. Instead of saving her, I let her drag me down into her world."

He scrubbed a hand over his face.

"The night she died. We fought worse than ever. She was high and incoherent and crazy. The neighbors all heard us. I knew someone would call the police again. I tried to find her stash, flush it, get rid of it. As if that would fix it all—but I knew she'd be right back out there tomorrow, buying more." He let out a ragged sigh. "She went nuts. Scratching, smacking, clawing. Like a wild animal. I was in the bathroom, dumping her shit. She came at me, I jabbed her with my elbow. Must've caught her in the face. I knew what it would look like if the police showed. I got most of her drugs in the toilet. Flushed. Then I got out of there. She screamed and ranted. The last thing I heard from her was screaming."

His grip on my hand tightened.

"I spent the night in my car, parked in some neighborhood. When I got back to the apartment the place swarmed with police. And I knew. I had this feeling. I knew she was dead." He took a long pause. "The neighbors had called. Heard a ruckus, screaming. I gave my story to the cops. No one believed me. The paper loved it. Splashed it everywhere. Former Navy sailor and his beautiful fiancée—they claimed I had PTSD, that I had a drug problem, that I'd beaten her up in the past."

"Oh, Ben…" I wanted to spare him the hurt of remembering. I wanted him to stop. "And they thought you'd murdered her."

He rubbed his eyes with the heels of his hands. "She OD'ed. They didn't figure it out until the tests came back. That warrant? It was an old one. Still not cleared out of the system, I guess. Her family still doesn't believe it. They think I beat her to death." He cupped a hand over his mouth. His eyes widened. "Oh, God."

Men cry differently than women. Their sorrow seems to come at them like a physical attack. A brutal blow to their gut. Buck had never cried. Not once. I'd only heard my stepfather cry when my mother ran off. That one horrible day of realization that she'd never be back. Never wanted to be part of the family they'd created.

I climbed into Ben's lap and looped my arms around his neck. I bent my head to his and felt his tears on my cheeks. I soothed with my presence. "You asked me once when I was going to stop living the life my father wanted me to live," I started quietly. "When are you going to live the life you want to live, Ben? When is that going to happen? Never? Hiding in a cabin in the middle of nowhere isn't going to change what happened to you. Running away from something won't make it disappear."

I stared out at the remaining jumble of belongings on the dredge I needed to pack up. My mind an equal mess of emotions. I wanted everything to be simple again, to stay in its neat little place and follow the prescribed formula of my life: dive, gold, eat, sleep. Although I hadn't experienced the same sharp tragedy that Ben had, I understood his pain. My life had been upended when Buck had his accident. The ugliness underneath had been exposed. The ugliness I'd been ignoring. What a fool I'd been.

*

"Do you want to take it out one more time?" Ben asked.

The sun shone coolly in a white-blue sky. A distant wall of clouds gathered at the horizon, but they would take hours to arrive.

"Yes." The weight of failure lifted for a moment.

Ben smiled.

I got up to start the engine.

He automatically headed aft to untie the dredge from the dock and coil the rope.

I backed out of the docks and aimed for the open water. He joined me in the wheelhouse. I set aside everything I'd been thinking about. The uncertain future, the loss of my father's dredge, the end of my diving and gold seeking, the map I'd left for Kyle at the police station. I let it all go and focused on the sun and water. The smell of the tides. The slap-slap-slap of the waves against the side of the

Alaska Darling as she made her final voyage. I was transported back to that very first summer when I was twelve. When I'd known nothing about gold dredging and had played the sidekick. I hadn't a care in the world. All I wanted was for my father to love me. And now all I wanted was Ben.

Ben swept the hair off the back of my neck and kissed the exposed skin.

I shivered.

"What do you want, Aurora?" Ben said in my ear. "What do you really want?" He wrapped an arm around my middle, and my stomach trembled.

I leaned into him, my back curved into his torso. "You."

He kissed down the side of my neck and lingered at a spot on my shoulder. The plaid shirt I loosely threw on over my tank top slipped. He tugged at the strap.

I steered the dredge around the jetty.

Ben palmed my breast.

I gasped. My legs grew unsteady.

Ben settled his hand on mine and took the dredge out of gear. The engine rumbled.

We drifted back toward the harbor.

"We'll crash," I protested weakly.

"Then we'd better be quick."

A rush of adrenaline and desire settled in my core.

He scooped me up as if I weighed no more than a feather and set me on the love seat. I kicked out of my shorts and panties. He unzipped his jeans. I straddled him. Our bodies met in an explosion of heat and need.

"Aurora," Ben breathed. His eyes so blue.

I kissed his neck and rocked in a slow rhythm, wanting it to last. Wanting the feel of him inside me to never end.

His hips raised upward. He shuddered to stay in control. He pushed up my tank top and rested his hand on my naked breast. My nipple hardened in his hand.

A wave hit the *Alaska Darling* crossways, and my torso tipped into Ben's face. I steadied myself by putting both hands on the back of the love seat. Our gazes met. I saw a new color in Ben's eyes. A deep electric blue. Desire. Intensity. Joy. All wrapped into one hue.

"I love you, Ben." The words escaped my mouth and blended with the soft sounds of the sea.

"And I love you."

We kissed and continued the motion of our bodies. The world outside forgotten. Everything I needed was right here, in this moment. And nothing else.

*

Ben and I stood on the bow of the dredge. We charted a course along the coastline, away from other miners. We enjoyed the cool breeze and the vast expanse of the water. Ben rubbed a hand across my back. Hard to believe the man I'd first perceived as 'the Beast' had been so gentle with me. I flushed at the recent memory of our lovemaking. I wanted more of it, and I wasn't ashamed to admit it. I leaned into him and took the warmth and strength he offered.

"You do have the skills for this, you know," Ben said softly. "You're not the cheater, your father is."

"How do you know?" A week ago, I might've bristled at the compliment. "I thought my father showed me how to dredge, but now I don't think I learned anything. He deceived me." It hurt terribly, but the only way I'd overcome it would be to deal with it, not hide it. I'd hidden the pain my mother caused for years, and it had only created a divide between my sister and me. "The things he told me about how to read the bottom, where to find the gold. He never knew a thing. He stole a map from an old man. The food I've eaten, the apartment I live in, the clothes on my back—all a lie built on someone else's hard work."

"Wait, Rory, that's not true." He took my hand and kissed it. He spoke deliberately. "The other day, when all those dredges were swarming, we found our own path, remember? A path *you* tracked on the GPS. That wasn't from any gold map. That wasn't anything your father had given you. That was you and me working the ground, looking for the clues, finding the gold through hard work. Not through cheating."

"That was pure luck." Knowledge of the map had knocked me down quite a few pegs. I'd been so confident the *Alaska Darling* was the best dredge on the water. Now I wasn't so sure.

"You have to believe in yourself, Rory. You have to believe you're capable. You can do this. Despite what your father and Nate did to get ahead, you weren't complicit in that." He captured my chin. "You didn't know what they were up to. Can't you see that?"

I shrugged.

"Come here." Ben led me to the wheelhouse and turned on the GPS. He clicked to the saved tracks. The purple track we'd started ourselves. "That is you and me, Rory. Nobody else. Just you and me. Don't ever let someone tell you differently." He traced the purple dots we'd plotted. "You and me."

I stared at the purple dots. My pulse beat slow and calm. A peace came over me. "You're right." To say the words took away the tension and stress that had rested on my shoulders. "We did make it happen." Even though my father had cheated his way to success, I'd uncovered my own instincts. My own knowledge boosted with the help of Ben.

"You said there was a mother lode out there," Ben remarked. "I've got some money saved. What if we partnered up, started our own operation and kept looking?"

"I wouldn't ask you to do that, Ben. I can figure out something else." I hadn't thought much beyond selling my father's dredge, giving Nate his half, and taking care of the financial burdens that remained.

Ben unzipped his backpack. He pulled out the carving he'd been working on when I'd been at his cabin. I'd thought he'd crafted a single owl, but he'd made a pair of owls next to one another on a branch. "*We* can figure out something else, you mean." He put an arm around my shoulders and kissed the top of my head.

I picked up the carving and ran my thumb over the details. In my mind, I roved over the bottom of the Sound. The gravel, the cobble, the sand, the rocks. I knew the terrain. I knew what to look for. All I'd needed had been the confidence to believe in myself.

"Yes," I blushed. "We."

No longer Rory Darling, daughter of Buck Darling, I'd become Aurora, Finder of Gold, Dredger Extraordinaire.

We cruised along the shoreline. Ice season would arrive soon, and Ben and I could start again. I connected my phone to the GPS and downloaded our purple plot points. Our work, our future. Together.

The End

ABOUT THE AUTHOR

K. J. Gillenwater has a B.A. in English and Spanish from Valparaiso University and an M.A. in Latin American Studies from University of California, Santa Barbara. She worked as a Russian linguist in the U.S. Navy, spending time at the National Security Agency doing secret things. After six years of service, she ended up as a technical writer in the software industry. She has lived all over the U.S. and currently resides in Wyoming with her family where she runs her own business writing government proposals and squeezes in fiction writing when she can. In the winter she likes to ski and snowshoe; in the summer she likes to garden with her husband, take walks with her dog, and explore the Big Horn Mountains.

Check in with K.J. at her blog: kjgillenwaterblog.blogspot.com or visit her website for more information about her writing, her books, and what's coming next. www.kjgillenwater.com.

If you enjoyed this book, K. J. Gillenwater is the author of multiple books, which are available in print and in eBook format through Amazon.

The Little Black Box

When thoughts can kill.

After the suspicious suicides of several student test subjects, Paula Crenshaw, research assistant in Paranormal Sciences at small town Blackridge University and budding telekinetic, suspects they may be connected to a little black box designed to read auras. Professor Jonas Pritchard, the head of the department and renowned paranormal expert, doesn't believe his precious experiment could be causing students to drop like flies.

Haunted by memories of a childhood accident, which she believes she caused with her untamed psychic abilities, Paula finds herself lured to the black box and its mysteries. But when her best friend, Lark, comes close to death after her encounter with the black box, Paula realizes her investigation might endanger the people she loves most. As the suicides stack up, she convinces her fellow researcher, Will Littlejohn, to help her solve the conspiracy. The closer they get to the dark truth behind who might be financially backing the project and why, the more dangerous—and deadly—it becomes.

The Ninth Curse

His blood for a cure. It's a cruel and deadly bargain...

Nine curses. Nine weeks to live. Joel Hatcher has inherited more than a family legacy. It's a time bomb that's ticking down to the inevitable: his own death. But the curse won't die with him. Unless he can find a way to break the cycle, his younger brother becomes the next victim.

In the throes of the third curse, the Painful Pox, Joel makes a last-ditch decision to seek the help of a young spiritualist.

One look into Joel's suffering eyes, and "Madame Eugenie" finds herself torn between doing the right thing and fulfilling her most secret wish—bring her husband Adam back from the dead. Joel's cursed blood is the missing ingredient in her resurrection rituals, and Adam's spirit whispers seductively that there's only one way to get it: steal it.

As Gen and Joel unearth his family's past to track down a cure, they come closer to each other, and to a horrible truth. To live, Joel must lose everything. Including the woman he has grown to love.

Warning: This book contains curses, sacrifices, a ghostly husband, a crazy cat and a love that defies all odds.

Acapulco Nights

ACAPULCO NIGHTS was a Write Affair finalist (Kensington Books) on Wattpad as an "Editor's Pick."

Suzie's fiancé, James, is pressuring her to pick a day for their wedding. She's cancelled three dates, and he's starting to wonder if she really wants to get married. But how does she go about telling her fiancé that she's already married to a man in Mexico? She needs a divorce, and she needs one fast. Her marriage has been a secret from her best friend, Janice, her fiancé, even her own mother, and she wants to keep it that way.

When Janice asks her to come along on an all-girl vacation to Acapulco, Suzie leaps at the chance. A search on the Internet gives Suzie all the information she needs to track down her husband, Joaquin, while out of the country and finally get that divorce.

Unfortunately, Joaquin won't give her up so easily.

When James appears in Acapulco unexpectedly, all hell breaks loose, and Suzie stands to lose everything she's ever loved.

Blood Moon

Werewolves are roaming Northeast High, and Savannah Black is determined to hunt them down.

When Savannah's academic rival mysteriously disappears, she enlists the aid of her two best friends, Dina and Nick, to solve the mystery. Football players with glowing eyes and razor sharp canine teeth may have fooled the faculty, but not Savannah and her friends.

These brave students are determined to eradicate a clan of deadly werewolves who threaten to take over their school. When Dina disappears right before the big Homecoming Dance, Savannah and Nick must act quickly to save her from the werewolf's curse. But will a straight-A student be able to master knives and silver bullets as easily as chemistry and calculus?

Skyfall

A science fiction short story collection of three flash fiction works.

Skyfall. A miner confronts a devastating future.

Time Travel. A failed engineer tinkers with a matter-energy transporter, which he plans to step into for the first time.

Torch. A man attempts to escape from a futuristic prison.

Nemesis

K.J. Gillenwater edited and wrote a story for this science fiction anthology entitled, NEMESIS. The idea for the anthology was this: Write a short story between 4,000 and 5,000 words using the word "Nemesis" as your inspiration. Ten writers participated (including K.J.). Here are the short story titles included:

Polarity by Holly Gonzalez
Superhero Comic Girl vs. the Litter Box by Steven R. Brandt
Last Walk by Jinn Tiole

Stagnant by Dave Cardwell
Three Shades of Black by Matthew Thrush
Disciple by Kristin Jacques
Outwitting Alexa by Jesse Sprague
Mordecai by Hannah Ansley
Guardian by Louis Williams
Star Log by K. J. Gillenwater.

The Man in 14C

A brand new science fiction short story anthology of three fiction works, which were all written using contest prompts.

Encounter. Two crew members must deal with a hull breach on a hauling vessel bound for a distant earth colony. Alone and desperate, they make a choice that might alter their lives forever.

Lucinda. A tv star in a dystopian America reveals her downfall from highly paid news anchor to a low-life host of a television reality show featuring everyday people being evicted from their homes during the worst financial crisis in U.S. history.

The Man in 14C. A cancer patient on a flight back from Tokyo passes through a wormhole and experiences time travel that transports him 20 years into the future. His life destroyed, he must reconnect with family and discover how he fits into an unfamiliar world.

Made in the USA
Middletown, DE
16 November 2020

24212830R00129